PERFECTION COMES AT A PRICE

by

Ulla Beattie

Dear Deborah
Enjoy the Phoberomys
Patterson particularly.
lots of love
Ulla

Dedicated to Susan

Chapter 1

"Mum, it's seven o'clock. Weren't you and Dad going to go to the pictures?"

"You bet we were. You got that one right, you Mr Know-All! That father of yours is a scumbag. Leaving me here to stew with a seven-year-old."

Eric flinched. Another horrible week-end was on its way. His father had no doubt gone to the pub as he usually did on Friday evenings. That was the pay-day. He worked as postman and he was one of the lucky ones who worked on one Saturday a month. Most worked every Saturday.

"Mum, shall I set the table?"

"Bloody hell, no! I'm not hungry. Bring me another gin bottle out of the cupboard. And a Tizer. When that man gets home, I'll have his guts for garters! What are you staring at, you stupid boy? Make yourself a sandwich and take it to your room together with an apple. Scram!"

The pale seven-year-old boy hurried to do as he was told and settled to read something. Not an easy task as his mother put on loud records and wailed along drunkenly.

After her fourth glass of gin, Barbara Flint broke into tears of rage. That horrible husband of hers had yet again broken his promises.

At quarter past eleven Barbara heard the key in the lock. The culprit had returned.

"Tom, you bastard! Where the hell have you been?"

"Oh, shut it, will you. I was at the Fox and Hare as usual."

"You drunken shithead, we were supposed to go to see the new film tonight. You promised we'd go to the pictures."

"I promised no such thing, Babs! I'm always at the Fox and Hare on Friday nights."

"You damned bastard! How dare you?"

She went to get the cleaning brush and started to hit her husband viciously.

"Ouch! Ooh! That hurt. Stop it, Babs, or I'll give you a black eye."

"It was meant to hurt. Tomorrow we'll go there without fail. And as for a black eye, you are the one to get it."

Barbara stood up. She towered menacingly over Tom. He was a slightly built man who knew that he was no match for his strong and buxom wife.

There was a movement in the corridor. Eric flitted quickly to the bathroom.

"Why is the boy still up?"

"He isn't. He's just going to the toilet."

"Shit! Make it fast. Then get yourself into your bedroom," Tom bellowed after the boy. His head began to spin." Ouch. I'm not feeling all that good."

With that Tom hurtled to the bathroom just as Eric was coming out. The two collided and Tom was sick all over the bathroom floor. Then he turned around and swiped the boy several blows.

"You vermin! It's all your fault. Babs!" he yelled and then retched again. The vomit flew all around. By now the mother had come to the scene.

"Look what you've made your father do!" she screamed and started to hit her son with the brush that she was still holding. "Because you went to the bog just then your father could not reach it in time. It's your fault. God, it stinks. You will clean it up. Now!"

The boy's eyes were wide with fear. He smarted from the blows he had received. He went to get the rags and mop and a bucket and started quietly to clean up the mess.

The neighbours, who had been wakened by this noise, were knocking angrily on the walls. The couple paid no attention but went into their bedroom to continue their quarrel.

When Eric was finished, he went into his bedroom to lie with his eyes wide awake for a long time.

It had been a typical Flint family day.

The following morning Eric got up quietly to make himself breakfast. On Saturdays and Sundays the family had bacon and eggs, so he boiled himself two eggs. He much preferred boiled eggs to the fry-up that his mother made, which swam in grease. Then he went out on his paper round. It helped to get him a few pennies. Unlike the other children on the estate, Eric did not get pocket money, though sometimes his father might give him as much as five shillings (a fortune for Eric) if he was in a particularly good mood. His other income came from doing the shopping for three old ladies. He saved furiously. Whenever he'd saved up to ten shillings, he went to the post office and changed the coins to a paper note, which he kept hidden inside the top cupboard in the kitchen. He put the notes carefully under the shelf lining-paper. He knew that his mother regularly snooped in his room, and any paper note would have vanished in a jiffy. A few pennies did not interest her.

After his paper round, he would join the other children on the estate who had come out to play. Eric's family lived in Southall in a block of flats. The area was mostly Indian but in the blocks of Eric's estate the people were mainly white with a sprinkling of Caribbean families.

Eric went home at one o'clock. He knew from experience that by noon his mother would have been up in order to prepare a lunch by quarter past one. His father would leave for the football or rugby before two, and his mother by two- thirty in order to be at the bingo by three. Between six-thirty and seven the parents would be back provided that one or the other, or both, had not gone out to a pub with friends. It was like clockwork.

That evening, just after seven, the parents were back. Eric's mother was purring, as she had won a set of hair-curlers as well as some costume jewellery. His father was a thundercloud because the home team had lost by a whisker.

"What bloody bad luck! The scumbags from West Ham won," he lamented loudly. To console himself he had come home with lots of beer.

"Stop ranting. I don't give a shit how your beloved home team does. They can't win all the time."

"You know nothing about football, Babs."

"No, I don't, and I intend to keep it that way. It makes me sick to think how grown men are interested in kicking some object round a field. Pass me some cheese, Tom."

There was a little lull while the family munched. Eric judged the moment right for what he was going to say.

"Mum. Dad. I hope you remember that on Monday there is the parent-teacher meeting at school at seven-thirty."

Eric hoped ferociously that this time his parents would be going as they had missed on any previous ones. Also his teacher had said that he particularly wanted to speak to his parents because Eric had done so well.

"What! What's the point of all that reading and swotting? You're working class, and you'll always stay that way. Don't give yourself airs," his father snapped and gulped a big swig of beer.

Eric was nearly in tears.

"Look, son, we've got other things to do than go to listen to lengthy blabber from your teacher," his mother added. "Now go to your room and leave us in peace."

And indeed, Monday came and went, and yet again Eric's parents had not gone to the meeting.

Mr Hargreaves, the deputy-head of the school was slightly annoyed because the Flint parents had not turned up at the meeting. He had told Eric specifically that his parents should be there. This was the third time those parents had not come. The meetings took place twice a year, and most parents came at least once a year.

He ruminated over Eric. The boy, born on the 26th of October, 1946, had started school in September 1952 when he was nearly six years old. A curious child. Very secretive. Very observant. Very competitive. He was slightly taller than average and had a beautiful face with fine bone-structure, a straight nose, full lips and most arresting large blue eyes. The boy would grow into a singularly handsome man, thought Mr Hargreaves. The future would indeed prove him right. But now, and what concerned the deputy-head, was the fact that he was beginning to see from the boy's advancing work that the school had a potential star pupil. Someone who would go far in life, provided that he managed to stick to his studies.

Home-life mattered as regarded studies. Encouraging parents was usually the key. Such parents could give a child the stamina needed to advance. A dysfunctional family could prevent any member from advancing. In a dysfunctional family, the parents often were two nasty, low types of pond-life who had no interest in furthering their offspring, in fact were hostile to see them advance. During his thirty years in teaching, Mr Hargreaves had seen only five cases of star pupils. In three cases there had been supportive parents, and two young ones, two boys and one girl, had gone into brilliant careers in life. In the other two cases, the parents had been vicious, jealous individuals who had prevented their offspring from advancing. It had resulted in two terrible tragedies. The one boy had gone with his father into petty criminality, with the result that he had been in prison on two occasions and had subsequently taken to drink. The other boy had committed suicide at the age of twenty-two.

Now in the case of Eric, a tragedy was the most likely outcome. Mr Hargreaves remembered the parents vividly. The father was a small, thin, rat-like man with a nervous gaze, and the mother...well! It was difficult to describe the woman. A terrible mop of dyed red hair, a cigarette dangling from a vividly painted full mouth, rouge that cried out loud and eye make-up that made her look like a panda with purple eyes. Mr Hargreaves shuddered. The woman had ruined her beautiful eyes, face and hair. She was permeated by a sweet and cloying perfume, a type of scent that would linger anywhere long after the wearer of it had left. The nails were those of a predator. Good Lord, she applied green nail varnish! Unheard of. Her hour-glass figure was well-advertised through clothing that was much too tight. Being a normal married man, Mr Hargreaves had not been able to prevent himself from taking in the deep cleavage of Mrs Flint, not to mention her well-padded buttocks. And the woman behaved like a man-eater.

With such parents, how would Eric fare? Mr Hargreaves had a yearning to help the boy forward. He decided to take a nurturing interest in the boy and help where he could. If the next three to four years went well, the boy would have the strength to get over the first hurdles and would be likely to continue. At least till thirteen or thereabouts. The next hurdle would come when the boy would be in the throes of puberty. A difficult period for any growing lad. So many of them wanted to quit school at that age and only waited till they were fifteen, when they could do so. Mr Hargreaves sighed. He had seen so many lives go to waste.

The door slammed.

"Shut your trap, you stupid man," Eric heard his mother's voice.

"You were flirting in the pub, I saw how the men ogled you."

"You saw nothing. It's all in your head."

"And no wonder. Your breasts are nearly bursting out of that blouse!"

"Shut it. I can't help it if I've got a fine pair."

"I won't have you parade yourself like that. Hitching your skirt up as well."

Tom stopped while he had a coughing fit and then burped. There was sound of breaking glass.

"Bugger! I've dropped a beer," yelled Tom.

"You fool. Get clearing it up this minute," shouted his wife. "If I get any glass in my feet, you'll be sorry."

"All right. All right. Where is the brush and dustpan? And newspaper? Come and help me, Babs."

Eric lay still in his bed listening to the commotion. It was not the first time his parents quarrelled on that topic. Eric was fully aware of the types of looks that followed his mother, they were amused, disapproving or suggestive. He had often heard people in the estate refer to her as "that hussy".

For the moment, his parents seemed to have forgotten about him, so all was well. Eventually the noise would die down when both of them were sufficiently inebriated and fell into a slumber.

Chapter 2

"Eight, nine, ten. I'm coming," shouted Timmy.

The children were playing hide-and-seek. The little group that usually played together, consisted of Eric, Timmy, Katie, Nandita and Helen. They were classmates, all having been born between October and December 1946.

Eric and Katie were hiding together behind the bicycle shed. Nandita was behind a small wall, and Helen was standing behind a tree.

"Don't think you can hide for long," Timmy continued shouting, "My nose will sniff you out."

"Yes," giggled Katie to Eric, "he reminds me of a spaniel."

"Shush, don't giggle, or Timmy will find us."

The game continued, and the five friends had a lovely time.

Timmy Day knew more than most of the others about Eric's horrible home-life. The Days lived next door to the Flints and were thus subjected to hearing the regular quarrels between the couple. They also knew about the beatings Eric suffered as they could not avoid hearing them.

Mrs Day was a large, jolly woman who managed her four children wonderfully. Her husband was a carpenter, a quiet man, who got on with working. Mrs Day would have liked it if Eric had come more often to their flat to play with

Timmy, but Eric preferred on the whole to hide in his room. He was conscious of the pitying glances of Mrs Day. Also he preferred her not to know how often he was hungry. As it was, whenever Eric had gone to play with Timmy. Timmy's mother had invariably made a pie or a cake. On one occasion Mrs Day had given him two portions to take home. That had turned into a disaster. Eric's mother had seen him with a small paper bag.

"What have you got there?" she asked.

"Mrs Day gave me two pieces of cake to eat later."

"The bloody woman. The cheek of it. And you stupid boy accepted that! All she is giving are handouts to the poor. As if we could not afford to feed ourselves. Don't you dare to accept anything again in the future. I'm going to go there and throw these back in her face."

Eric felt terrible, he felt humiliated. That kind woman was being paid back in the nastiest of ways. Oh why had he not thought about that before? Never again would he bring anything back home.

Helen Brown was a quiet girl who always seemed anxious. And indeed she was. Her parents were divorced, a disgrace in the fifties. Her mother worked in the local council in a secretarial job. She was a disappointed woman. Her husband had left her for a widow who had a house. No doubt the man was comfortable there, so comfortable that he did not often come to the estate to see Helen. The girl

14

missed her father. Well, thought Mrs Brown, at least the alimony came regularly and any presents to Helen were always of quality.

Nandita Patel was an Indian girl. She was Katie's second best friend after Eric. She was an only child, a fact which was a thorn in the side of her paternal grandmother. Her father, a tailor, had married for love, against his family's wishes. However, the family, which consisted of his mother (his father had passed away when he was only sixteen) and two younger sisters, had had nothing to say. Mr Patel adored his wife and was as proud as a peacock of his only daughter. His mother could fuss all she liked about the fact that there was only one child and a female to boot.

"But, mother, our daughter is not just any female. We have our Nandita, the most wonderful daughter there ever was."

Anyway, they lived now in England, not in Bombay. Mr Patel had no intention of ever going back there; no, he loved England. He was a good tailor and he was determined that sooner or later he would have his own business. His wife was an excellent needle-woman, and she helped her husband.

Their flat had only two bedrooms, but they were big. Mr Patel had made a separation wall and an extra door to one of the bedrooms so that Nandita could have her own room and not have to share with her grandmother. Their lounge was their shop. There were two sewing machines, an ironing board with an iron, a cutting table and many shelves. In one corner was a cubicle for changing with a long mirror. There was a long moveable railing. Their kitchen served as the family room with its table for six. All was practical. They lived frugally and saved every penny they could. The business flourished.

The fifth in the group was Katie. She was very close to Eric. She came from a happy family. Her parents were devoted to each other and to their child. Despite efforts, Katie had remained an only child. Her father, Mr Smith, was a rarity in the estate, as he was only occasionally to be seen in the local pub. He went there only when his friends really insisted.

Katie was aware of Eric's home-life. That was because Mrs Day was best friends with Katie's mother, and Mrs Day talked thirteen to the dozen. Often Katie's mother would put her finger across her lips in a sign to keep the sound down, as she wanted to spare her daughter from hearing too much about the Flint household. Eric himself never told anything about his home-life. On occasions, Katie would hear snippets from Timmy. And marks of contusions appeared regularly on Eric's body. Some time ago Katie had noticed two particularly bad contusions.

"Eric. Your parents have been beating you. You must be in pain. Why do they hit you so often?"

"No, no. I just fell down awkwardly."

"Don't lie to me. Timmy mentioned yesterday that his family had heard some dreadful noises coming from your side. They had heard you cry."

"Please, Katie, don't tell anyone else."

"No, I won't."

Katie's heart was bursting with sadness for Eric. When she'd get some nice tit-bits from home, she would give them to Eric.

"But what about you?" Eric would ask.

"I've already eaten all my goodies, Eric, I'm quite full. Those are just for you," she lied.

Her heart would swell with joy to see Eric wolf down her offering.

Chapter 3

For the past few years Eric had managed to advance well at school in spite of all the obstacles. Mr Hargreaves was highly satisfied. He paid a lot of attention to the boy but did it surreptitiously. Just the odd times after a class when he'd ask Eric to stay for a moment or two. Sometimes outside school when he'd see the boy. Then he would have a little chat with him.

Eric had no idea that he was being singled out. Mr Hargreaves had decided that Eric would not be awarded any prizes till he was at least eleven years old. The child needed to be a child whilst he was one and have the freedom that went with it. Where Mr Hargreaves had failed was to get the parents to attend any meetings. There he had to concede defeat.

When Eric was nine and a half, he slowly began to assess what his life was about. So far he had only been as far as West Ealing from his home in Southall. He began to want to see more of his surroundings. Thus one Saturday afternoon he took the bus to Ealing Broadway. He enjoyed seeing an area new to him. Another time he went as far as Hammersmith. He walked to Chiswick, and there he came across Chiswick House and park. How lovely. He admired the fine building and the cedar trees beside it. Later he would learn that the architecture was Palladian in style. The high road in the area was full of cafes, restaurants and shops. So much to see. There was one place called The Old Cinema which had been turned into an antiques shop. Apart from the china, glass, porcelain figurines, lamps and so on, there was a lot of furniture. How lovely. The antiques really appealed to Eric, it was so different from his home. The beautiful wood and the carvings he found fantastic.

What struck Eric particularly was the difference between the areas. Southall, West Ealing and Hammersmith seemed rough areas compared to Chiswick, where the people seemed better dressed. Only after he had been more to the centre of London, in Kensington, did he really notice the difference between classes. In Kensington Gardens a lot of smartly dressed people took their afternoon walks. He realised with a shock that he was wearing frightful clothes. He had never liked the second-hand clothes that his mother bought for him, but now he became deeply ashamed about his appearance. He looked every bit the tenement urchin that he was. Because of his sufferings in his home life, Eric's senses had become honed; he had become observant and noticed all kinds of details.

He winced in agony. He had gone all pale and had to hold himself against a wall. A kind woman stopped.

"My dear boy, you are looking very ill. Can I help you? Do you live far away?"

Eric was mortified. It remained to pray that the woman could not read his thoughts. Eric forced himself upright.

"Thank you very much. I am feeling better now. Don't worry, I live just around the corner."

It was infuriating how he had let himself down. Getting faint did not help him forward one iota. Action was needed. He would have to change himself, and that he promised himself he would do.

He started to go to different parts of the city centre and every part was an eye-opener to him. Hyde Park made him feel almost as if he was in the country-side. There were paths for horse riders. The people who lived in the smart buildings surrounding the park had even horse riding available at their doorstep. The boats on the lake were fun to watch. He had asked about the price of hiring one, but they were too expensive for him. What a superb large green area right in the centre of a big city, he thought. From there he discovered Green Park and admired the building of the Foreign Office, and near it, the Horse Guards at one end. Seeing soldiers in uniforms impressed him. When he saw Buckingham Palace, he was bowled over by its size. He wandered how they kept the soup warm during its journey from the kitchens to the dining room. Anyone in a hurry there would need a bicycle! And again the sight of soldiers in their colourful uniforms filled him with awe. He was astonished. He discovered the Thames, the Houses of

Parliament and Westminster Abbey. The very first time Eric had been there a priest had asked him if he had come for the Evensong, and if so, he better hurry as it was about to begin. The priest guided him to the choir stalls. Eric thought he was nearly in heaven, so beautiful did he find the service. This started a life-long love of going to the Evensong. In the centre there were often groups of tourists and a guide. He would latch himself to a group and listen attentively to the guide in order to learn about the places.

On Saturday, he had time from around two or two-thirty (depending when his mother went to the bingo) till seven. During that window of four and a half to five hours on Saturdays he could do anything unobserved. His parents assumed that he would be playing with various boys on the estate.

Bus fares were very cheap, but it took an hour and a half to get to the centre. Thus he learned to use the underground. That was much quicker. He would go by bus to Ealing Broadway and from there with the Underground. The District Line took him to places like Chiswick, South Kensington, Westminster and Tower Hill. He was particularly interested in The Tower, that historical place of fate. The place gave him an uneasy feeling. He knew that two of the six wives of Henry the Eight had been beheaded there. The Central Line took him to Shepherd's Bush, Notting Hill Gate, Oxford Circus and St Paul's. In St Paul's he found the luminosity wonderful. The place was enormous and he felt like an ant. The cupola was ever so high up. Everywhere the colour and beauty of the paintings impressed him. The world was full of wonders.

In town he studied the shop windows. He saw that he would have to change his wardrobe completely. In order to do so, he persuaded his mother to let him get his clothes himself. She would give him a meagre sum. This was where his savings in the kitchen cupboard came in useful. Even in the second-hand shops there were price-ranges. Eric bought only one item at a time. A jacket was the first one. A dark grey wool jacket that was a little too big for him. He took into account that he would be growing. Next came a blue shirt. Then a pair of grey trousers.

The colour scheme was more or less what he already had, but the quality, the fabric and cut were totally different. With his new second-hand clothes he suddenly looked smart for those who had eyes to see. His parents noticed nothing. Neither did his friends. The most expensive item was a pair of black lace-up shoes. Those he could not get second-hand so he had to count on luck to find them at some sale. His luck held.

There was one person on the estate who did notice the changes in Eric's wardrobe. That was Mr Patel, the tailor who lived on the ground floor and whose windows Eric had to pass when he was going out. Both Mr and Mrs Patel were observant and curious.

"I've noticed that Eric is changing," said Mr Patel to his wife, "He has begun to look smart. Good tailoring has gone into those clothes, and the quality shows through. Yet he gets everything second-hand."

"You are right," his wife answered, "and have you noticed that he only wears those new clothes when he goes out on Saturday afternoons? As soon as his mother is out sight, he hurries away. Regularly. I wonder where he goes?"

"I also wonder. Apart from the quality, cut and style change, he looks much the same as before. I should doubt whether anyone else in our estate has noticed anything."

No, nobody had.

As for the change in Eric's behaviour pattern, there was one other person who had noticed it. And that had been by chance. That was Mr Hargreaves. On one afternoon in August he had had business in the centre, and as he was near the Houses of Parliament, he suddenly saw Eric with a group of tourists. The guide was just explaining about Big Ben.

"May I join you?" asked Mr Hargreaves, patting Eric on the shoulder.

The boy went all red and directed a pair of anxious eyes at the deputy-head.

"I'm not really eavesdropping," he stammered with a red face.

Mr Hargreaves smiled and put a finger across his lips to indicate silence. Then they both stood and listened till the guide finished.

"Eric, that was very sensible to join the group to learn about Big Ben. I had no idea that you came to the centre of the town."

"Mr Hargreaves, sometimes I like to travel to different areas of London. It's so big. Till last Spring, I had no idea about it at all."

"I'm so glad you're exploring the city in which you live. I suggest that you go to the school library and get out a book on London. That way you can plan your journeys."

"Oh thank you for the suggestion, Mr Hargreaves, I'll do just that."

"I'm glad to have bumped into you this afternoon, Eric. Good bye for now. Enjoy the rest of the afternoon."

"Good bye, Mr Hargreaves."

As Mr Hargreaves walked away, he had a distinct feeling that Eric had gone out to town in secret from his parents. Good. The lad showed curiosity about life and places and he had started to find out about things in practice. This boded well. He would see to it that he occasionally suggested to the boy places which he should see. The youngster needed a rounded education apart from merely school-work.

Chapter 4

As Eric was growing, he became more and more aware of his miserable home-life. He was an unloved and unwanted child. His mother had become pregnant at the age of nineteen and that had necessitated a hasty marriage. The couple was very quarrelsome. They had frequent shouting matches and the vocabulary was unrepeatable. More often than not, their attention turned to Eric who then got the brunt of their fury.

Mr Flint was a dour type of man who was only interested in football and rugby. At the end of the week, on Fridays, he was regularly to be found in the pub from where he swayed home at closing time. Eric's mother never stopped talking. She went on and on relentlessly. Her interests in life were local gossip, the gutter press and bingo. She smoked like a trooper and kept gin bottles in her wardrobe. Food was what it was. Dinner time depended upon her return from various cleaning jobs. She gave herself airs and graces and pretended to be a Fine Lady. Had she but known it, the whole estate giggled behind her back. It was rumoured that there was more to her cleaning jobs than met the eye. Eric was mortified. On occasions, when she was in an alcoholic soppy mood, she would have Eric sit next to her while she caressed his hair and gave him the odd pat. It was terrible for the child who was in need of affection to see that his mother never did that when sober. Eric often cried himself to sleep.

By the time he boy was ten years old, he had started to wash the dishes in order to make sure that they were clean. He washed and ironed his own clothes. He kept his small room neat and tidy. His mother was contented because thus she has less to do.

Eric's savings depended upon his little earnings. He saved diligently and the sums mounted steadily. That was what enabled him to buy the second-hand clothes, added to the small sum his mother gave.

Under the covert guidance and help from Mr Hargreaves, Eric continued to blossom in school. To his parents it was of no interest at all.

It was a warm September day. The nearly twelve-year-old Eric had been to Kensington Gardens. It had been wonderful. Before setting back home, he decided to go into one of the smart cafes and order a pot of tea. That made him feel quite grown-up. He had hardly got settled with his tea when two smart ladies entered the café with loads of parcels and they sat at the table next to his.

"Georgina," said the dark-haired lady to the blonde one," we've got some splendid stuff. Your new two-piece is out of this world, and that negligee is to die for."

"I agree. I had not expected such success. But you did very well yourself in getting two pairs of heavenly high-heels. I am particularly taken by the light-grey suede ones with the white trimmings. Most unusual."

"After our coffees, shall we pop into one of the kitchen departments? I am in need of a fancy tray."

"No problem. Oh Lizzie, I wanted to ask you about that new Jazz quartet that you went to see. Are they good?"

"Yes, Georgina. They were excellent. I can thoroughly recommend them. Even your Tom might appreciate them in spite of his penchant for classical music."

"Lizzie, how are Lucius and Emma? Will you be taking them to a pantomime again this year?"

"Of course, I am. Now at seven and eight they will appreciate the humour in the pantomimes better. It is very funny when they use those dreadful working- class accents and expressions. They were five and six when I first took them, but they could not follow all of it at the time."

"Now that my Sarah has turned six, I think I'll give her a start with a pantomime, just like you did. To give her an idea what it feels like to be in a theatre."

"Do, Georgina. For the time being, the odd Pantomime is enough. Plus children's films. Mine like Walt Disney. When they are ten, an amusing theatre play might be good, and when they are twelve, I think that music should be added. By fourteen they should be introduced to operas, operettas and concerts. Carefully chosen, of course. That's when it starts to be fun for us parents as well."

"As we are on the subject of education, we must remember the museums and fine arts as well."

"Of course. However, before dragging them there, they've got to have a base. That base is the Good Book. That is why going to church and taking part in the Sunday School is so vital. Without a thorough knowledge of the Bible, how would they know what they are looking at? As for the museums, what I do once a month is to take Lucius and Emma to one section only and stay no longer than half an hour or so, after which it is the play park. This works wonders."

"Indeed, not to overdo it is the key. Look, Lizzie, we better hurry with our coffees and continue on our way."

Eric had been listening to the two women intensely. What he had heard had appalled him. He felt diminished into a sewer rat. It dawned on him in one fell swoop that fine clothes were not enough. No way. He felt hot under the collar. Thank heavens nobody knew how utterly shameful his life hitherto had been. He knew now that he was in a social abyss thanks to his parents. The shame of it was unbearable. A whole education was needed. Here he was, nearly twelve years old and he had visited no museums, no theatres, he knew nothing about music or art or literature, plus he had never opened a

Bible, the very book upon which his culture was based. And good heavens, he was bound to have one of those dreadful working-class accents of which he had been unaware till now. He was crying inwardly. He sat in the café, drinking his tea and his brain was furiously turning somersaults. A new program had to begin, a new orientation had to be started. He would change his life. He swore to himself right then and there in that café that he himself would not remain a moron, no, he would do whatever it took to lift himself up from that abyss to a position of honour. Mercifully he was still young enough to be able to catch up on education and learn everything needed.

The two women had left a newspaper on one of the chairs. Eric picked it up and turned to the entertainments section. He wanted to know what was playing in the theatres. He had just had the bright idea to take Katie to a show for her twelfth birthday. Oh yes, as from beginning of December, they were showing Dick Whittington at the Richmond Theatre. He had money saved and he would take Katie to see Dick Whittington. He was sure that her parents would give permission. Thank goodness for the money he had saved.

When Eric approached the Smith parents with the request to take Katie to Richmond Theatre, they were truly astonished. It was quite unheard of. From where on earth had Eric come to that idea? But they were delighted that their Katie would have a posh outing. Eric had bought expensive seats, on the sixth row in the front. He would remember this, their first outing, till the end of his days, and he wanted it to be perfect. He wore black trousers, his grey jacket and a cream shirt. His old winter-coat had to do but he had bought a fancy new scarf to spruce it up. Katie wore a pleated skirt with a new bright-blue twinset. Her mother had lent her a small silver pendant.

Katie's father gave Eric one whole pound "to get ice-creams with". That was more than generous, but Mr Smith had realised that it must have been very difficult for Eric to save up enough money for theatre tickets, and thus he wanted to help the boy by his over-generous ice-cream offer.

Both youngsters were most excited and they felt very posh indeed. It had been an unforgettable occasion. To be in a real theatre was a heady experience for Eric. During the interval they had their ice-creams. For both of them it had been more than a Very Special Occasion.

Chapter 5

At school, on the Monday after the "Lucius and Emma Episode", Mr Hargreaves got an inkling that some major changes were happening in the boy. As a result Mr Hargreaves paid more covert attention than ever. A new intensity had come to his eyes, a kind of determination. A week later the boy approached him at the end of the day when most people had gone home.

"Mr Hargreaves. The school library does not have a Bible."

"Good heavens, Eric. That is quite scandalous."

In Mr Hargreaves' mind it occurred that the school probably assumed that everyone had a Bible at home, and thus they had not thought of providing one.

"Should I go to the main library, Sir?" asked Eric.

"I have a very good solution to this, Eric," said Mr Hargreaves. "As I happen to have several Bibles in my home; I could give you a small one. It is more convenient to handle than the big ones, Yes, it would be your very own. In that way you can dip into it at home whenever you like. Otherwise, by all means, get a library card at the main library. It could be useful for the future. By the way, If I may suggest, you will find it the easiest if you read first Genesis, then Exodus and then jump to do the New

Testament. Afterwards to continue with the Old Testament."

"Thank you very much indeed, Mr Hargreaves, you are very kind. May I ask you another question?"

"Please do."

"Do I have one of those dreadful working-class accents?"

"Well, Eric, yes you do. How could you have anything other? However, you do pronounce your words properly, unlike some."

"What can I do about changing it?"

"You would need elocution lessons. But don't worry about that now. Later you will have opportunity to change it if you want to. What would help is if you listen carefully to the news readers on the radio and if you keep a little list of difficult words. Then come to me from time to time"

Mr Hargreaves watched Eric walk away. He felt like a question mark personified. Eric wanted to read the Bible! How had that come about? It was the best thing the boy could have done. Apart from the spiritual guidance, it would teach the boy what his culture, and that of his country, was based upon. Had somebody said something? But who? The boy and his parents did not attend church. Mr Hargreaves burned with curiosity.

The reason he had suggested giving Eric a small Bible, was because most probably the boy would not want his parents to know. The young one had realised that anything he undertook to do or to learn had to be kept secret from his parents. Otherwise they would step upon any of his efforts. What a horrible way to live! The fact that Eric would be reading the Bible was bound to influence him thoroughly. Yes, the future would show that the power of the Bible to convert was there. Eric did become a believer, and later in life he would join the church.

He, Mr Hargreaves, would point the boy towards various volumes that would help his general knowledge. The boy wanted to know, to find out, to instruct himself. It was like sweet honey to Mr Hargreaves.

Eric started a gruelling program. But for him it was no heavy weight because it was the way that would provide him with the wings with which to fly into the future. It was the fuel for his little plane of life so that it could reach its destination. It was also the runway from which to fly. His parents should have provided it for him, but in his case he had to build it himself. He was fascinated by it all. Life with knowledge was worth living. To be cooped up in ignorance was death. He read the Bible steadily and it opened up his mind and his spirit. He set out to find out about other things as well, such as painters, composers and literature. When his parents were not at home, he listened to classical music on the radio. On his outings, now he visited churches and museums and galleries. All of these activities he kept a great secret, even from his best friend

Katie. For the time being, the secrecy was imperative because it was only by small steps at a time that he advanced. Each step made him realise how utterly uneducated he was. This he could not divulge to anyone else as he was unable to divulge it to himself. He did not want anyone to know how like a sewer rat he felt. Once he was beginning to see daylight, he might tell Katie something.

There were, however, two people who knew what Eric was up to. One was Mr Hargreaves whom Eric had encountered once in St Paul's Cathedral and another time in the National Gallery. The other was Mr Patel, who had once seen Eric at the V&A Museum when he had been taking his family around. As soon as Eric had seen the Patels, he had run to hide. Mr Patel realised that Eric did not wish anyone to know about his outings. Indeed, mused Mr Patel, Eric's parents would have beaten the lad black and blue had they known that their son frequented places like the V&A.

He, Mr Patel, took his family regularly to museums and galleries in order to give them the best education there was. He did not wish any member of his family to be regarded as "some stupid Indian". The Flint parents, unfortunately, were the opposite.

Chapter 6

When Eric turned thirteen, he was hit by puberty. His voice broke and went up and down. His body started to react in a manner that he could not control. Like the other boys who were entering puberty, he started to avoid girls. Katie could not understand why her former "buddy" now avoided her and no longer came to collect her to play. Katie's parents explained to her that at that age it was the normal course of things. It would last three or four years and then there would be a change. When Katie, at the age of fourteen got her period, she began to understand nature.

Eric was with groups of boys. They were all mainly interested in sports. Rugby left Eric cold, but he was keen on football and also gymnastics. He was a member of a gymnastics team. Car-racing he found fascinating, mainly because it was considered to be an elite sport, just look at the life-styles of the racing drivers! Another interest with the boys was cards. As Eric excelled at school in maths, physics and languages, it was his grasp of numbers and how they worked that made him an excellent card player. He liked cards, any card games, and he had a real sense for them. He was good at reading body language and he enjoyed taking calculated risks.

What was particularly important was that his intelligence dictated to him that winning too often would make him unpopular. Thus his aim was to control the games without the others having any inkling thereof. He engineered that Jack and Peter became the main kings of the games. As for himself, his steady losses were invariably small, but his infrequent winnings were large. Due to the occasional stroke of luck, of course. In this way he had a fairly steady income in secret.

In the winter when Eric turned fifteen, his frustrations with his life were taking a certain toll on him. His grades dropped. He discovered beer with the other boys. It was some of the new boys among the card players who had instigated the beer. They also wanted the stakes at play to go higher. The new boys were slightly older and had left school already. Some of the boys started to owe money to these older ones.

"Eric," said Timmy one day," Can I ask you for help? I owe a full fiver to couple of these guys. I don't know what to do. I only have three pounds."

"How dreadful, Timmy. Have you asked anyone for a loan?"

"No, not yet. I wouldn't know who to ask."

"Then don't. I'll lend you the two pounds but you must not tell anyone who you got it from. If, and I mean if you can pay me back someday, fine. If you can't, consider it an early birthday present."

"Eric. You are a real pal! I owe you one."

"You don't owe me anything," laughed Eric, "just don't get into debt again.

Sometime later Jack got into trouble. He appeared in school with a black eye. He had lost in the card games, and the big boys wanted their money. A nasty streak had slithered into the formerly harmless games. The older boys knew full well that the younger ones would not have the money to pay them.

This brought the first steps of petty thieving. The older boys suggested some dishonest methods. Small pilfering thus became the preferred method of raising money among some of the boys. Why not join them, it was all extra income? Even Eric had been influenced by the bigger sums that were being played with. He gained more steadily though seemingly he was forever losing small sums. He was not considered to be a danger. With the added money, he began to want some expensive items. Everyone seemed to be pilfering, so why should not he? The situation began to grow like mushrooms. At a certain stage the headmaster announced to the whole school that a number of items had gone missing. He urged their return so that he need not inform the police about it.

Mr Hargreaves had been vigilant. He had noticed the dip in Eric's work and he had looked with a jaundiced eye at the type of boys Eric was mixing with. The boy was at a stage where he was floundering. He would have to be guided back to form. What had prompted the address by the headmaster was the fact that the wrist-watch of one of the masters had disappeared, and also an expensive pen of another had gone missing. During that address, Mr Hargreaves had observed a smug look on Eric's face.

Alarm bells rang in Mr Hargreaves' head. The boy must be involved. That had to be stopped before it all got too serious. He would see if he could sleuth out the truth. The following Saturday afternoon Mr Hargreaves followed Eric to town. The boy went to an Evensong at Westminster Abbey. Once the lad was seated in the choir stalls, he went to join him and pretended pleasant surprise. Afterwards Mr Hargreaves invited Eric to a café for some tea and cakes. As the wily teacher had guessed, it was Eric who had taken the master's watch. There it gleamed, on the boy's wrist. He could only wear it out of school.

"Eric," said Mr Hargreaves," I see that you are wearing Mr Turnbull's watch."

Eric went pale. A pair of anxious eyes looked up at Mr Hargreaves.

"Dear Eric. I'm not going to turn you in. I can only hope that you will return it to the staff-room. You are the star pupil of this school, and I have been following with great pride your advances in your education. Armed with knowledge, your intelligent brain will make you fly into success. A splendid future awaits you. It will be a long road, but it will be worth it.

However, if you are involved in petty pilfering, when the law gets on to it, you will get a record. An indelible one at that. A brush with the law will prevent you from advancing in the future. You are playing your entire future against a watch. Is it worth it?"

"Thank you, Sir, for putting me right. I am so sorry about it. You are right. It is good to know that my future matters to someone. I am so grateful for your caring words. What shall I do?"

"Give me the watch, and I will slip it onto Mr Turnbull's desk. He will be pleased to have it back, and nothing further will follow. None of the masters wants the law in."

"Here you are, Mr Hargreaves," said Eric, passing him the watch. "I will no longer follow that set of boys, I have learned a lesson."

"May I bother you with just one more matter? It has come to my attention that you boys have discovered beer. Cigarettes as well, no doubt. When one lives in very difficult family circumstances, it is true that the odd beer too many can relieve the immediate distress. But it does not remove the problem.

When you grow up, if you feel the need to drink, it will be to your benefit if you did so only in your own privacy. A drunk puts himself into a vulnerable position. Various home-truths can leak out. Not good. No swaying in pubs or in parties. Do you understand what I am saying, Eric?"

"I do, Sir. By the "home-truths" you mean my horrible family life. You are quite right, that truth must never come out in the future. If I am to make it in the future, my past must be dead and buried. And I must study properly. I am sorry that my grades have dipped lately. I will put it right."

"I am so glad that you will turn over a new leaf, Eric, I am in the background and I'll help you in any way I can. Very discreetly, as you already know. Now eat up that cake. I think it is time for you to hurry home."

"Oh yes, indeed. Thank you again, Sir. Good bye."

"Good bye, Eric."

Chapter 7

In the Spring of 1961, when Eric and his friends were fifteen, Helen's mother, Mrs Brown, organised a dancing course at the council. She had persuaded many parents that it was a good thing and as a result most parents of Eric's year and the year above enrolled their youngsters into the course. Nandita's parents were among the exceptions. Her parents felt that it was not the right thing for young Indian girl to attend. Nandita had been furious and had felt that it was not fair. Especially as she would have been a shining star thanks to her training in Indian classical dance. But her parents had been adamant. There were boys there and western dance meant that a boy would hold a girl by the waist.

"My parents are being horrid, Katie, by not letting me join the dance course!" she raged to Katie.

"Why not? Almost everyone is going."

"It's this thing about boys being there."

"What does that matter? They're there also at school."

"Ah, but my parents say that the boys will be touching the girls by the waist," explained Nandita, "that is what my parents won't allow. If I attend the course, they won't be able to find me a husband."

"How annoying for you. Do you have to marry someone your parents choose?"

"It is customary in India that the parents find a spouse."

"How ghastly. But you are not in India. Maybe you could find someone yourself. You are very pretty," said Katie, looking admiringly at her friend.

"How am I going to find anybody when I am not allowed to go out anywhere?"

"Well, that is a problem," said Katie.

It had been the dancing class that had brought Katie and Eric back together. The worst turmoils of their changing bodies had been overcome by then and a natural interest for the opposite sex had set in.

Katie had started to daydream about Eric. He had now begun to look like the handsome man he was to become. At fifteen he was five foot eight inches tall and he would grow to reach six foot one. The down on his upper lip and chin had begun to turn into hairs, and he had started to shave. He hated the stubble and wanted to avoid a "shadow" which his beard growth gave as it was two shades darker than his blond hair. His love of gymnastics had developed his muscles and he had a fine masculine shape with broad shoulders. Katie's eyes followed him covertly everywhere, and she tried to be where he was.

Eric had noticed Katie's interest in him. He was mightily pleased because he fully reciprocated her sentiments. But for the time being he did not show his feelings too overtly to her. It was mainly manifested during the times the two of them danced together. He would hold her slightly closer than necessary, and occasionally he let his head touch her hair. The odd squeeze of hand also spoke volumes. Their nearness to each other was so important that they did not speak, their bodies and their instincts relayed the messages of affection. On the odd time Katie would sigh, give a little smile and whisper, "Eric."

Katie was aware that most girls were sweet on Eric. In fact there were no fewer than five other contestants for his attentions. He was charming to them all, but Katie knew that he was only interested in her. Thank heavens she was very pretty. She had an oval face, flawless skin, large grey eyes with thick lashes and long, luxurious light-brown hair. She was five foot six in height and had small hands and feet. Her body had developed curves where curves should be. She sensed that Eric was not indifferent to her.

"Oh, Eric. Kiss me. Kiss me," she repeated in her mind.

It had been at Helen's sixteenth birthday party that Eric had finally kissed her. What bliss. It was as if a fire had been lit inside her. Her whole body yearned for Eric. From then on he asked her out at the week-ends. They went for walks and sometimes to the cinema. Eric always got tickets at the very back so that he could kiss her in peace. They were two playful puppies.

"Oh Eric. Do you think we could have an evening alone?" Katie had sighed, hugging him as closely as she could. At her words she could feel him tremble.

"Eric, I want to be all your own," Katie continued.

"If you are sure, then I'll arrange it," he said, smiling at her dreamily.

He did indeed arrange it. Nandita's sixteenth birthday party provided the ideal opportunity. They planned that Katie was to go to the party briefly and leave after an hour, pretending to be unwell. Then she was to come to his flat. Eric would be there alone as his parents were visiting some relatives overnight. A type of Christmas visit, and they had no wish to pay for Eric's rail fare. That would leave the youngsters alone till midnight, the hour when the party officially ended.

The planning thereof made Eric somewhat nervous. He had gathered that Katie might be keen to go further. That meant they might end up in bed. Eric certainly wished for it fervently, but would under no circumstances push his advantage. For he truly loved Katie. She meant the world to him. Also, his knowledge about such matters was restricted to the talk among the boys. That was no good. He better inform himself upon the subject. Thus he went to the library and hunted under the medical section for any information on human sexuality. He found a volume and then proceeded to peruse it in the library. No way would he take out a book of that ilk. Somebody might see it and then the fat would be in the fire. A good job that he had read the book. There were practical issues to be considered. A pregnancy had to be avoided at all costs. More ruin was not to be added to two already ruined lives. He'd not go to any of the local chemists, no, he'd go to town to get the necessary. He went to Soho where he had no embarrassment about his purchase, only a knowing wink from the sales assistant.

On the day of the party, Katie was at Eric's place by eight o'clock. Eric had cleaned the whole flat, the lights were low, and a bottle of wine was on the table as well as some peanuts and chocolates. He had not got the cheapest bottle, no, he had wanted quality. Thus he had given a reasonable sum to Timmy's cousin who was twenty-three, and thus would be able to buy it.

"Oh Eric, this looks lovely," smiled Katie, "fancy you getting a bottle of wine! And my favourite chocolates. You are a wizard."

"Katie darling, you are so special to me," said Eric and then he embraced and kissed her.

"Now let me pour the wine for us," he said.

Katie was bursting with happiness.

"How was the party?" asked Eric.

"I could hardly wait to get out of there," replied Katie, "but the Patels had done wonders with their lounge, that is, their tailoring room. It had been cleared of most of the stuff and lovely Indian tit-bits were on offer. Nandita was dressed in a new pale-green Sari and she wore some gold jewellery.

She looked lovely. She was most disappointed when I left. Never mind."

"Let's dance, Katie. I have some records of Ricky Nelson, Pat Boone, the Everly Brothers and Buddy Holly."

He knew that Katie loved to dance. So did he. He had an excellent sense of co-ordination plus rhythm and thus was a very good dancer. They were both in bliss. He put on first the faster pieces and then started on the slower ones. He held Katie closer and closer. From time to time he stopped in order to kiss her. They refilled their wine glasses.

"Katie, I love you. I have always loved you."

"Eric, I love you too. I only want you."

"Katie, I would so like to be even closer to you. To make love."

"Oh yes. I want that too. I want to be yours completely."

"Darling, my darling, let's go into the bedroom."

Katie took off her shoes, as did he. Then she took off her dress. Eric took off his shirt. Partially clad they approached one another. They embraced. Eric's hands were caressing her breasts. It felt wonderful for both. Then they divested themselves of the rest of their clothing, sat upon the bed and caressed one another.

"Are you sure?" whispered Eric.

"More than sure. I love you, Eric."

The wonder of being together engulfed them. To Eric, Katie's skin was softer that the softest silk. Her tresses were like a cascading waterfall. Her body was sweet beyond belief. He realised how enticing a female body could be. As Katie lay down to recline and receive him, both their eyes were locked into each other's and an intense joy and desire filled them both.

For Eric the experience had been earth-shattering. The power of sex really hit his senses. But what was more and what elevated the situation into the sublime was the fact that he was making love to the girl he truly loved. It was a union of both body and mind. The same was true for Katie. She did not feel that they were doing anything wrong, never mind that society frowned on pre-marital sex. She was now his, she would always be his, till the end of time.

They lay together for quite a while quietly, just feeling the other's presence. Eventually they dressed again, filled the last glasses and just sat there on the sofa, holding hands. There was no need for conversation. They knew they loved one other.

Thus started the romance between Katie and Eric. They went out regularly and made love when they could. Where there is a will, there is a way. It was usually at his place on a Saturday afternoon because his parents were out like a clockwork, his father to a football or a rugby match, his mother to play bingo. However, they never stayed for long in case his parents came back early. On Saturday evenings they went to the cinema or to dance. Both sets of parents seemed pleased with their friendship. They felt that theirs was a budding couple.

As Saturdays were now taken up by Katie, Eric went on his cultural expeditions on Sundays. He thought it would be good if he included her in them as well, so every second Sunday he asked if she would like to come with him. Ever since he had turned sixteen, his parents were not worried where he was or what times he kept. As long as they did not have to shell out any money in his direction, they were content.

Thus Eric took Katie to a sung mass at a fine church or a visit to a museum. He shone as a guide, and she was amazed at how much he knew.

"Katie, let me take you out to town next Sunday."

"Super. Where shall we go?"

"I want this, our first big outing, to be special so I thought we'd go to see Buckingham palace so you can see where the Queen lives. But I don't want it to be talked about on the estate."

"Understood."

The trip had been a success. Katie had been impressed by the magnitude of the palace. They giggled when Eric said that the first time he had seen it, he had thought that they needed bicycles in the Palace.

"Or at least all the staff on roller skates!" chuckled Eric.

"It is just as well that the Queen cannot hear you," smiled Katie.

Sometime later he had suggested the British Museum. However, after a while Katie had yawned and said,

"We've been here now for well over an hour. Why don't we go and have some tea? Then head homewards. This place has too much stuff for me."

They had done so and Eric had made a mental note not to stretch outings with Katie beyond an hour.

Another outing had been to St Bride's church. The choir there was renowned. The acoustics were superb. That was not a true success because Katie, who had not been brought up with any religion, found it rather alien. She was bored, and it showed. She felt that it went on forever.

"The choir was wonderful, wasn't it, Katie?"

"If you say so."

It left Eric somewhat deflated, but he understood that he would have to be patient and introduce Katie even more slowly to his world.

When he had taken her to the National Gallery, it had been painful to watch how she had no idea about the paintings. She really did not know what she was looking at. Well, Eric did not feel that it was his place to suggest some Bible study to her. He began to feel that he would have to concede defeat as to their cultural outings together. What a pity.

However, he could not stand shops. His next suggestion had been to go to Westminster Abbey, but Katie had said that she wanted to go to the shops in Kensington High Street. She had been in bliss, and Eric had patiently dragged his bones from shop to shop. He had found it gruesome. The only respite he got was from the toy departments. He found those truly riveting. What a wonder world they were. Oh, if only he had had some of those toys when he was small!

The crowning horror had come when Katie had lingered in one of the women's lingerie departments. Quite unnecessarily, thought Eric. He had felt acutely embarrassed there. The worst had been when a smartly dressed middle-aged man had spoken to Katie.

"Ah, madam, I see that you are admiring our negligee collection. I can help you there if you have any questions. I am the buyer-in for ladies' lingerie. What in particular has taken your fancy?"

"I like the cream ones with the black lace. They are heavenly, but also expensive."

"They are indeed rather splendid. They are quality goods and thus are not cheap. Is the young man your husband by any chance? Do bring him to take a look."

"We are actually not married," said Katie quite unnecessarily.

"That is no problem. You would look most fetching in this."

Eric fled down the shop floor with Katie following.

"That was horrible," he panted.

"Don't be so uptight. The man was only trying to be helpful."

"I don't think I can cope with any lingerie departments. You'll have to go to those with your girlfriends.

"All right. All right. I did not think that you were such a prude," giggled Katie.

"Well, I am and that's that. Now let's go and have some tea."

What a surprise Katie got when she opened up her Christmas present form Eric and found in it the wonderful cream negligee with the black lace and a nightdress to go with it. Katie was over the moon.

Chapter 8

When school finished, Eric came out with straight
A's in all of his three A-levels. He had done
History, French and Mathematics. His teachers had
expected no less as he had passed all his six O-
levels with straight A's. The headmaster had said to
his parents that their son was university material,
but hey had been against the idea. On no account
would they undertake any expenses because of Eric.

"You are working class," they had said, "and
working class you will stay."

Eric had been appalled. His parents did not
want to give him any chances at all! And that he
should contribute to the finances if he stayed at
home! As if he would stay there. Anywhere but. He
would definitely leave the moment his school was
over. He had been planning for it during the last
eighteen months of school. Being seventeen he had
been able to take on a portering job at a hospital on
Sunday afternoons from three till eight. It paid the
rate of double time because of the Sunday. That
money he put into his Post Office savings account
where it grew into a tidy sum. His parents had no
idea what he was doing on Sundays. They assumed
he was busy with some gangs of boys. Or with
Katie. It did not matter to them.

A month before his school ended, Eric went
to look for a job and a cheap bedsit to rent. He

chose Hammersmith as the area to go for because of its good transport connections. The area was not too distant from the centre, yet it was cheap. He found a small bedsit in King Street with a small kitchenette and a shower room/WC. Cheap and unfurnished with peeling paint. Luckily the block had central heating. At the same time he found a job at an Estate Agents, only minutes away. Good.

He had asked Katie's parents if they could lend him a few items for a short period of time. He needed a mattress, some bedding and some kitchenware. They had been happy to supply him with that. The mattress was only an old padded blanket, but it did not matter to the young man. It was end of July, high summer, and the weather was sunny. Good for drying paint. After he had cleaned the place thoroughly, he set to paint and to decorate it. And to do repairs where necessary. He had to pay a plumber to unblock the shower and the kitchen plughole plus renew the taps and the shower. The toilet mechanism was also renewed.

Katie came to help him whenever she could. They both enjoyed making the place nice. As a colour for the living room Eric had chosen pale yellow in order to get the feeling of some sunshine and for the kitchenette and for the shower room he had chosen a muted pink. His worldly possessions were in three large cardboard boxes.

Another surprise awaited Katie.

"Darling," said Eric one day, "I've something important to tell you. I have approached the local priest here and he will give me some lessons in catechism, and later I shall be baptised, confirmed by the bishop and join the church."

"Why? What on earth for?" Katie was a question mark.

"When I was twelve, Mr Hargreaves gave me a small Bible, which I have been reading ever since. In secret from my parents, of course. It has shown me the way. I am ready to join the church. Would you like to know more about it and perhaps join with me?"

"What good would that do? Why are you mixing yourself with all that mumbo-jumbo?"

"It is not mumbo-jumbo. I need a spiritual life, Katie. Don't you sometimes wonder about life? Why are we here, and so on? What happens when we die?"

"Definitely not. When we die, we die. We are dead meat. We must hope for as long a life as possible. Does it matter why we are here? I know that I am here to love you. Our togetherness has meaning for me."

"For me this is an important step. As you know, I like going to churches. And I've always enjoyed the Evensong. It has taught me a lot."

"You can join the church if you like. But please don't start to drag me to services. It is not for me."

"I won't drag you to anything you don't want. I can only suggest. But now let's get on with the painting."

When the painting was dry he fixed two stout hooks at either end of the room on which he could put a thick cord to hang his clothes on their hangers until such time as he would have obtained a wardrobe. The same cord would serve as clothes line for his laundry. It was the only solution. Not too much at a time would keep the room from getting damp. He was also getting out books from the library on antique period furniture. As he had over the years enjoyed going to look at antiques of all descriptions, including furniture, he now wanted something really nice for his little home.

At the beginning of September he made his first purchase, an antique mahogany double bed with beautiful carvings. It was a superb item, a connoisseur's delight. Eric had got for a song from a junk shop in West Ealing. He got a new mattress and bedding. Proper wool blankets and a real eiderdown. At last he would be able to sleep properly. The ironing board plus iron came at the same time as he needed them to keep his clothes neat for his job. Then followed a small round Regency table with two rosewood chairs, all from the same junk shop. After that came the kitchen necessities so that he could return to Mr and Mrs Smith what they had lent him. As curtains he used newspaper stuck to the windows.

For his job he had bought two good quality suits, one dark grey and one blue. Two white shirts and two cream ones followed as did two pairs of

Church's black shoes. Those had come with a cost. But he needed to be smart.

By the beginning of October he had found a wardrobe and a writing desk. He bought nothing unnecessary, but when he bought something, it had to be quality and precisely what he wanted.

In September Katie started at the Secretarial College. Her parents had put money by for her further education. During that study year she would live at home with her parents and when she got a job, then she'd move out to rent a room in shared digs. That was what young people did in those days. She was to look for a husband if she found herself unable to hook Eric. That was what her parents had indicated. As if she'd want anyone else ever! Unthinkable.

When Eric had first moved to King Street, Katie had been horrified by the frugality of his bedsit. However, when it was finished by Christmas, the bedsit of early days was unrecognisable. The big change had come when he had had sumptuous light-green brocade curtains made with a bedspread to match. There were also two small early Victorian armchairs upholstered in pale green velvet. In between was a pink marble table. There was a crystal ceiling lamp and a Tiffany lamp on the writing desk. Any china he bought was only for two people, but all of it was special: cut crystal and Wedgewood.

For Eric this process had been primordial. When he got in and closed the door, he could forget Southall, his portering job and the Estate Agents. He was in the type of world he wanted to be in. Katie purred together with him. She loved his surroundings, they were so Eric. Total opposite from Southall.

His first guest, for a Christmas drink, had been Mr Hargreaves. The old deputy-head had been very pleased that Eric had kept in touch with him. So, the young man had chosen Hammersmith to live in. Not a smart area, but practical because of its relatively close location to central London. Mr Hargreaves was boiling with curiosity. Hopefully all was well.

The door opened and a smartly dressed Eric stood there.

"Good evening, Mr Hargreaves, it is a great pleasure for me that you were able to come. Please step in."

"Good evening, Eric. Thank you for remembering me."

Then he stopped to take in his surroundings while Eric helped him out of his coat.

"My! Your place is beautiful. So stylish and elegant. You have an excellent taste in antiques. This is another world from King Street."

"I am glad you like it. I feel relaxed here in my surroundings. I have worked hard to be able to achieve this, and I'm glad I've succeeded. Now, Mr

Hargreaves, what can I offer you to drink? I have a good Madeira or a single malt whisky or some orange juice if you prefer. There are also walnuts."

"I am tempted by the Single Malt."

The two men settled themselves in the Victorian armchairs.

"May I ask what you are doing now, Eric?"

"Since August I have been working at an Estate Agents just round the corner. It pays reasonably, and I also get commission. And on Sundays I continue my portering job at the hospital which I started while still at school, as you know. It has been invaluable."

"I am glad that you have settled so well. I see Katie sometimes and she talks about you."

"You mean that Katie and I are a couple?"

"Well, I ..."

"Don't worry, Mr Hargreaves, you have always known that Katie and I have been close. And yes, we are a couple. At my age, with no career or future to offer, I cannot ask anyone to marry me. I would on no account put my future wife to suffer any hardships. Without sufficient funds, marriages can shatter."

"Dear Eric. Those are wise words. It is for a man to first settle himself before he can undertake the burden of family life."

"I am not yet sure where I want to go. At this moment my two jobs are only a springing board. I need to get some funds behind me. Apart from taking Katie out, I am not spending on anything. Can I top up your glass, Mr Hargreaves?"

"Yes, please. It is a joy to drink such a good malt. There is something I have been wanting to ask you, Eric, but you don't have to answer if you don't want to."

"Please go ahead and ask."

"Remember that time when you came to tell me that the school library had no Bible. What had brought you to ask for it?"

"Oh, it was the story about Lucius and Emma. Let me tell you the details and the results that that tea-time at the cafe had."

Eric told the story about the two lady shoppers and what they had been talking about. How it had galvanised himself into action and how from then on he had started to really educate himself. He also told how he had slowly become a believer through reading the Bible and the moment he had left home he had approached a priest who had helped him and had got him baptised and confirmed into the C of E. Mr Hargreaves was smiling and nodding his head in approval.

"I am eternally grateful to you, Sir, for your help as regards the pilfered watch. It was a complete revelation to me that there was actually somebody who cared about me. Who was interested in me and my life. Who had been secretly helping me all the along. The warmth of it enveloped me, and I became changed. Also let me tell you that I have found out about elocution lessons and have enrolled myself as from January in a course."

"Dear Eric, you give me great joy by your successes. You have stamina and courage. Also I am glad that you have your childhood love to stand by you."

"I am wondering where I should aim my future to be."

"For a little while, why not stick with the Estate Agents for perhaps a year or so, and at the same time start to look into different possibilities. I have a suggestion that you could look into."

"Do tell me."

"Why don't you find out whether you could get into the Diplomatic Service? It won't be easy, but if you can make it, then you can have a truly glorious career. And one which would suit your personality down to the ground."

"What a wonderful suggestion. Now, may I tempt you into a third glass of malt?"

"Well, I may as well. But then I must be on my way. Before I go, I would want to give you a present. Please open it after I have gone."

The two chatted for a while, and then Mr Hargreaves got up to go.

"Will you keep me posted as to how your life goes, Eric? Some news from time to time would give me such pleasure."

"Of course I shall, Mr Hargreaves."

When Mr Hargreaves had gone, Eric opened the present. It was an expensive Parker pen. He was delighted. Foxy old Mr Hargreaves had known exactly what Eric would really like. Bless the old man.

Chapter 9

Eric mused about Mr Hargreaves' suggestion. During the months at the Estate Agents it had become clear to him that there was no future career in it for him. He made enquiries about the Diplomatic Service. There were two main streams of entry: the top stream, the "A" stream, for outstanding university graduates who would start at a higher level and then there was the lower stream, the "B" stream, which started at grade 9, for less brilliant candidates who would start at a more junior level. Then there was the possibility of starting at rock bottom as a clerk. Those without degrees could start at the rock bottom. However, it seemed that anyone had the possibility to climb to the top if he showed aptitude. He would have to start at the bottom and hope that in the long run what stream you entered in would make no difference.

By the autumn he had made up his mind to apply. For his level there were examinations in March every year. There would be a comprehensive written test lasting a whole day and if that went well, then it would be followed by a later interview. That would leave Eric seven months in which to cram himself with the type of knowledge the Foreign Office would be requiring. He would prepare himself with more detailed knowledge on Britain after the war. He followed the daily news like a hawk. He listened to discussions on the radio.

All was sure to turn out to be helpful, but he had to prepare himself for a whole host of unexpected questions as well.

He would tell Katie very little about it till it was in the bag. Yes, Katie. He had to consider what he was going to do as regarded her. His hitherto uncomplicated thoughts about her suddenly began to blur. Why on earth was that? Her sunny disposition did him so much good. He himself was prone to dark and despairing moods. She had the knack of making his "chest feathers swell up with pride". She understood him, she fulfilled his needs. He was aware that Katie was dreaming of marriage with him, but that thought did not fill him with joy. It should have, but it did not. This he kept well hidden from her.

He had done well in the written examination. Now he had to wait for the interview at the end of May. He felt very nervous. It was a Friday and on Saturday lunch-time Katie would come as usual. He had tonight free. Somehow his footsteps led him to the Off Licence. He got a bottle of whisky. Upon his return he opened it up at once and poured himself a good portion. He settled himself into one armchair broodily. Why were his parents suddenly in his mind? Any thoughts about the estate made him want to vomit. His dark mood got darker and darker. He poured another triple portion. He knew that he should make himself read something in order to change his thoughts, but somehow he had no energy for that. All that mattered was the bottle.

Then suddenly he heard the key in the door. It was Katie.

"Darling, somehow I just could not wait till tomorrow. So I came this evening. You look strange. What is going on?"

Eric was truly annoyed that Katie had appeared without telling him first. He had wanted his privacy – and now the girl was there!

"I am drinking. I hate that Shithall! It has blighted my entire childhood. Shit- Shit- Shithall…"

"Good heavens, Eric. How much have you already had?"

"As much as I want, and I want more."

Eric slurred his words slightly as he poured another big portion for himself.

"Drink never solved anything…."Katie began.

"Oh shut up. It is now solving my problem. No, you are not having any of that bottle! If you want a drink, get yourself a beer from the fridge."

"You don't have to be so rude. You know from your own parents that…" she got no further.

"You bloody leave my parents out of this. How dare you mention them?! They have ruined my life. I hate them, I hate Shithall, I hate everything…"

Suddenly Eric burst into tears. Tears of rage and frustration and disappointment. The tears were as much a surprise for him as they were for Katie. Eric was overwrought.

"Darling Eric, you are right. I'll pour you another one. But surely there is enough in a bottle for me to have some also? Don' forget, I too come from Shithall."

"All right, sobbed Eric, "you are a fellow sufferer. Come here and hold me."

Katie went to embrace him. She let him wail till he calmed down. Then she helped him into the bathroom and then to bed.

It was the first of such incidents that Katie would witness over the years. She understood that from time to time, Eric needed to drink himself silly when something triggered thoughts of Southall. He never drank much in public. He heeded the words of Mr Hargreaves about home-truths leaking out.

The next morning Eric woke with a hang-over. He drank several cups of tea with honey and ate a piece of bread. By midday he was feeling fine and both he and Katie had a nice time. Neither mentioned the night before. That night they went dancing. As was their routine. Every two weeks Eric took Katie either to a cinema or to dancing.

May had come and gone and the interview had been done. He was unable to guess whether he had passed or not. His gut feeling was that it had gone well. And so it was to prove. In June he got the results. Yes, he had been accepted at the clerical level and he was to start at the registry in September

65

as a grade 10. Eric got the news on a Tuesday. He was glad that he had a few days to digest these news before seeing Katie. She would be delighted for him, that was for sure, but it was bound to produce an expectant type of look in her eyes, a look that he knew all too well. It was that of an expectant bride! It made Eric cringe and feel guilty.

When Katie came on the Saturday, he greeted her with a song.

"I'm taking you for a meal today. I've passed the exam, my love," sang Eric to the tune of the Teddy Bears' Picnic. He was jubilant.

"Congratulations. I knew you'd pass. You were quite unnecessarily worrying about being a "greenhorn". This is a great relief. I've noticed that since March you've lost weight. It's the stress. When do you start?"

"In September. If I do well at the job, then after about two years I will be able to take the crucial test to see whether I qualify as a grade nine. After that it should be plain sailing."

Katie was doing some mental arithmetic. They were now in June. Eric would start in September. Then, most annoyingly, there would be another two years wait till Eric would obtain the desired grade 9 and feel that he was now launched in life. She knew that he would not propose till he had reached that stage. She sighed. It meant another two and a half years of waiting!

Chapter 10

In September 1967, the nearly twenty-one year old Eric started his job at the Foreign Office. The salary was much lower than what he had earned at the Estate Agents. There the commissions had helped and Eric had managed very well because of his personality. He had been wise enough to build up a nest -egg. He would keep his portering job for a little extra. He was not even on a proper payroll there but somehow under the general portering as a part-timer. He was paid weekly in cash. For him this job was worth its weight in gold. There was usually very little to do, and he got most of his reading done there.

When he started his job at the Foreign Office Katie had been most excited. She was so proud of him. To Mr Hargreaves Eric penned a letter about his success, thanking him for the suggestion he had made.

When Eric started at the Foreign Office, he found himself in a different world. A world totally new to him. Thank heavens he had the two decent suits, in fact he would need some more. With horror he realised that he still had some remnants of the working-class accent in spite of the elocution lessons, however, to a much lesser degree than before. How dreadful. That would have to be corrected with more lessons. He needed to pay real attention to his pronunciation. Otherwise he would show that he was working-class. There was a book on etiquette (the Foreign Office, in its wisdom, made sure that their young diplomats knew how to behave), and he realised that he would have to cram that information into himself as well. It was what one was taught at home in society. Knowledge and accents were not sufficient to raise one up. Manners had to be learned. If someone held their knife and fork in an incorrect manner, nobody would comment, but that person would not be getting a second invitation. The worst was that they would not know why.

As regarded his parents, he had said that his father was employed by the Post, making it sound as if the man was in a senior position there. Two other new entrants were also in the Registry. They came from middle class families and Eric felt that he was the one and only low class entrant ever. All was well as long as nobody knew, and he would see to it that nobody ever would.

He had thought that his French was good. Now he realised that it would have to be bettered seriously. He enrolled himself into a Foreign Office course (those were available in all languages and they were excellent) and started to make headway. He liked the French language and what he knew of Paris had always made him wish to see that magnificent city one day. In fact he fervently hoped for a posting there in the future.

The large registry was pleasant. The head of the registry, Richard Bracknell (known as The Handbag behind his back) was a kind and patient man. He explained to Eric what the job would entail. The letters that were sent to the relevant desk officers from the countries they had been assigned to look after were then sent to the registry. In the registry these letters were to be read and then a short synopsis was to be written on the covering paper folder (or "jacket", as it was called), a heading was to be given, and then the jacket and the paper were to be sent back to the desk officer for further action. When the paper had been finished with, it was to be archived in the relevant file. In the first instance it felt like a very cumbersome and work-intensive way of doing things, but after a while it became obvious as to why the method was so very practical. The skill of the officer could be seen in the synopsis of the content.

Another new entrant at grade ten was Horace Grant, who in spite of coming from Oxford, started at grade ten. He had come out of Oxford with a fourth in Geography! He had wanted to have fun in Oxford and had succeeded in his quest. He had spent his time eternally rowing and was considered a star. The actual fact had been that the board who were doing the sifting out of the candidates, had found him intriguing, and he had done well in the exams. Also, what weighed heavily in the scales was the fact that Horace was fluent in Mandarin. He himself suspected as much. The Foreign Office needed Chinese speakers. When Horace was a child, his parents had been for nearly eight years in Hong Kong. From the age of five to eight, He had been put into a Chinese school. He had learned both Mandarin and the colloquial Cantonese. He had also been taught how to write Chinese! At the age of eight, his parents had put him into the English school but had kept a special Chinese tutor for him in order for him to continue his proficiency in Mandarin.

Eric and Horace became great pals. They loved to crack jokes together and were very good at inventing office jokes where The Handbag was at the butt of their humour. They both adored their boss. Horace was one of the few who got invited to Eric's bedsit. In fact, Horace had invited himself.

"Eric, where do you live? I want to come to visit you."

"Do you? I live in darkest Hammersmith. Can you manage such a trek? Better put on your country clothes."

Horace had come and had loved the place. He was also a good companion for Eric's outings to the concerts and theatre.

"Have you got a girlfriend, Eric?"

"Not just at the moment. I have one from time to time, but nothing serious."

There was no way that Eric would tell anyone about Katie. That was a secret. To Katie herself he did not mention that he had any special friends at work. She would otherwise become curious and would want to meet them.

Eric's other close friend was Malcolm McGregor who was good at bridge. The two often played as partners. The third was Cecil Pemberton.

One day there was a party for the Ambassador to one of the countries for which Eric's department was responsible. The Ambassador had come home for an international conference in London and Eric's Head of Department thought it would be a good idea to include some of the junior staff, so as to broaden their experience and get them to help with looking after the guests.

This, the first party he attended, had happened far earlier that he had expected and that had been an eye-opener. Elegant people in good clothes mingling with ease and holding amusing conversations. Thank heavens he had a good repartee and a natural sense of humour. Intelligent and amusing comments were required at receptions. One had to have thorough general knowledge. He discovered champagne. How wonderful. Elegant sips from a champagne glass suited his style well. As everybody in those days smoked, he got himself some cigarettes and in public he would smoke perhaps two or three. Just to show that he could afford them and that he fitted into the crowd. In reality he hated cigarettes because they reminded him of the eternal blue haze of his childhood home where his mother puffed endlessly.

From the library he continued to take out books on politics, commerce, biographies of famous people. And so on. He crammed knowledge into his head. As a result he was never bored. At his job in the Registry he was excellent. His capabilities began to shine through and the this was realised by his superiors. Eric got noticed as someone who had the makings of a good career.

Katie followed Eric's development.

"Eric, you have begun to speak different. Sort of posh. With me you can speak as always."

"No way. You will have to cope with my "posh" accent, Katie, I am not reverting to the estate accent in any situation. I did offer you an opportunity to do the courses in elocution as well but you felt you did not want them. I know it can be a bit of a bind. But, you know, I can't afford to stand out in the Foreign Office because of a poor accent. Call it snooty, if you like, but there is a point to it. Be so kind as to allow me to croon to you in a posh accent. My love for you has not changed, it's only the accent. So stop fussing."

"All right, dearest. I'll at least try to speak clearly in return. You know that I like to please you, my love. Tell me, is there anything special going on at work?"

"As you are asking, you know the fact that Alexander Dubcek was elected the First Secretary of the Communist Party of Czechoslovakia might cause severe problems for that country."

"When did that happen?"

"Only two weeks ago, on the 5th January."

"Is that something we should worry about?"

"Yes, it is. The Soviet Union is making unhealthy noises about it. Communism is throwing its weight about."

"But Russia is over there far away."

"Yes. Thank goodness. We don't want it encroaching any further."

When they had got to March, even Katie had heard about the student riots in Paris. She felt for the students.

"Eric, at last the French will have to listen to their students. They want their rights. They are willing to fight for it."

"I myself find it lamentable. All that stuff about free love! Sex galore! To think that 1968 will be remembered for such a reason is pitiful. Those students are far too young and lack any real knowledge about anything, and any political spouting by them is only a disguise for fornication. They want to be allowed to get into the sack when and with whom they please. This is a follow up from the hippies who clamoured about free love, free drugs, anything goes. It augurs badly for the future."

"But Eric, we want free love just like them."

"No, we don't. I certainly don't. I do not agree that we should each jump into the sack left, right and centre with whoever we please at a moment's notice. Ours is a serious relationship, not a bit of pastime."

"Well, when you put it like that, I think you are right."

There was yet another side of Eric that was unknown to Katie. Since planning to join the Foreign Office he had started a program of theatre, concerts, ballets and opera. He would buy a cheap ticket so that he could afford to go often. Thus every three weeks saw Eric at the performances during a weekday evening. He did not want to pay for Katie to join him because there would have been no point as she was not interested in such things. Among his colleagues, Eric had noticed that they all had had good theatre educations, not to mention concerts. He needed to catch up and to be able to talk about various performances with knowledge.

He invariably bought a program which he kept in a box on the top shelf of his wardrobe in secret from Katie. That secret box gave Eric an uneasy feeling, for it had echoes of his home where he hid his money. Why should he now, as a grown man, have to keep a secret box? He realised it was because his relationship with Katie was not straightforward and easy. How he wished that it had been so, but he had no right to force Katie into a cultural tumble-dryer. For that would have been her reaction, secretly, of course. To him she would have pretended that she was content.

In all this came also the question of hobbies. One had to have interests. It was natural that he would choose cards. Thus he had enrolled into a famous bridge school. It was the best thing he could have done. He was born to be a bridge player. He advanced to the top class, and as a result he got many invitations to smart dinner plus bridge evenings. Most people in the Foreign Office were bridge players, it was such a good way of mixing with people.

Chapter 11

Eric usually went to the bridge club on a Thursday evening from eight to eleven. The timings of the club were from 10am-1pm, 2.30-5pm,5-8pm and the last session was from 8-11pm. This seven days a week. On one occasion he had missed a Thursday, so he went on Saturday at 2.30pm while Katie was busy with some girlfriends. He noted that on Saturday afternoons most players were women. At his table was a very pleasant woman called Philippa Saunders. The name rang a bell. Only recently he had seen it mentioned in The Times. Ah yes, it came to him, Sir Philip Saunders was in the Royal Society.

"Are you a new member, Eric? I've not seen you before."

"I've been a member for some time, but usually I play on Thursday evenings. This is my first time on a Saturday, and it is only now that I realise what I've been missing. All the lovely ladies. I shall have to come here on more Saturdays in order to enjoy their company."

As he said that, he looked rather pointedly at Philippa and gave her his foxy grin. It was his dimple on the left-hand side that created that foxy look. Women found it irresistible – and Philippa was no exception.

After that Eric did notice that on every second Thursday evening Philippa was at the bridge club as well. He would have short, polite exchanges of words with her. He also decided to go on Saturdays from time to time. When the right moment occurred, Saturdays allowed for the possibility of asking a lady to linger for a coffee at the club. There were a couple of sofas for that purpose. Ideal for the beginning of a relationship.

Katie was most disappointed by the bridge.

"It is very annoying that you are so often invited on a Saturday evening to a bridge party. That should be our time. We only have the weekends."

"Look, Katie, it is important for me to respond to these invitations. I am getting to know people. You have never liked cards, that cannot be helped. Otherwise I would have suggested that you learn it with me. Also bridge enables me to mix with higher classes of people which I might not otherwise be able to do. I am still at the bottom of the pile. However, if I am at bridge on a Saturday, then let's arrange for you to come already on a Friday on those week ends. All right?"

"Oh yes, that would make it better. I just want to be with you all the time. Soon I hope we will be able to do just that."

"I am always home by midnight. I never stay late. I tell my hosts that I need to leave by eleven the latest. They are happy with that. It is for you that I hurry."

"It's still very boring to sit here all that time on my own. There is nothing to do."

"You could read."

"Not the type of books that you have here. If we could afford a television, it would be marvellous."

"Well, we can't yet. I'm sorry."

"One day we'll be able to afford it. You are doing so well. You will get promoted, and then we won't look back."

The office had been busy. A lot of paper was created by the Commonwealth Immigrants Act 1968 which reduced the number of immigrants from the Commonwealth countries.

"I think I must have been a donkey in another life," complained Malcolm.

What makes you think you were a donkey in another life?" piped in Horace, "You could have fooled me, though you are awfully good at braying."

"Who is good at braying?" asked Cecil who had just walked in.

"Don't let it worry you, Cecil," said Eric, "it's only Malcolm and Horace at each other's throats."

"I'll load our donkey with a few more papers to cart. To make sure of speed, I'll put some nettles under his tail. This stuff needs to get to the relevant desk officers as of an hour ago. If you don't get moving, The Handbag will snap."

"Will it indeed?"

The voice of Mr Bracknell came loud and clear. The culprits turned and reddened.

"I gather that among worthy literature you have come across Oscar Wilde. That aside, the situation is beginning to calm down, so it'll be more relaxed next week. Meanwhile, would Ernest start in earnest to fill those latest jackets," said Mr Bracknell pointing his finger at Horace and then going out with heaving shoulders. The three young men were so amusing and likeable.

The following day was a Friday.

"Malcolm," said Horace, "I am penitent. I come with gifts to soothe your ruffled feathers."

"What do you mean?"

"I've got four free tickets to the Lyric theatre for tonight where they are showing "Lady Windermere's Fan". Any of you interested?"

"Definitely," said Malcolm, Eric and Cecil in unison.

"The Lyric is just round the corner from you, Eric, isn't it?" said Horace.

"Yes, it is."

"Right, boys, we'll go afterwards to Eric's place. You must come and see his seduction couch."

"Good heavens, you've got me all curious," said Cecil.

"Fairy tales, as always," said Eric. "After work let's go straight to the theatre. They've got a café where we can get sandwiches."

The play was good. The four young men enjoyed it thoroughly. When they got to Eric's, the other two were as impressed as Horace had been when he first saw it.

"Hmm. This is indeed a seduction couch," said Malcolm, "who is Eric seducing?"

"None of the office secretaries, though they are, one and all, panting with passion after him," said Horace, "with Eric's looks, you better ask him how many has he on the go."

"I haven't time for too many frivolities. Now, what would you like? I've got a bottle and a half of whisky and a bottle of dry sherry."

"Whisky, please," came the answer from all three.

The atmosphere was full of jokes. The odd cigarette was smoked. At one stage Horace went to the loo, and when he returned, he had red rouge circles on his cheeks and he was wearing lipstick.

"I've discovered Eric's make-up kit," giggled Horace. "I'm wearing Orchid Blush rouge and Red Berry lipstick."

"A dark horse, you are, Eric," mused Cecil, "only a real girlfriend would leave such items behind."

"I occasionally do have some love-life, but let's not harp on that. Why don't we concentrate in finding you, Cecil, a sweetheart? Your eyes are forever roving round the typist pool."

"Yes, let's," said Horace.

The party went on till past midnight, and then Eric piled his three friends into a taxi. He cleaned up, aired the room and then sat for a while resting. He was not drunk, has had only pretended to sway. From then on he would check before going anywhere that any tell-tale signs of female presence were removed.

They had got to April. Then a mighty upheaval was caused by the Rivers of Blood speech by Enoch Powell. It launched Eric into a speech to Katie.

"Such a direct speech is going to cost the man dear."

"Will there be rivers of blood? And when, Eric?"

"I have no idea, Katie. Maybe yes, maybe no. Sometime in the future. But this is creating racial tensions. There will be major reactions from many parts of the world."

"Is he right?"

"He may be. I can think of situations where this prediction could indeed become true. But before that, a lot of changes would have had to take place. We are not there now."

"Then let's not dwell on it. Let's think of your holidays. How are you going to spend them? Could we go on a coach tour?"

"Yes, we could. At the end of July I am allowed two weeks so we could go for a week to

Wales. How does that sound? The other week we could stay in London and enjoy it here."

"Brilliant, Eric. I can't wait."

Eric was sitting at his portering job at the hospital. He was not reading. He was just sitting and thinking. It was becoming more and more clear to him that Katie was waiting for him to marry her. She often referred to the two of them as "we" in the sense of a couple. He shuddered when he thought that he had nearly asked her to marry him before last Easter. When the bedsit had been nearly done. But then Mr Hargreaves' visit had made him pause. That had made a complete difference to Eric's thoughts. What he had said about having no funds nor future to offer to a potential spouse he firmly believed. For a short moment he had toyed with the thought that money would be enough, and provided they had sufficient money, he and Katie could live "happily ever after". As soon as Mr Hargreaves had mentioned the Diplomatic Service, Eric's eyes had opened to the fact that he needed a real career if he was going to be fulfilled. Only that could really change his life. From then on a veil had come down between him and Katie, he no longer felt he could confide in her entirely. His actual plans had to be kept secret in order not to hurt her, but that was no solution because in the end there would be the hurt. Both to her and to himself. By the beginning of summer, he had begun to think actively about finding a suitable spouse. This had had its kick-start that first Saturday when he had gone to the bridge club.

Now that he was in the Foreign Office and saw what a different world there was to achieve, he saw how wise Mr Hargreaves had been. The old man had correctly read Eric's character and had spent time in thinking what would be the best future for him. How right the man had been. Eric might eventually have stumbled into that career, but Mr Hargreaves's words had precipitated the issue, and now Eric had an early opportunity to start a forward move.

They were now in September. What had started Eric's ruminations that Sunday was that he could not get away from the fact that Katie could not follow anything that he was really involved in. When, on the 21st of August, the Soviet Union had invaded Czechoslovakia, the Foreign Office had buzzed like a beehive. Activity was overflowing. There was pressure everywhere. Eric loved the buzz. It did not matter to him if he needed to work late. He had had a stroke of luck because of The Handbag. The man had had a nervous breakdown because his younger brother had been diagnosed with advanced pancreatic cancer in July with a very poor prognosis. The doctors spoke of weeks rather than months. They had been right, the patient lived for only five weeks till the first days of August. This had taken its toll on the elder brother and the Office had given Richard Bracknell three months compassionate leave. This at a time when they needed all hands to the pumps. So Eric had been singled out to help at one of the special units that had been set up to deal with the crisis. It suited him down to the ground. It gave him a chance to be noticed with his future in view.

Marriage with Katie sank into the background. She was so beautiful, so warm-hearted, and she adored the ground he walked on. Their sex life was perfect. And he loved her. However, he was interested in everything he could possibly learn in this life. She was interested only in him. That was the big problem. Even though she had been there to see his progress, she had not really taken it in. She did not understand properly his need for advancement in order to change his entire life-style. She was there to observe it, but she had not got the point. Eric felt that he had given a fair amount of effort towards trying to encourage Katie forward in life. It had not worked, and he could not force-feed her with culture. She only basked in the idea that a marriage between them would make them automatically happy forever. She would be the little woman to cook and clean for him.

No, that was not enough. Eric had learned that diplomatic life needed a lot from a spouse. Input by a spouse was invaluable, and the Office regarded a husband and wife as a team. A smoothly working team. Cooking and cleaning did not come into it. A diplomatic wife needed to be educated, speak languages, have read books and be on top what was going on. She needed to be a hostess at formal occasions and know about seating plans and topics of conversation, and also to know how to keep up appearances. She could not produce gaffes. A difficult or stupid spouse held a man's career back.

Oh dear, oh dear, oh dear! Katie did not live up to par. Not even near. She had remained a back-street girl whilst he, Eric, had kicked the shackles of his back-street persona well away. Katie would only flounder while he had come out on top. His past would stay a secret from the world. Nobody should ever be able to guess it. In order to keep up appearances, he could not marry Katie. She would show him up. With Katie by his side she would only hamper all his promotions. With a heavy heart Eric realised that these were now the last days of their relationship. When he got the desired promotion to a Third Secretary, then he would no longer be able to have Katie around. He would then set to look for a wife who would enhance him. He still had time with Katie but from then on his mind was actually made up. He only pretended to himself that such was not the case.

Eric's first year had gone well. Nothing as earth-shattering as the Prague Spring had occurred in 1969. At home some very positive things had happened. The Victoria Line had been opened by the Queen. That eased the Underground travel, and it opened new areas to the commuters. Then there had been the television documentary, "The Royal Family", which had attracted a record number of viewers, over 30 million! Eric and Katie had been among those to watch. Both had been riveted by the program.

"We are so fortunate to be a Monarchy," said Eric, "this program really showed how involved in everything our Queen is. She has an enormous work load on her shoulders. But the others, too, are active. I am impressed."

"Oh Eric," sighed Katie, "the Queen's jewellery is wonderful. It was a magnificent colour pageant. I love the horses and the carriages. No other country has them like us."

"We are lucky indeed," said Eric.

Not long after that there was the televised investiture of Charles, the Prince of Wales, with his title at Caernarfon. Eric and Katie had been glued to the box.

At the office, the four friends were still together as none of them had so far been posted anywhere, pending of course the crucial exam.

The four were sitting at lunch in the canteen. It was cheap and cheerful.

"We've all been in the Office for nearly two years. Soon we will have our exams. If all goes well, where would you boys like to be posted?" Malcolm asked.

"For me it would be China, I love the East," said Horace.

"For me the ideal would be Italy," said Cecil, "with my parents we have toured up and down that beautiful country, and the girls are lovely."

"Trust you to think of that," said Horace with a grin, "our skirt-chaser has not changed his spots. However, should you not get the land of your dreams, there are skirts to be chased everywhere. The ladies will no doubt swoon in bliss as soon as they see our Seducer-en-Titre arrive."

"Oh shut up," mumbled Cecil through his sandwich.

"For me it would be America," said Malcolm, "North or South, I don't mind. I have been on the Portuguese courses in the hopes of getting to Brazil. I thought that you, Cecil, were panting to go to Russia since you have been labouring heavily with that language."

"Russian women are said to be sexy," crooned Horace, pouting his lips in imaginary kisses, "but on to other things, don't you find it extraordinary that none of us three has been taken by the much-raved about hippy culture?"

"We didn't get into the Foreign Office for being birdbrains. Hippy culture stands for nothing, delivers nothing, enhances nothing. Their constant talk about love is nothing but hyper-exaggerated self-love – that of the sponger. Sponging on parents, sponging on society. For them the expression "hard work" is nothing but two four-letter words to be avoided at all costs." Eric had got on his high horse.

"Boys," crooned Horace, "wouldn't you just love to vegetate?"

"Right. You've just invented your own nickname "The Vegetable," said Malcolm, picking up a carrot on his fork and holding it up.

"I'll write a poem in Chinese called "For the Love of Vegetables". I have a ready market at once: the vegans. The poem will be translated into thirty languages. I could continue…"

"Eat up, oh thou Vegetable. We must go back to the coalface," said Eric, "we musn't worry The Handbag. We don't want to be the cause of any further nervous breakdowns."

When Christmas approached, Eric took Katie to see the sixth James Bond film "On Her Majesty's Secret Service" which had just been released. As they had enjoyed all the previous James Bond films, so they enjoyed this one.

Christmas itself Eric would celebrate alone. He had done so ever since he moved to his bedsit. Katie was naturally with her parents and they had asked Eric to come but he had declined, as he had always done. It was beyond him to be at the estate for Christmas. He would, in the New Year, pay his parents a visit. For Christmas he liked to go to the Midnight Mass and then loll about on Christmas Day, tucking into cold cuts and downing a bottle of good wine.

In January, Eric was told that he would be taking the crucial examinations for grade 9 in April. All was going as it should.

In March there was another flurry in the Office which got Eric involved. It was because Rhodesia declared itself a republic and thus broke ties with the British Crown. At home the government refused to recognise the new state as long as the Rhodesian Government opposed majority rule. Being so busy at the emergency Unit, Eric had no time to worry about his coming exam.

Chapter 12

In September 1970, three months before his twenty-fifth birthday, Eric was appointed to the desired grade 9, the starting point of the "B" stream. He would now cease to be a Registry clerk and would have the chance to rise to the top of the Foreign Office. He could now say that he was a diplomat. All his efforts at getting somewhere, ever since nine years old, were finally beginning to bear fruit. He had sighed an enormous sigh of relief. He would be taking a desk officer's job in September. All this showed what a concentrated effort at educating oneself could do. It had been a hard road with not much free time. But then, as everything interested him what would he have needed more free time for?

Katie was over the moon. She went to her parents to brag.

"Mum, Dad, Eric has been made a grade 9."

"What exactly does that mean?"

"I don't quite know, but it means that now his job is secure, and he will get foreign postings. This will now mean marriage."

"Has Eric proposed to you?"

"No, he hasn't, but he will. You'll see. I have been patient all this time and now I'll get my reward."

"Just don't count your chickens till they've hatched," said her father. He was by no means convinced about the matter. In his opinion the relationship between Katie and Eric had gone on for too long. He felt that if Eric really had intended to marry Katie, he would have done so long ago.

"Well, I shall confront him about it. I'll tell him it's about time," said Katie.

Thus, on that October day when she confronted Eric about the question of their marriage, Katie got the shock of her life when he said that no, he was not going to marry her, in fact he was ending their relationship. He had been meaning to tell her these last days, but she had beaten him to the post by her words.

"You have been stringing me along all these years, making me believe that you were going to marry me!" she yelled.

"Please calm down. I have not been stringing you along. I have never mentioned marriage to you."

"You have told me over and over again that you loved me. That means marriage. You bed me as if I was your wife."

"I have bedded you because I love you, Katie. Believe me, I really do love you. I have always loved you."

"You say that you love me! Rubbish. That can't be true because you don't want to marry me. You are a liar and a cheat!" she continued to yell.

"You know that that is not true. It hits me heavily that I shall not marry you, and when you have calmed down a bit, I'll explain."

Katie started to sob.

"I'll tell all and sundry how badly you have treated me, I'll tell...." Sobs racked her and for a while they were all that could be heard.

"Why? Why? What have I done?"

"Katie. As I have decided that I shall not be marrying you, I must end this relationship now. It is not fair that I should "string you along" any further, as you say. I have given it considerable thought, and I have come to the conclusion that a marriage between us would not work."

"But we love each other."

"Yes, Katie, that is true. But here is more to marriage than just love."

"What! No. There can't be anything more important to a couple than love."

"I would be unable to make you happy. The type of life that I envisage to lead would only cause suffering for you. I know that with certainty."

"I would be willing to suffer anything for you, Eric."

"Maybe so, Katie. But I would not want that. I would not want to watch by your side and see you suffer. Especially as I would have no means of alleviating anything. It would be torture for me as well as for you."

"I don't want to live in that case!" screamed Katie, "I don't understand what has happened to us. Is this happening? How can it be? Have you fallen for someone else?"

"No, I have not. During all our time I have been faithful to you and I can assure you that I love no-one else. But I will not ruin us both in a marriage."

"Oh my God! What am I going to do? Eric, what can I do?"

"My very dearest Katie, you should concentrate on your family and your friends. They lend you support. Especially Nandita. Get on with your work and go out to meet people. Make new friends. Out there is surely the right man for you to marry."

"I love only you, Eric."

"At the moment yes. But you will fall in love again. After today I shall not be seeing you nor shall I answer any calls. I believe that a clean break is best. It enables both of us to calm down and get a grip on ourselves. Believe you me, it is as hard for me as it is for you."

Eric took Katie home in a taxi. At the door he kissed her forehead and then turned, without looking back.

Katie cried herself to sleep. The next morning she woke up with a heavy head and a terrible anguish. The worst had happened to her. Eric did not want her. He was not going to marry her. She felt as if the floor had fallen from under her feet. She could not fathom it. He was not going to marry her because it would make her unhappy. That just wasn't true. She might not have understood everything, but as she knew she made him happy, of course happiness would have followed in a marriage. She would not have demanded anything; she was content for him to rule the roost. He knew better anyhow.

There had to be some hidden reason for him not to want to marry her. She knew and felt that he loved her. Was it perhaps something connected to those deep, dark moods of which she had the odd glimpse on the occasions when he had got drunk in her company? The depth of those dark feelings had frightened her. She realised that she knew only patches of his character and what drove him on.

To the world he was jolly and superficial. What had he wanted? Now that she thought about it, Katie remembered how at the beginning he had tried to interest her in history, art and music, but seeing that she did not have the same enthusiasm, he had given up on that. He had tried to teach her card games, but she had no card sense, and it had had to be given up.

It began to dawn on Katie that Eric probably wanted someone who had similar interests to himself. It was an understandable wish. But as for wives, no wife would be able to fulfil everything. Eric seemed to want perfection. Well, that was something Katie could not provide.

Hitherto she had had no worries about her own self. Now with a sudden pang she became aware of having a whole host of deficiencies. Good God, how many were there? She must be full of them! The more she thought about it, the more she realised that she excelled at nothing. She was not really good at anything. An average, bordering on below average, that was a good description of her. How dreadful!

She could now see that she was not good enough for Eric. She agreed with that thought entirely. Why should such a brilliant man want a nobody as a wife? A massive inferiority complex overwhelmed Katie. She was appalled at herself. That was the worst. Eric had seen that she was untrainable. Of course he would not want such a wife. She was a low-brow nothing. Her looks were immaterial, they paled into insignificance. The love of someone like herself was worthless. It was already a miracle that Eric had loved her at all and had given so much of his time to her.

No, she would not embarrass him with her presence. He had not deserved that. Like the sewer-rat that she was, she would skulk back into her sewer.

For a good three weeks, Katie could not bring herself to tell anyone about the end of her relationship with Eric. Then she finally told her parents.

"Katie darling," said her father, "I think I told you over three years ago that it would come to nothing. As your relationship stretched longer and longer without any talk of marriage, it somehow lost its power. Don't look so desolate, my girl, Eric did love you. It could be clearly seen. If you had insisted on marriage as soon as you both had jobs, it might possibly have taken place."

"Oh Dad," interrupted Katie, "we had been together since we were sixteen. You know what I mean."

Her father was truly astonished. He had had no idea that such things had been going on at such an early stage.

"I am sorry to hear that. I can only conclude that by such behaviour you removed any hunting instincts from the man. You were like a rabbit that sits in front of the hunter. Dear me."

"But I loved him so much." By now Katie was sobbing. "I still do."

"Sure you do," her mother soothed her. "It is not possible to turn affections on and off like taps. Either they are there, or they are not. It is possible that it was a kind of puppy-love for Eric, and it changed as he matured."

"You are still young, my darling," continued her mother, "You will fall in love again."

Katie did not reply.

When she went to see Nandita in December, her friend managed to clarify many things to her. Nandita at the age of twenty-six was much more mature than Katie. For five years she had been a married woman. She and her husband lived in a nice house in Earl's Court. From time to time Katie and

Eric had been invited to a dinner there. Eric had been most impressed.

After finishing school, Nandita had trained as a nurse. Her great interests in life, playing the sitar and Indian classical dance would not provide a job. She trained at Hammersmith Hospital. When she had become qualified at the age of twenty-one, she was offered a job there. That is when Cupid struck. A new young ear, nose and throat specialist had come.

The young specialist, Dr Ishan Desai, fell hook, line and sinker for Nandita as soon as he set eyes upon her. The man was called Ike in the hospital. His passion was returned. In no time at all he asked Nandita if he might court her and asked to see her parents. She was delighted by this proper approach.

Meanwhile the Patels had moved to Ealing. Mr Patel had managed to buy a house. His business was on the ground floor and the family lived on the two upper floors. Mr Patel had done wonders to have achieved this.

Never in their dreams would the Patel parents have thought that their daughter would marry anyone but an ordinary Indian, much less that she would find a young consultant who was well off. Dr Ishan was welcomed with open arms. He did not allow his parents to dissent in any way, and as an only son, they did not want to lose him. He had been born in London and spoke English without an Indian accent. He was very conscious of being

British and welcomed the fact that Nandita felt similarly. The wedding was a colourful Indian one. Katie and Eric had been invited to it. They had been very happy for their friend.

Ishan and Nandita were very well suited to each other.

When Nandita opened the door, she could see at once that something was terribly wrong with her friend.

"Katie, my dear friend, what is the matter?"

"Eric has left me."

"Oh no. How terrible. Come here and sit down. Now, tell me all about it, if you can."

Katie started talking. She burst into fearful sobs and Nandita held her and patted her. She wisely let her friend cry and did not try to hurry her. The whole tragic story came out. Nandita turned out to be much more astute than Katie.

"Dear Katie," she said, "I know all about feelings of inadequacy. Don't forget that I am an Indian in England. But this is not about me. Tell me, did you not notice how Eric kept changing? Already when he was but nine years old, he started to wear quality clothes. My father, since he's a tailor, noticed it immediately. It was underplayed, but Eric began to look smart.

Remember the Richmond Theatre. The whole estate talked about it for months. He was beginning to reach out. On two occasions I saw Eric in a museum. As soon as he saw my family, he quickly disappeared from the scene. My father explained to me that the boy did not want to be seen. I always assumed that you knew about his outings."

"Oh Nandita. I did not. How stupid and blind I have been. He did try to drag me to some cultural events but he saw my preference for cinema and dance. I am paying for it now."

A new wave of tears followed.

"No wonder he did want to marry me."

"Now, don't be disparaging about yourself. You are a different personality from him, and you have different needs."

"I only need Eric."

"That is probably part of the problem," pointed out Nandita, "to be too needy of another person puts pressure on him, and eventually he starts to resent it. He begins to feel that it is his duty to be with the other person, rather than a free joyful wish to be with her. In a marriage such a situation can occur if one is not careful. Often the needier spouse puts the heavy pressure of duty upon the other so as to prevent him from escaping instead of looking into herself and then correcting her own behaviour."

"If I had started to learn the same things as Eric, I might not have lost him. What do you think?"

"Most probably you would not." Nandita found it necessary to lie for her friend's sake.

She felt very sorry for Katie, who saw Eric only through rose-tinted glasses. In her opinion Katie had actually been lucky to have escaped

Eric's clutches! That man was all out for perfection. Poor Katie would have suffered constant orders from him as what to do or not to do, what to say or not to say, what to wear or not to wear, which books to read and which not to read, and so on. The list was endless. Katie would have become a nervous wreck in such a marriage. Eric was the type never to be satisfied and Katie the type to take all the blame upon herself.

With an upper class wife, proud Eric would be the underdog who would not dare to complain about anything. Such a one would serve him right. The man was a boot-licker and a cunning and ruthless one at that. Of course he was exceptionally intelligent and exceptionally handsome.

"Nandita," Katie was saying, "how is married life after five years?"

"Ike and I are very happy, and I shall see to it that it stays that way. I have not brought any Indian element into our marriage. I dress and behave like a western woman. I live in England. I do not allow India nor my Indian relatives to encroach upon my marriage. I have India when I visit my parents and then of course I wear a sari to please them. Gujarati I will teach to any children of ours as all languages are useful. By the way, Katie, I am three months pregnant."

"Congratulations, Nandita, how wonderful."

"My parents sighed with relief. Nearly five years of marriage without a child is difficult for Indians to understand. I wanted time for us two to cement our marriage first. And Ishan agreed. A child is not necessarily a uniting force.

Katie and Nandita prattled on for a while and Katie started to feel better. Before Katie left, Nandita said, "Dear Katie, do try to go out and meet people. And another thing, you have always had a beautiful singing voice. Why don't you join a choir? That way you will have a new activity and a new set of friends. Think about my suggestion, will you."

A month later, in January 1971, Katie joined a choir.

Chapter 13

As for Eric, it had been with a heavy heart that he had ended his relationship with Katie. As hard as he might try, he saw no way for them to be able to attain happiness in a marriage. By pushing her away, he knew that he had wounded her mortally. It would probably make her uncertain and mistrustful of any men for life. He could only hope that she would meet someone who would love her and make her happy.

It was an evening with the whisky bottle. He poured himself a good dose. He would get drunk that night. The next day was Saturday, the usual day for Katie to come to him, and now there would be a void. He poured another drink.

By his action he had doomed himself to loneliness. He knew for certain that among the upper classes he would never meet someone to whom he could open his heart or who could understand his personality. Katie had been the only person in whose company he had had no need to pretend. She knew all about his background as she shared it, she knew the horrors he had had to endure, knew his struggles and his advances. What she had failed to grasp was how deeply it had affected him.

It was a terrible shame that all his efforts at trying to educate her had come to nought. It was unfortunately beyond her. He felt that he had made a fair number of tries, only to fail to get her interested. Her interest lay in him, Eric. It was flattering but of no use to him in his future plans. He wondered whether he should have left her already as soon as he joined the Foreign Office. That had been the time when he really knew that he would not be able to marry her. He had not had the heart to do so any earlier that absolutely necessary. He so needed her. As she needed him.

She fulfilled one half of him: his past. She was unable to fulfil the forward- moving half of him. Whichever way he turned, he would only ever be half fulfilled. However, under no circumstances would he choose to remain with the backward-looking half. It was his duty to himself to strive forward the best he could. He would not compromise anything.

Katie would always fill one half of his heart. He would have to find somebody else to fill the other half.

He already had someone in his sights, Philippa Saunders, the only child of Sir Philip Saunders, the eminent scientist, whom he had met through the bridge club. She had fallen in love with him the moment she had seen him. That had been clear to Eric. While he was still with Katie, he had not approached her except to say hello and be with her at the occasional play at the same table. But he had noted the potential that the club offered for striking up an acquaintance. Now the situation had changed. He was free and at the stage where he was sure of himself. He was handsome and charming; he had what could be called "the gift of the gab", and by now he was educated and at the beginning of an important career. A nobody no longer. Women were not indifferent to him. He had for some time now had all the opportunities to play the field widely, but he had had no interest in doing so because he had had Katie.

Philippa Saunders had all the qualities he needed. To look at she was nothing special. She was not ugly, only somewhat plain in a Spanish manner. She had long dark hair, somewhat sallow skin and a long, prominent nose, just like her father. She was six years his senior. It was evident that she had not had many takers so far in spite of the monied background she had. Eric had well noticed how she paid covert attention to him. It augured well.

He would start a courtship. His first move was to suggest to her that they occasionally play as partners. She was most flattered as she knew that Eric was a superior player. At the bridge club to which they both belonged, he sometimes suggested that they meet a bit earlier and have a coffee together. She was there invariably at least half an hour in advance. That was to make sure that she would not miss one minute. It catered for any delays on the Underground. On one occasion Eric had made himself late on purpose so that he arrived just as the play was beginning. He had seen from her face that she had been most disappointed. Good.

The lady was definitely keen on him. Then he invited her to a lunch. That clinched it. Philippa could not disguise how pie-eyed she was as regards Eric.

He calculated that his prey was in the bag. Well and truly to be expected was that her father, once in the know, would speak vehemently against Eric. He would surely go through Eric's life history with a fine toothcomb and what he would find would not impress the man. However, Eric felt certain that in the end Sir Philip would have to buckle under to his daughter's pressure. Surely he would not want his only child to end up as a sour spinster? Would he not care for the possibility of grandchildren? Surely he would appreciate a husband with a career? As for Eric's roots, Sir Philip would end up in hiding that past as effectively as he did himself.

The time had come for a dinner invitation.

"Philippa, at what time would you like me to come to pick you up? I've booked a table for seven fifteen."

"That's not necessary. I'll meet you at the restaurant."

"But I would pick you up in a taxi."

"No, no. I shall be coming from my dressmakers," Philippa lied.

It amused Eric to see how she avoided her parents from knowing him. It told him that she wanted to be sure of him before she did so. He really mattered to her, otherwise it would not have mattered whether her parents knew anything at all. He needed to act fast but not to make it seem so.

Eric was well in time at the restaurant. He rose when he saw Philippa.

"How lovely to see you. Let me help you with your coat. I'll see that it's put into the cloakroom."

"Thank you Eric."

"Let me escort you to our table. I have chosen one towards the alcove, I think it's cosy, but if you would prefer to sit elsewhere, just say so."

"It looks just perfect."

As they lifted their menus to read, Eric said,

"Would you like an aperitif? A sherry perhaps?"

"No, thank you, Eric. But I may like a digestif."

"Would you like a hot first course or a cold one?"

"A cold one. In fact, I'd like some salad."

"For the main course, would you like meat, fish or poultry? That will determine the wine."

"I would like some fish, please. I am fond of a filet of Dover sole."

Eric did the ordering. He looked admiringly at the elegant woman in front of him. Philippa knew how to dress and how to apply make-up, a little touch here and there gave a splendid result. A light foundation took away the sallowness of her skin and a bit of greenish eyeshadow accentuated her light-brown eyes. Her lipstick was a soft coral colour. She did not use nail varnish. Thank goodness. Eric hated claws with varnish, they reminded him of his mother.

"Philippa, you look lovely. I'm so lucky that you agreed to come to dine with me. I've been wanting to get to know you better."

"It makes me very happy that you sometimes partner me at bridge."

"I cannot hog all your attention. I'm only a humble diplomatic seedling."

"I'm not sure you're using the correct language here. It's well known that to get into the Diplomatic Service is a big hurdle. Not many actually make it."

"Thank you for those nice words. It is true that I have worked hard. I am now at the stage where I would like to start to consider the serious sides of life."

"Like what?"

"A woman in my life. But I tend to be a little shy and slightly frightened."

"You don't need to be frightened of me, Eric. Is there a woman in your life?"

"You know full well that there is. Have you not noticed that I have feelings towards you? I just haven't dared to say anything."

Philippa took Eric's hand.

"I have noticed, but I too am a little shy. And I return your sentiments."

"Philippa, I am falling in love with you. I really want you. For me you are the most wonderful woman in the world. No, don't shake your head. It is what I think that matters. The opinions of others are totally unimportant. You fulfil what I want in a woman."

"Oh, Eric. I love you." She blurted out.

"And I love you too. I am the luckiest chap alive! Philippa, that you should love me is an intoxicating thought. Let's get intoxicated with some champagne. This needs to be feted. Darling, my darling, how happy I am."

Eric took both her hands and kissed them with meaning. His eyes bored into hers. He also stroked her hands. Philippa was in bliss. The unbelievable had happened. Eric wanted her. Her.

The champagne arrived and they sipped it.

"To our future," said Eric.

Philippa was head over heels in love with Eric. He took his time before he kissed her properly. He knew that she was waiting for it on tenterhooks and on many occasions he had made it seem as if he was going to do so, only to pull back at the last minute and leave her with a peck. His technique had the desired effect. Philippa was on fire. When at last he did kiss her, he knew that she was ready to eat out of his hand. He made no attempts to bed her – she would only have her cake upon marriage. He gave her passionate looks and made poetic love declarations but kept all decorous. It was driving Philippa mad!

Oh my God! At last there was a man in her life. And a clever and handsome one at that. Did she dare to hope? She was frightened by her passion for him. Did he feel the same? She did not feel that he loved her only intellectually as had been the case with Hermann, after whom she had panted for four years in her mid-twenties. He had bedded her at her insistence but never with any enthusiasm. She had always had to instigate anything. Worse, she had been reduced to having to ask as to whether their relationship was leading towards marriage.

"Good heavens. This is sudden. We are still far too young for such a serious step. Your father would under no circumstances approve. He does not approve of me anyway. It is such early days. Why spoil the moment with something too serious? Matrimony is to be considered at length and many aspects weighed up carefully. Time is needed for discussions. This is all too sudden."

It had been nothing but pure verbiage. The answer had been crystal clear: he had no intention whatsoever to marry her.

"I get it. You have never had any intentions whatsoever! I see no point in continuing this relationship."

"You are so right. I shall get my stuff immediately and hurry out of your life."

It was a terrible humiliation for Philippa to see how Hermann had sighed with relief and had hurtled out in a hurry. Grim.

She had raged and cried torrents in her father's arms.

"For four years he has led me on. He has behaved disgracefully."

"That is not quite right. It has always seemed to me that you were the one taking any lead at all."

"That's what I mean. He never suggested anything, and if I had not insisted, we would never have had a relationship."

"Perhaps you should have taken some cue from him. There has to be at least some effort from both parties. Hermann had no go in him at all."

"I did try to put some backbone into him, but I failed. I did all I could."

"What a terrible statement. Do you realise what you have just said? 'I did what I could.' Please, Philippa, do not ever use those words again. And you did not fail. In the case of that individual there was nowhere to go. A wet, boring type if ever. Not worthy of you in any way. I did try to indicate to you that your hunt was hopeless and definitely not worth the time, but you steadfastly refused to listen to me. Because you had all that passion, you assumed that Hermann felt the same way."

"I have been told that love has to be worked at. Oh Daddy, I so hoped that I would succeed. You know full well that as I am not particularly pretty, I have not had many takers. And I don't want you to buy me a man."

"No, darling. I did not think that you would want one to be bought. You are only thirty-two, you are young. The right man will come along."

"If only. I know that mother and grandmother keep lighting candles to Our Lady with that hope in their minds."

Her father had seen it all coming. His poor daughter. What a pity that she had inherited plain looks. She should have been a Spanish beauty, as were her mother Estefania and her grandmother Conchita from his side. She was a clever girl and had a responsible job at a research laboratory. If only her love-life had been in order! That dreadful Hermann, around whose neck she had hung for so long, had been a wimp. And boring wimp at that. A typical dry accountant. What his daughter had seen in the man escaped Sir Philip. All he knew was that the wretched girl had pursued him relentlessly. On the two occasions when Hermann had been trotted in front of his own eyes, Sir Philip had glared at the man like an enraged bull. As he was a large man with a ferocious temper, Hermann had been terrified of him.

Sir Philip had sighed with relief when the affair with Hermann was finally over. However, it had been heart breaking to see how disappointed Philippa had been. Before Hermann there had been only one boyfriend of note, and that had ended in ridicule. Philippa had pursued the young man for nearly two years, using all her ruses, till finally he had had to tell her that he was otherwise inclined.

Philippa had felt idiotic. Her romance had been reduced to a farce! At least then there had not been those torrents of tears which followed the Hermann debacle. His daughter had the knack of choosing the wrong man.

For the past three years, as far as Sir Philip knew, there had been nobody in Philippa's life. Now, however, since a few months, it had seemed to him that she might be seeing someone. There was a glow about her, and she did not say where she had been.

One Saturday, Sir Philip had been in a taxi going past the V&A when he had spotted his daughter in front of the museum in the company of an elegant, handsome man with blond hair, obviously younger than her. The expression in her eyes had been pure bliss. The protective fatherly instincts of Sir Philip were immediately roused. He would start to observe his daughter more closely in order to see where this might be leading.

"Steffi," Sir Philip called as soon as he got home, "I think our daughter has found a new man."

"Madre de Dios! Gracias! Oh Philip, if only this time it would hold. How do you know this?"

"Coming home in a taxi, I saw her by the V&A with a handsome fellow."

"We must keep our fingers crossed, Philip."

"Keep lighting those candles, my love."

Sir Philip was correct in his surmise that his daughter had fallen in love again. This time Philippa said nothing to her parents about Eric's

112

courtship. She would only tell them if something came of it. She did not want to advertise that yet again somebody had dropped her.

At last that wonderful frosty January Saturday had come. Eric had taken her for a walk in Chiswick House gardens and then had asked her to tea in his little den. She had been delighted that at last she would see where he lived. The block of flats was not smart, but when Eric opened the door, Philippa had gasped in surprise. His place was wonderful. Tasteful and elegant. Her trained eye could see at once that all items of furniture were quality antiques.

Eric served tea and cakes at the table and when they had finished, he escorted her to one of the armchairs. Then in an old-fashioned way he bent one knee and proposed.

"Philippa, my darling. I love you. Will you marry me?"

"Yes, Eric, I will. I am the happiest girl alive."

"And I the happiest man."

Eric kissed her and cuddled her for a long time.

"Beloved Philippa, you are my one and only. I knew it from the start."

More kisses and cuddles. Philippa was beside herself with happiness. She could but whisper "Oh Eric" over and over again with tears of joy in her eyes. He let her sob against his shoulder for a bit and then gave her a clean white handkerchief with an embroidered little E.

"Now, darling, calm down. We are going to be married. I must get you an engagement ring. What particular stone would you like? That's better. A nice smile. I must also ask your father for his approval. If I get his approval, when would you like to get married?"

"As soon as possible. As soon as it can be mustered. A big wedding, that is. I want a real celebration and I know that my parents would want one too. As for the ring, I like classical. A square cut white diamond would be lovely. Oh, you have made me the happiest of all women. Of course you'll get father's approval. My parents will be delighted. And I'm dying to meet yours."

"All in good time. Your father might not approve. I come from a very humble background. It has taken me enormous efforts to get to where I have."

"Your background can be anything, as far as I am concerned. For all I care, your father can be a wandering gypsy. I am not marrying your family, I am marrying you."

"Well, darling, families do sort of loom large when it comes to matters of marriage. And they are right to do so. A marriage is the union of two family lines. All parents are most anxious about future members. We will cross our bridges when we need to. I must also tell you that I do not have very much money so I won't be able to keep you yet in the style you are accustomed to. I will work to give you the best I can. I do have a career in front of me and as I advance, all will be well."

"Look, dearest, don't worry about the money side. Let me deal with it," said Philippa, deciding then and there that her father would prop them up for a proper start in life. Her parents were rich, they had from what to give. What else would they be keeping their money for?

Eric sensed that Philippa would badger her parents into submission and obtain the necessary financial assistance needed for a brilliant future.

Chapter 14

Philippa hurried to her parents' house in Knightsbridge.

"Mother. Father. I'm engaged to be married."

"This is very sudden," said her father, "do we know him?"

"No, you don't, but soon you will. His name is Eric Flint and he is a young diplomat at the Foreign Office. He has asked if he may come to see you, father, in order to obtain your approval."

"Has he indeed! Of course he may come to see me. Whether he obtains my approval depends on what I see."

"Eric is tall, handsome, blond…"

"It is not his looks that interest me," said Sir Philip, thinking back to that day when he had seen his daughter with a tall, handsome, blond man.

"He has a career to look forward to. I might yet become a Lady," purred Philippa.

"Good heavens, you are going fast," said her mother, "Are you marrying him in order to become a Lady?"

"Mother! Of course not. Eric is the man of my dreams. I am so incredibly lucky to have met him. He is a gentleman through and through."

"I should hope so. But what do you mean?" said her mother.

"He has behaved correctly and not tried to seduce me. More's the pity. He believes in a proper order of events. The way to his bedroom leads through a well-lit church," laughed Philippa, quoting Empress Eugenie.

It was arranged that Eric come to meet Philippa's parents that coming week on Thursday evening. He could have his talk with Sir Philip first, and then they would have dinner. This was of course assuming that all went well.

Eric arrived punctually at seven with a dozen pink roses for Lady Saunders and a box of chocolates for Philippa. He was indeed a singularly elegant and handsome man, even better close up than from a distance thought Sir Philip. The man had a charming manner. He was the type to melt most women's hearts concluded Sir Philip. Dear me, would he turn out to be skirt-chaser? What had attracted him to Philippa? Money had to be the answer.

Once the two men got into Sir Philip's study, Eric got to the point at once. He had been blessed with the ability to read people's characters, and he had seen that complete and brutal truth was necessary if he was to get on with Sir Philip.

"Sir Philip. I come from the gutter. I am a back-street boy, well and truly one of them. I grew up in some tenement flats in Southall. My parents are working class of the gutter level. My father is a postman and my mother a cleaning woman. Violence and swearing and cruelty are what was meted out to me. I am lucky that I live in this century, otherwise my parents would have put me to work for some fishmongers at the age of six or seven. They had no education, just enough to be able to read and add up, and they wanted none either. They were proud of being in their gutter. Shall I continue?"

"Please do."

"They were not interested in the fact that I was the best pupil the school had had for a very long time. They never came to the teacher and parent meetings. They never turned up for any prize giving, though it was I who was getting the first prize regularly. "Don't give yourself any airs and graces," they said, "you are working class, and working class you'll stay". However, I was made of a different metal from them."

"You must have been. Otherwise you would not be where you are now. I am astonished at what you are telling me."

"Already by nine I had begun to see what a quagmire I was in. A burning wish to get out of it was born inside me. It burns to this day. It is that fire that is pushing me forward to realise my full capabilities. I will let nothing stop me. I would like to forget my background entirely, but that is impossible. It will always haunt me somewhere in the back of my mind, but I will not let it ruin my life. By the way, Sir Philip, Philippa knows nothing of this."

"That is very wise of you. My girl is only full of happiness."

"That is how I want it to stay. But to continue. At school there was a "guardian angel" for me, a Mr Hargreaves. He helped me over various hurdles and guided me into more and more interest in my surroundings and raised an intellectual curiosity to learn and gather knowledge. Bless that man, I am eternally grateful to him. Thus I educated myself into knowing first and foremost the Bible, then the museums and art galleries, classical music, literature, and so on. I changed my style, my surroundings, my accent, my all."

"How did you manage it? Moneywise, that is. Even bus fares must be paid for."

"I took on, from about the age of seven, a paper-round, did some shopping for old ladies, helped out anywhere in small jobs. And then saved. Had to hide it all from my parents, of course. At the age of seventeen I had the great luck of getting a portering job at a hospital for Sunday afternoons. That was a God send. I still have it."

"Good heavens. Why?"

"Somehow it seems my safety net. Sounds funny, that. Maybe that shows my insecurity, I don't know. Anyway, when school finished, I moved out of my parents' place and moved to Hammersmith where I got a job at an Estate Agents'. Then came the Foreign Office, where I entered as a clerk at Grade 10. I have now been promoted to a Grade 9 with very good promotion prospects, and from now on it is forward in life and in my career. I know that I am going to do well.

119

There is no point in showing you some false modesty in this frank talk. That is why I permitted myself to ask Philippa to marry me. I do have something to offer."

"Eric. You have been astonishingly honest about yourself. I fully appreciate that. It does you honour. You have guts and go. Now, I am obliged to ask you that banal question, why do you want to marry Philippa? Your type of man can have his pick of the ladies. Do you love her?"

"Sir Philip. I have great affection for her, I admire and respect her. As for soppy Hollywood type of love, no, that I do not feel. I am actually convinced that the so-called "love" is one of the worst reasons to get married. Love needs time to blossom in a nurturing environment. I am convinced that our two characters are compatible and that we would support one another well. Naturally I am aware that Philippa has a romantic passion for me. That I should be so lucky! I appreciate that very much indeed, and it fills me with happiness. I don't think it would do her any good were I to indicate to her that perhaps I am not as romantic as she is. I want to cosset her and let her bask in her romantic thoughts if it makes her happy."

"You are confirming what I think is the case. I think you are planning to build your marriage on a sound base. It should go well."

"It will go well. Have no doubts about it. And another hidden question, to which you may want to have the answer, is that of other women. In the past

I have had no time nor inclination towards useless affairs and flirtations. Nor will I have. I had one girlfriend for over eight years, a childhood friend of mine. However, as the years advanced, we grew in different directions. I had to put an end to it. It was as painful for me as it was for her, but reality had to be faced. A marriage cannot be conducted on love alone."

"Thank you, Eric, for being so truthful with me. None of our conversation will go back to Philippa. I can see that you have had to surmount mountains to get to where you are. You have courage and determination and I admire your efforts. I am happy for you to marry Philippa and I welcome you into the family. Now, Eric, please drop the Sir. Just one more matter, if you should need any financial help, I should be more than happy to give it to you. Forgive my forwardness."

"How very considerate of you, Sir, I mean, Philip. I am not too proud to accept some help for Philippa's sake. If I could have a small loan, I would be eternally grateful. That would enable us to get a better dwelling to start life in. Otherwise we would have to start out in my bedsit. I assure you that I will pay you back every penny. Now I shall have no spare money for a while because I need to get an engagement ring. Philippa wants a square cut white diamond…"

"What!" interjected Sir Philip. "The silly girl, what an expensive wish."

"She shall have it. My savings will go into it, but that is fine by me."

Sir Philip looked at Eric with new eyes. He was pleased with Eric. The young man would go far. And Philippa was besotted with him, quite understandably so. His daughter had at long last chosen well. As she was already thirty-two, her child-bearing years were dwindling. Eric seemed to have made real efforts to put their coming marriage on a firm and happy ground, and with his type of determination, that was bound to prosper. Why should Sir Philip snatch away from his daughter her possibly only chance of happiness? Of course not.

He patted Eric on the back.

"All is well. Now let us go and join the ladies."

Chapter 15

The wedding was planned for July of 1971. It was the fastest that a big wedding could be done. Philippa was agog with happiness. Her parents were happy with her. They turned out to be more than generous. As a wedding present they bought the young couple a three-bedroom house in Chelsea with a large garden. The young ones were to choose the colour schemes and the furnishings. It would be ready to move into by the end of June. After their planned honeymoon in Florence, the young couple could move straight into their new home.

The present of their new home showed how caring Philippa's parents were. Eric could hardly believe his luck. As for his portering job – Philippa had put that to bed. She was under no circumstances having her new husband away on Sunday nights. No way. With her dowry, they had no financial difficulties so the job was not needed. Eric capitulated gracefully.

He saw Philippa as often as he could. That meant twice a week certainly, sometimes a third time. When there had been the Rhodesia affair occurred, he had had to phone her occasionally to say that he would be late. That had not worried her in the slightest. That had given great relief to Eric. From the very beginning of their relationship Eric had decided that though they were going to be a married couple, he would see to it that they did not become like Siamese twins, tied at the hip. Both he and she would remain persons apart from being spouses. He would have some friends of his own whom he would see privately and have some outings with, and she should have the same. He explained it to Philippa.

"There needs to be a certain amount of absolute personal freedom and privacy if a union is going to be happy. To even think of having to spy on the other one is already a sure sign that the relationship has broken. If so little trust is given to the other, why bother with a union? And before starting to blame the other one, a good look into one's personal behaviour would be salutary. Do I make sense?"

You do, Eric. I agree with you entirely. It is good that we touch upon such matters before marriage. I have seen too many of my girlfriends fret about every minute they are not at the side of their boyfriends. Not good. They stifle their men. They become jailors. Nobody ever loves a jailor."

"On occasion when I've been a bit late, it has been so refreshing that you have not nagged about it."

"Darling, you have a responsible job. I want to support you in it and encourage your efforts. But, on another subject, I learn that Dr Paisley was in the news recently. Problems again."

"Yes, ever since the Bannside by-election, which occurred as long ago as April 1970, we are lumbered with that man. What a dreadful creature. A real agitator. He is responsible for much."

"He incites trouble wherever he can. He makes sure to inflame tempers when he sees the slightest opportunity to do so. Is that causing some flurry in the office, my love?"

"It is, and it will continue to cause flurries regularly. That problem is not going to go away quickly. If ever."

"It is wonderful how in your job you are encountering so many different world scenarios. The busier you are, the better you look."

"You've sussed me out, my sweet. Now, come and sit next to me so that I can cuddle you."

Everything had been wonderful except that terrible visit to his parents. Philippa, like all women, was curious and so had insisted that she meet Eric's parents. He had tried to say that she would find nothing in common with his parents, they were an ordinary working-class couple.

"I can't avoid wondering why you are so unkeen on them. I'd want to meet them at least once. I find it all very strange."

"Why on Earth are you so curious about them?"

"Because they are your parents. I find it absolutely normal that I should be interested in your background."

"Is not what you see enough? Enough to have made the decision that you will have me? This curiosity of yours makes me think that you may have doubts."

"I don't have any doubts. I'm marrying you because I love you."

"You might be put off me by my parents. Any thoughts like "the apple does not fall far from the tree" – and you'll run for cover."

"Let me be the person to make up my own mind. I am not marrying a pig in a poke. If I decide to marry the pig, it will have been my free decision. A poke is out of the question."

"Very well. But don't say that I didn't warn you."

Eric was seriously displeased by this turn of events. There was a lot of wisdom in the saying "let sleeping dogs lie", but women were infernally curious. What if his parents succeeded in frightening Philippa away? That would be a blow. Not to the heart but to the purse. Eric knew that he loved money and fine things, and he knew it came from the deprivations of his childhood. His ambitions were the driving force in his life.

Was he as selfish as his parents? Had he inherited that characteristic? Most probably yes. And as for his ability to "pull the wool over people's eyes"? That was an euphemism for the plain verb to "lie". That ability had developed in Eric because it had been a necessity for his survival. From any visit to his parents, Philippa was bound to learn at least some things. He decided to talk to Sir Philip.

"Philip. Philippa insists that she come to meet my parents."

"You really don't want that, do you?"

"Hell, no. But she said that she would not marry a pig in a poke. She might marry the pig but not in a poke."

Sir Philip's shoulders heaved as he was trying to subdue his mirth. Eric found nothing funny in the matter.

"It was not the nicest not the most accurate of comparisons. Just a turn of phrase. She only used it to justify her curiosity."

"She could go off me."

"I can see that that would be a blow to you from many points of view. I am not criticising you, Eric. Ambition is not the worst quality for a man to have. No, Philippa will not go off you. I can guarantee that. She is in love with you to the deepest fibres of her being. It is as strong as her love for me, only in a male/female way. As a father I know this. So please stop worrying."

Eric sighed with relief.

"I suggest you do it," continued Sir Philip. "My Philippa is as curious as the next woman. Otherwise she will nag you to death. No wonder there are fairy tales like Bluebeard's Wife! It's too close for comfort."

Eric did not prepare Philippa in any way. He felt it would be better for her to have it "right up front". So the two had gone and had spent the compulsory hour in the flat. Philippa's eyes were watering in the haze created by Eric's mother's cigarettes. The place reeked. The mess was unbelievable. Had it ever been dusted? The TV blared in the background. Eric's mother's jersey dress was tight as a sausage skin, leaving no room for any imagination. Her war-paint covering the face was thicker than ever, and she had changed her hair to a deep purple colour. Eric had felt mortified and also unendingly sad. His mother had insisted that they all drink sherry in honour of the occasion, that is, the engagement.

"This has been a bloody surprise to me. And here's me thinking that Eric was going to marry one of the local gals. Thick as thieves they were. I bet Eric was in her knickers at an early age."

"Mother! Please!"

"What's surprising about that? Hell. Most gals are pregnant by eighteen. They get hitched up early. How old are you, Philippa?"

"I'm thirty-two."

"Lord! You are pushing it! I did think that you were a lot older than Eric. If you hurry, you might just be lucky enough to get pregnant. When's the wedding? I like parties."

"Mum, we have not yet decided on the date. In fact we feel that we don't want any fancy ceremony. We would prefer just a trip to the Town Hall with two witnesses."

"What nonsense is that? You think I'm an arse-hole? I don't believe that your fancy bit of fluff doesn't want a wedding! Tom, don't you think I'm right?"

"Sounds like porkies to me," her husband replied giving a loud burp.

"Eric. You little turd! Listen and listen to me well. I want a party, get it? You can have the knot tied in an outhouse if you so wish. But I want me drink."

"Mum, we don't need to decide anything now. I've brought you a large bottle of gin. And a Tizer. Plus a pack."

"Hmm. That's at least something."

The couple fled. Philippa had been appalled. She had been truly shocked. Now she fully understood why Eric avoided his parents. She would help him to avoid them even more. Eric's life must have been sheer hell. She was silent on the way back. So was Eric. Philippa glanced at him; she could see how he was suffering. Eric indeed was suffering, but that was because at the estate they had come across Mr and Mrs Smith, Katie's parents. He had greeted them politely, but only in passing and had not introduced them to Philippa. The sight of Katie's parents had brought back the old times to his mind. Inside him, he missed Katie terribly. Luckily for him, his silent pensiveness was interpreted by Philippa as having its cause in his parents.

When they got back, Philippa decided to take the bull by the horns.

"Eric, I have no words to help you in this matter."

"Darling, I knew it would be a shock for you. It can only be believed when seen. Try to forget it, my love."

"But what about the wedding? I don't think…"

She collapsed into sobs.

"That my parents should be invited," Eric finished the sentence for her, "Well, neither do I."

"Oh Eric, I'm so sorry…" she stammered.

"Don't be. Calm down, my sweet. We shall not have our wedding day ruined. My parents won't be there. To the guests we can say that my parents are unfortunately in quarantine because of mumps."

"What a good idea."

"Also, darling, please don't fret about my parents. You don't need to see them again. I will pay them a visit on my own from time to time."

"Eric, you are so understanding."

"You have such a soft heart, my love. You have led a sheltered and happy life basking in the love of your parents. That is the greatest fortune anyone can have."

Eric's face clouded over. For the first time Philippa saw how the childhood trauma which he had endured had caused deep wounds. Wounds that would never heal. In some way parts of Eric would remain shackled to his past and prey to inner turmoil. No matter how much she loved him, in that pain she was unable to help him. Oh Eric, oh beloved – you suffer and I can't help you. Her feelings overflowed and she burst into desperate sobs clinging to him.

He soothed and cuddled her and eventually managed to calm her a bit.

"Darling, I think the best thing at this moment is for you to go home. Will you be able to go alone in a taxi? You can. Good. I'll get one right now."

Once Philippa was on her way, Eric telephoned Sir Philip.

"Philip, Eric here. I have put Philippa into a taxi, and she is on her way to you. She is in a frightful state because of that visit to my parents. It has hit her really hard. I've done what I can, but I think she needs her father's advice."

"Thank you, Eric, for alerting me. You've done the right thing."

When Philippa arrived, red-eyed and pale, her father said,

"Good heavens, sweetheart! Red eyes! Have you already got to your first quarrel with your intended?"

"No, Daddy, certainly not. It's a long story. I need a drink."

Her father poured her a brandy. Philippa started to tell about her terrible experience. Sobs started to rack her again.

"Come and wail on my shoulder, my dearest. Let it out. It has been a real ordeal for you, has it not?"

"Oh Daddy. It doesn't matter about me. I don't know how to help Eric so his childhood wounds will heal. I have no way of soothing them. To see him suffer is intolerable for me. What can I do? Oh, Daddy, help."

She was wailing by now. Her pain was terrible to see. Her father patted her.

"Daddy. I love him so much. And I think he loves me."

"My child, calm down. Eric is devoted to you. He truly wants to make you happy. Don't start to spoil things by excessive worry. It is clear that wounds received in childhood do not always heal. However, they need not ruin the future.

If I may be so bold as to advise my intelligent daughter, I would suggest that on occasions where you notice a brooding reticence in Eric, do not try to poke about with questions. Instead, leave him to ruminate in peace. He may even wish to get drunk sometimes. Let him. Let it pass over, and should he crash down in the guest-room, don't make a song and dance about it. Next day behave as if nothing had happened. He will be ever so grateful to you and love you all the more for it."

"You are so wise, Daddy. You have always helped and supported me. I am so very grateful for everything."

She embraced her father. For a long time they sat quietly together with father stroking the long silken hair of his daughter. They were both in bliss. Father and daughter had always been like two peas in a pod.

Chapter 16

In March, Nandita asked Katie to come to see her. Nandita was six months pregnant but she was small, and the bump hardly showed. She looked radiant. The two friends settled in the lounge. After the usual exchanges, Nandita said,

"I have news for you, Katie. Eric is getting married in July to Philippa Saunders, the only daughter of Sir Philip Saunders. I know this because Beatrice Brockley-Doone, the wife of Ike's colleague Dr Benedict, is the best friend of Philippa. She is a former Wycombe Abbey girl as is Philippa. They came to dinner with us last week and my ears pricked up when she started to say that they had been invited to a big society wedding, that of Philippa Saunders and a young diplomat called Eric Flint."

The colour drained from Katie's face. The news hit her like a dagger. So, Eric had already forgotten her!

"He dropped me at the beginning of October. He's getting married in July. He must have been with Philippa while he was going out with me. That two-timer!"

"Not necessarily. He would have known her, yes. Don't forget that they both belong to the same bridge club. But I am quite sure that he would not have done any courting before he had ended his relationship with you."

"Still, he jumped pretty quickly from my bed into another."

"Oh no. That's not the case. I encouraged Beatrice to talk about her friend and the coming wedding. We women love to talk about romance. Apparently, the bride is head over heels in love with the groom, and is waiting impatiently for the marital embrace. The groom has been behaving properly, much to the frustration of the bride. Beatrice giggled as she was telling this to me. So, Katie, Eric did not jump from one bed into another."

Yes, Katie could well believe that. She had begun to see that everything in Eric's life had to take place according to accepted norms and in no other way. The only reason why Eric had started an early physical relationship with her, Katie, was because he had been so young. Nature drives the young strongly and at that time he had not yet matured into Mr Perfect! Bloody Perfection! Curse it!

The plans for the wedding were advancing at record speed. Lady Saunders had what seemed like a whole army of people dealing with the arrangements. It would be a grand society wedding. The religious ceremony would be at the Brompton Oratory. Philippa was a Catholic as were her Spanish family members. Sir Philip was an Anglican and thus Eric as an Anglican was well accepted, provided that the couple brought up their children as Catholics.

As for the wedding announcement in The Times, it had to be carefully worked out. Southall could not be mentioned. Eric and Sir Philip thought of a ruse. Eric's mother's grandmother came from a village in Lincolnshire called Sleaford, conveniently near to nothing. The announcement would mention that Mr and Mrs Flint of Sleaford, Lincolnshire, and that would solve the problem. Nobody would be the wiser.

"I hope this will work, said Eric, "We are forced to put that announcement in."

"We are indeed force," said Sir Philip, "and of course people are curious. But not to that extent. If there is any mention by anyone about the subject at the party, skim over it and change the subject."

"I'm thinking more of the danger of someone from Southall seeing the announcement and then running to my parents."

"But they already know about your engagement and they have met Philippa. On top of that, the announcement does not tell the where or the when of the coming nuptials. It only mentions that an engagement has taken place and there are no exact addresses, only Knightsbridge is mentioned. The word Sleaford is unlikely to worry them as your parents know that your mother's mother came from there."

Why not use the ruse, mused Sir Philip, he had seen so many times in his long life how people who craved for distinctions were involved with bogus titles, and bogus orders of chivalry complete with robes, ribbons, costumes and decorations to the point of folly. There was actually a huge market for such things. Oh vanity of vanities! The absence of the groom's parents would be mentioned at the beginning of the dinner. They had been struck with a bad case of mumps and so were in quarantine.

Over two hundred people had been invited. Philippa's parents were not sparing any expense. Eric was inviting three colleagues, Horace Grant, Malcolm McGregor and Cecil Pemberton. His best friend among the three was Horace who had been asked to be his best man. Philippa had been introduced to his friends some time ago and she got on well with them. All three thought that she was a wonderful woman and that Eric was lucky indeed. Quite a number of friends from their bridge club had also been invited. The main guest from Eric's side was Mr Hargreaves. He and his wife were both so pleased to see how wonderfully Eric's life had turned out. The old man felt a warm glow in his heart that he had succeeded in turning Eric's life from misery into happiness and success. Eric knew that nobody would learn anything from Mr Hargreaves, who understood fully the fact that Eric wanted his past to be as dead and buried as possible and the shackles of Southall to fall away. He would not divulge anything untoward about Eric.

Because Philippa was half Spanish, a Spanish theme had been chosen for the occasion. There was going to be dancing. A Spanish group had been engaged with a particularly good guitarist. Philippa had been trained in flamenco since a child. Eric found that fascinating and at her instigation, had started to take lessons in it. With Philippa he was learning the sevillana as they would be opening the dancing with it. Philippa was most contented that her future husband was one of those rare men who liked to dance and was enthusiastic about it. Sir Philip did not like dancing, but he had learned the main dances and to please his wife twirled her as the occasion demanded. Philippa had also started to teach Eric Spanish so that he would get a feel for the country. This, because she often visited her Spanish relatives, who lived in Malaga. And as a married couple they would be going there together. Another thing that Philippa had instigated was driving lessons for Eric. He needed to have a driving licence. Philippa had been given only recently a smart orange-coloured MG sports car as a present from her father. She much preferred that Eric should be in the driving seat. So he laboured at getting yet another skill, and by April the precious licence had been obtained.

The wedding day, Saturday the 10th of July, 1971, was gloriously sunny. The ceremony was to start at noon but already at eight o'clock the make-up artist and the hairdresser had arrived there. Philippa had woken up just before seven, before the alarm went off. She felt very nervous. One of the guest-bedrooms had been turned into a beauty parlour. The make-up artist was like a magician. He turned Philippa into a beauty. By carefully plucking the underside of her thick eyebrows, he opened up her eyes to give prominence to her naturally long eyelashes. By a heavier use of the eye-liner he brought out the Spanish element in her eyes. A light-brown golden-sheen shadow gave allure without looking too artificial. A luminous foundation changed any sallowness in her skin, and a clever use of some pale rouge lessened the impact of her large nose. The lipstick was a pale rose colour, imitating a natural look. The results were breath-taking.

Her hair was parted in the middle and was put up in a bun, to accentuate her Southern looks. It fell in soft waves, not having been pulled tight but to give a frame to her face. The style held the intricately made antique comb made of mother-of-pearl to which the veil was attached.

The dress was in flamenco style, with flounces at the sleeves and three layers of flounces in the skirt. It was a creation of white lace with a flower motif. With it came an underskirt of several layers in very pale-purple silk. The idea was that when dancing, there would be an effect of a seductive colour which would swish from time to time. Philippa's mother had had that idea. The shoes were white Flamenco ones. The end result was stunning.

Philippa was superstitious enough to want to have "something old, something new, something borrowed, something blue". The dress was new, for "old" she wore a garter-belt in purple which she had had for some time and which had been bought with seduction in mind. She borrowed from her mother a tiny enamel brooch which was mainly white but which had a small blue enamel ribbon at the bottom. This she attached to one shoulder. For jewellery she wore an antique diamond bracelet, given to her by her father.

When Eric saw his bride advance towards him, he was bowled over. His bride was everything he could want. It was sweet to see how she could not help herself from hurrying towards Eric with an excited smile on her lips.

"Decorum, Philippa," whispered her father.

"Oh come on, Daddy," whispered Philippa, dragging her father faster.

It was clear to the whole church that the bride couldn't get quickly enough to the groom, she was hurtling at speed. Amused and indulgent smiles were seen. Love was definitely in the air. It felt like an eternity to her till finally she reached Eric, who gave his bride one of his foxy grins, as Sir Philip handed her over. Happiness reigned supreme.

Chapter 17

The young couple had hardly got back from their honeymoon when Eric had the news that he was being posted to Paris in November. They started to prepare themselves in earnest. Eric was sent to the tailor. The obligatory black tie, white tie and morning coat were ordered plus four other suits and a sports jacket and trousers. For Philippa, among other things, a black mourning outfit in case a period of court mourning should be announced. Like most young couples, they made the mistake of procuring a fancy dinner set and glasses for twelve. After their second posting, and after a number of breakages, they got pretty, but cheap crockery and glass. Like everybody, they learned as they went along. They would be provided with a central flat with three bedrooms, all furnished.

To go by train or by plane, that was the question.

"I'd favour the train," said Eric, "because it would make more of the journey itself. We would have a first class compartment, and I hear that the food in those trains to Paris is super. What do you think?"

"What a good idea. I've always liked train travel. From the practical point of view, it allows us to have a fair amount of luggage."

So, the train journey was decided. They were greeted at the Gare du Nord by a colleague of Eric's who had also invited them to dinner that evening, together with two other couples from the Embassy.

Parisian life suited them both down to the ground. Philippa had been there before on several occasions with her parents, so she was a good guide for Eric. She spoke fluent French, having been tutored in that language from childhood on. On their very first Sunday Eric had wanted them to go to Notre Dame. It had fulfilled all his expectations. After the service they had wandered around a bit as the weather was sunny, and then they had gone to a small, cosy restaurant. They had not been disappointed, the food had been a joy to the palate.

On their second week, the officer in charge of the furnishings had come along with the inventory. Everything was counted and noted. The condition of all items was carefully described, so that at the end of their stay they would only be responsible for what they themselves might have damaged. It was a good system.

When Eric had got to the Embassy, he was introduced to the Ambassador. Later Philippa would also be introduced. Eric didn't show it but he was on tenterhooks. However, the Ambassador was a pleasant and friendly man, so Eric sighed with relief. As to the Councillor, with whom he would have more contact, it was rather the reverse. A short man with thick glasses. Eric sensed that the man had not taken to his type, so he prepared himself mentally to be particularly deferential to him and walk on eggshells as needed. He would see to it that the man would have nothing to complain about, Eric knew that he could pull his own weight. Later in the office it would soon become apparent how difficult the Councillor was. His secretary was a nervous wreck. The poor woman often had red eyes which she blamed on hay-fever, but no-one was fooled by that.

Already on his second week at work Eric had witnessed a painful scene. Miss Wilson, the Councillor's secretary, had been explaining to Eric some points that he ought to know.

"Miss Wilson," the Councillor's voice was heard to boom. Then a red, livid face appeared, "you are here to work, not to spend time in prattling to newcomers. Your work is more than haphazard. You forgot to book that restaurant. I was embarrassed in front of my guest, the Chief of the Police. There was no table, and we had to find elsewhere to dine. Now get to your desk, I must dictate a letter of apology. And make sure it does not have a single mistake."

Miss Wilson burst into tears.

"Miss Wilson, stop snivelling and get on with the job," growled the Councillor, after which the livid red face disappeared into its lair.

Philippa was fascinated by the elegance of the French women. They really knew how to dress themselves. During their stay in Paris, her wardrobe would grow quite considerably. To ease their life they shared a maid with another couple from the Embassy. She came to them on Wednesdays and Fridays. The days had been carefully planned by Eric. When they gave dinner parties, which they did about once a month, it would be only during week days. Week-ends were sacrosanct for family life, for the French as much as for themselves. So they gave dinners either on a Tuesday or on a Thursday, so that the maid would be there to clear everything up the next day.

Once a month Philippa took part in the big coffee morning given by the Ambassador's wife for the Embassy ladies. She herself gave a small coffee morning for her French acquaintances once a month. With cocktails and receptions, they went out around twice a week.

It was really Eric's skills at bridge that got them into different layers of Parisian society. That had to be carefully planned as well.

"Philippa, when we play against a French couple, depending who they are and what they are like, I suggest that we don't go for the kill every time. I'll steer the game. I'm pretty good at it, as you know. If I make some bad moves, like a bad opening lead, it will be with a reason. If I forget to count that a last trump is out, it will be with a reason."

"I think that is a good policy. I have gathered that our role here is to kow-tow to the French and please them."

"You've got it in a nut-shell," grinned Eric.

They had noticed that the Parisians tended to be a bit snooty and here was Eric, only a humble Third Secretary. His skills at charming the ladies played its own role. At parties the women tended to gravitate towards him like homing pigeons. If there was a gaggle of ladies with one man in the centre, it was usually Eric. The women found it fascinating that here was an Englishman who had just as much charm as any Frenchman.

Philippa looked on benignly. Eric had the habit of their having a little night-cap together when they got home from any function. Then he would set himself to really charm his wife. He flirted with her as if she was a young girl. Philippa often wondered how long it would last. She needn't have worried. He was to continue that pattern all through their marriage. She would often watch her sleeping husband and thank her lucky stars that he had chosen her.

He was most unpredictable.

"Philippa, this Friday I have booked us a table at the famous Moulin Rouge."

"Good heavens! I'm astonished. I'm not sure that it is respectable."

"Sure it is respectable. The Parisians pride themselves on the Moulin Rouge. I'm sure we will be most impressed."

"No doubt you will be impressed. What I gather about it is that it is full of naked ladies."

"Sure they will be there. That is the whole point. But it will be done in a very elegant way, believe you me."

Philippa had been somewhat apprehensive, but once they were there, she could but agree that the program had been exceptionally good. And the women had performed in such an elegant way that their scanty clothing had not mattered. In fact it had been a necessary part of the performance.

Chapter 18

At the Embassy, a lot of work was being caused by the lingering negotiations about Britain joining the European Economic community. The French were being very negative about it. In June Britain began new negotiations for EEC membership in Luxembourg. One rather satisfying thing for Eric had been that, during the first receptions they had attended, the French expressed incredulous admiration of the British expulsion in September of 90 Russian diplomats for spying. The year 1971 would be remembered forever. At the Paris cocktails and receptions, the amazed buzz still filled the air like champagne bubbles.

"That will teach the French, among others, that we are not just a piffling inefficient nation," Eric had said with feeling.

Finally, in 1972, the French approved of the enlargement of the EEC to include UK, Denmark, Ireland and Norway.

As regarded themselves, they were glad to be on a posting away from the UK where unemployment had reached a million, and a three-day working week had been declared by the Prime Minister, Edward Heath. To take their thoughts away from it all, Eric bought the new novel by Frederick Forsyth called "The Day of the Jackal". The last best seller that he had bought had been

Germaine Greer's book "The Female Eunuch", which had made his hackles rise.

The couple had no major quarrels, Eric saw to that. He could not bear the thought of any shouting matches, no, he had had an ample sufficiency of those in his childhood. There were only occasional tiffs.

"Eric, I've seen a heavenly two-piece in one of the fashion houses."

"Oh no. Not again. We really can't afford anything this month."

"But we are not short in any way, my love."

"I am more than aware that we are not short," grumbled Eric, "but I do feel that we must try to live within my income. We already owe such a lot of gratitude to your parents. I am not a sponger, Philippa."

"I know that. I'll squeeze into something else."

"Please don't. I seriously mean it. We could have had an income from the house if we had been allowed to let it out, but your parents were dead against the idea."

"Father was quite allergic to that suggestion. And so was mother. We actually could not go against them. Also, mother gets so much joy out of going there once a fortnight to run the taps, settle the lighting and so on. She feels like the queen bee presiding over the cleaning team every two months."

"Don't I just know. It's over the top."

"No, it isn't. We are all a family. We pull together in everything. Don't take that pleasure away from them."

Eric, again, could but capitulate gracefully.

Sometimes they had disagreements about politics. Philippa's Spanish family were rabidly pro Franco. That man could do no wrong. Eric saw it differently.

"I wish you'd be a bit more positive about Franco," said Philippa somewhat petulantly, "Spain would have been nowhere without him."

"I do not approve of dictators in any form," replied Eric, "Yes, Spain has come a long way thanks to Franco, I admit, but at what a cost in bloodshed."

"Without him there would have been even more bloodshed," pursued Philippa, "the Spanish could not get their act together without a strong man. Just like the French needed Napoleon after the revolution."

"Oh, let's drop this harping on the subject. I'll go and do some reading."

It was early August. When Eric got home from work one Friday, Philippa said to him,

"Darling, we need to celebrate."

"Sweetheart, I celebrate every day because I'm married to you. But what is this in particular?"

"We are expecting."

Eric clapped his hands in flamenco rhythm, shouting, "Ole, Ole," and then lifted them up to be the bull's horns while with one foot he dug in furiously.

"I'm the great Toro of Toros. A father. Or shall I say the Boar of Boars since you once likened me to a pig. Our clan is enlarging. Hip, hip, hooray!"

He made a few snorting sounds like a boar. Then he laughed and patted Philippa's stomach gently.

"Philippa. How wonderful. You are a treasure. When is our baby due?"

"In February next year, between the 17th and the 20th, says the gynaecologist. I am two and a half months pregnant."

"I shall pour myself a good cognac in view of the celebration. You can have no alcohol. I'll pour you an orange juice. Put on a slow waltz, I want to twirl with the mother of my child."

She did as he requested and then the two were engrossed in their dance.

"Father will burst with pride," said Philippa.

"I bet. I can really see your father in the role of a grandpa. He will launch himself into it with gusto. I fear that he will be far worse than any children."

"I don't want to dampen our celebration, but I must ask. What will you do about your parents?"

"Tell them nothing. As any children grow up, they shall be told that my parents are dead. As you know, I go nevertheless twice a year to see them. They are under the impression that I still work for the estate agents. As far as they are concerned, you are barren. It is remarkable how little interested in my life they are. That hurts me to this day and it will always do so."

"You are right, Eric. We won't talk about this subject again."

"Indeed, my love. Now let me put on a real crooner and we can sway to the dulcet tones. I shall leave you to tell your parents about our news."

When Sir Philip and Lady Saunders learned that Philippa was pregnant, there was no end to their jubilation. Sir Philip was over the moon for his daughter. He blessed his son-in-law. That man had truly made his daughter happy. And now the family was enlarging. Sir Philip felt that he was born into the role of a grandfather, he looked forward to crawling on the floor, playing in the mud, building sand-castles on the beaches and tucking messily into ice-creams. Bliss awaited him. Eric's predictions came true, in the future photo-albums it could be seen that Sir Philip was the messiest and most crumpled-up "child" of the gatherings!

The future grandparents went immediately on a visit to Paris. This time they could still stay with Philippa and Eric in their guest-room. During the following visits they would be staying in a near-by hotel because the guest-room would become the nursery and the other spare bedroom would be for the nanny.

One afternoon, mother and daughter had gone shopping, leaving Eric and Sir Philip at home. The two were sipping a light white wine.

"My boy, I thank you for the happiness you are giving Philippa."

"No need for thanks, we are very happy together. Ours is a love that is slowly growing. I am waiting so eagerly for our child. I love the idea of being a real family man."

"There will be real competition as to who will be allowed to push that pram. I volunteer as number one," laughed Sir Philip, "However, there will be sacrifices to be made."

"I can't think of anything."

Eric was flummoxed.

"It's the car, my boy, the car. The orange MG two-seater is not designed to carry children. You'll have to get a family car."

"By Jove. What a thought. We shall have to become worthy. There will be a number of my colleagues who will quietly cackle when they see me in a… a..."

"Austin Maxi," laughed Sir Philip.

"Yes, in an Austin Maxi. The orange MG has got the odd jealous glance. We'll have no problem getting rid of it. There will be a queue of potential purchasers."

"By the way, have you thought about where the birth will take place?"

"Yes, indeed. Philippa will come to stay with yourselves two months before. For the just in case. When anything begins, phone me, and I will be on the next plane to London. Door to door should take no more than six hours. I am told that a first labour usually lasts well over twelve hours, so I'll be in time to pace the corridors with you."

Chapter 19

After the family Christmas in London, Eric had returned on his own to Paris. It felt a bit strange without Philippa, he had got used to her. At least he had been able to celebrate New Year 1973 with the family. They had a good marriage. They tended to enthuse about similar things like world happenings, new books, new plays, and so on.

At the Embassy, the dreaded Councillor was leaving in May. Whatever the next one would be like, he could not be worse, so life was looking up for many in the Embassy. Eric's policy of being especially deferential had paid dividends. He himself had not had any unpleasant encounters with the man.

One Saturday evening in late January, Eric had been reading and listening to some pop-songs on the radio. He became aware that they were playing "Pretty Woman" by Roy Orbison. An acute pain hit him. That was Katie's and his song. He switched the radio off like a scalded cat. It was too late, his mood had changed. His feet carried him to the drinks cabinet.

"Oh Katie. If only you were here. You are so much part of me. I don't want to forget, but I don't want to remember. How can I solve this?" murmured Eric to himself as he slowly got himself drunk. The last time he had had that insurmountable urge to drink had been a week before the wedding.

He was beginning to see that he would always have those bouts from time to time. For with the thought of Katie came the thought of Southall. The two were intertwined and inseparable.

On the morning of the 18th of February, there was a phone call at 5am. Eric knew instantly what it was about. Philippa was in labour. Eric left a message with the night porter at the Embassy. Everybody had been alerted to the fact that the baby was due sometime between the 17th and the 20th. Eric had been given two weeks' leave from whatever date the birth happened.

He got on the 7.40 flight to London and by eleven he was at the hospital. Philippa was overjoyed. Sir Philip was already a bundle of nerves. His wife tried to calm him down but without much success.

"Philip. Calm down. Women have been giving birth since time immemorial."

"I am aware of that interesting fact, Steffi. But this is our Philippa. I remember as if it was only yesterday when she was born. I was a nervous wreck."

"That was evident to the whole hospital. You got intermittent hiccups. It was dreadful. Don't get them now. You are supposed to prop Eric up. I see that he is the type to be quiet when nervous."

When at eight o'clock in the evening Philippa was wheeled into the inner sanctum to give birth, Eric could not sit still. He paced the corridors together with Sir Philip. Lady Saunders sat reading a book.

Just before nine they were called in. Philippa looked neat. She had on a fresh nightie and her hair had been combed. The baby was in swaddling clothes in her arms.

"May I congratulate you on a fine baby boy," said the obstetrician.

When Eric saw his little son, the iceberg in his heart melted. A new feeling filled him, a feeling of a strong protective love which gave him a happiness he had never expected to have.

"Philippa, my treasure, I can't thank you enough. Our baby boy is wonderful," said Eric and took his son into his arms.

Philippa saw in the eyes of her husband an entirely new expression, one of deep, deep sentiment. For Eric, the baby was the first thing he had ever loved with purity and selflessness. Everything that he had ever lacked, he would give to his son. He would be called Lucius, that he decided at once. The little one would have all the chances like the other Lucius about whom he had listened all those years ago. Dear Philippa, she had given him the most precious thing on earth.

Sir Philip had gone to kiss Philippa, but now he turned to Eric.

"Please, let me hold him now for a while."

"Yes, surely."

"Have you thought of a name yet?"

"Daddy, we haven't. I would like Eric to name our son. Darling, what shall it be? Have you anything in mind?"

"He shall be called Lucius, Lucius Philip," pronounced the proud father very firmly, "and now it is time for the grandmother to get him."

The doctor approached them.

"I am very glad to see such a happy family reunion, but now it is time for the new mother to have some rest. You will see them again tomorrow."

Chapter 20

It was through Nandita's friendship with the Brockley-Doones that Katie learned about Eric. It was March and she had gone to see Nandita. Hardly had she arrived when she asked,

"Nandita. Any news about Eric?"

"Yes, and big news at that. He has got a son who was born in February. He is said to be over the moon."

Katie's face clouded over. Her loved one now had a son, he was a family man. He would be over the moon. Katie instinctively knew that the child would mean the world to him. Whatever he felt about Philippa was no longer of importance, it was the child who mattered. For Katie it was an irreparable loss.

"Katie, for heaven's sake, don't take it so. It is not the end of the wold for you. You are only twenty-six. You've got your future before you."

"I know. I should have. But I can't ger over Eric. He really was the love of my life. And I fear it will stay that way. Since we broke up, I have not gone out with any men. I have no incentive."

"This is beginning to sound like an obsession. Do at least accept some invitations and go out. At least have a look at what is available. You don't have to start any relationships unless you want to."

"My dearest friend, you are so wise, as you know, I took up your suggestion about joining a choir. That has turned out well. There is a good crowd. We are twenty-eight in all, twelve men and sixteen women."

"What about the twelve men?"

"There are four in their thirties, three in their forties and the remainder are fifty plus. Three bachelors, who I suspect are the other way inclined and the rest are all married."

"Well, there are always friends of friends. See how you get along."

"Will do. Will at least try."

As for her job, she was still in a typing pool of a big concern. There were two junior managers and another two in middle-management who were all keen on her. At least they were all single men. But they were nothing like the sainted Eric. What Nandita had said made sense, so she decided to accept some invitations and see what might ensue.

She still lived in shared digs with two other girls. She got on well with them. They had realised that Katie was no threat at all to them as regards their men. One of the girls was twenty-nine and the other was thirty-three. The latter had got somewhat desperate during the last two years. She saw her chances dwindling seriously year by year. She was always in a relationship but none had lasted even a year. They knew that Katie had had a relationship but that it had ended a few years ago, but they did not know with whom. They had noticed that Katie had become a bit reclusive and they had suggested she take up a new hobby in order to meet people. They had suggested pottery.

Pottery, indeed, thought Katie. She felt no inclination towards it. However, why not, she thought in the end and enrolled herself on a course. It was a revelation to her that she actually enjoyed mucking around with the clay and that she turned out to have a real talent in it. It was a serious course where the different techniques of making clay were gone into and what different shapes could be created by the use of different clays. Ancient history of the use of clay was gone into, that of the Egyptians, the Greeks and the Chinese. Katie lapped it up. She loved especially ancient Egyptian art. The course was one of the best things she had ever done in her life. And most wonderfully, doing pottery fulfilled her inner longings.

As she sat there playing with the clay, her thoughts, as always were upon Eric, and lo and behold, her inner feelings came out in the clay. Most beautiful and intricate shapes somehow created themselves. It was love in the form of clay. Her teacher was most encouraging; not often had he come across such a talent. Katie took her time in learning the techniques and finesses of the art. It was to become a life-long joy to her.

Chapter 21

Philippa came back to Paris with baby Lucius after Easter 1973, together with the nanny. The nanny was really an au-pair girl as Philippa had no wish for a real nanny to take over her child. They basically needed a baby-sitter for when they were going out. Also, they wanted to go on short holidays without having to drag a baby with them.

They liked two to three night tours to different areas of France, so as to get to know the country really well. It was usually over a Saturday, Sunday and Monday which meant that Eric only needed to take one day off.

By November, Philippa was pregnant again. The baby was expected sometime between the 22nd and 26th July, 1974. Eric's chest swelled up in pride. Sir Philip enthused endlessly.

There was so much romance in the air. At the end of November, back home, Princess Anne had married Captain Mark Phillips in Westminster Abbey. Both Eric and Philippa loved watching the ceremony on the television.

"Princess Anne is wonderful," said Philippa, "but I wonder whether that marriage will be easy?"

"I don't think such a union can be easy," replied Eric, "he is in the military, his career, for the moment, but he will find it impossible to continue. Being married to the Queen's daughter puts him on a different pedestal from the rest. Should he need to leave his chosen way of life, what would he do? Would that make him happy or would it bring frustration? Most likely the latter."

"I feel the same. If a man can't have his career, then it does not augur well. For the moment, though, everything is like in a fairy tale. By the way, my parents would like to come for a week's visit. They wonder when it would suit us."

"Anytime, my darling. When they come, the nanny can have time off. Your father won't want to go anywhere without the little one."

It was then decided that the parents come for two weeks for Christmas.

Sir Philip was sitting cosseting Lucius. He was tireless.

"You've been in Paris for just over two years now," he said, "how much longer do you think your posting will last?"

"Not much more than the summer, I'd think. I expect to hear about it soon in the New Year."

"How do you feel about that, Eric?" asked Lady Saunders.

"It has been a wonderful first posting in which to cut my teeth, however, neither of us is making the mistake of thinking that we belong here in any way. Home is London and home is best. I don't know whether the next posting will be at home or abroad."

"Which would you prefer?" asked Sir Philip.

"No real preference, but perhaps a home posting at this stage would be good. We shall see."

As Eric had foreseen, at the end of January he was informed that from May onwards he would be joining the Western European Department at home.

In Paris, the fancy receptions again buzzed like champagne bubbles. There had been the opening of the new Charles de Gaulle airport in Paris on the 8th March. The pride of the Parisians knew no bounds. At the dinners and lunches it provided an interminable subject of conversation till suddenly the topic changed to that of the death of the President, Georges Pompidou. That had been sudden and unexpected. Now the bets had got to between Francois Mitterand and Valery Giscard d'Estaing.

"Who do you think will win, Eric?" asked Philippa.

"There is no way of knowing these things. It will be very close, I'd say. My bet would be on Giscard d'Estaing."

As it turned out, Eric would have won his bet.

To return to the UK, Eric and Philippa had again chosen to travel by train. It was easy to settle back into their house, all it needed was to remove the dust covers. They had arranged for their second child to be born in the same hospital as Lucius and for Philippa to be under the care of the same obstetrician. The labour started in the early hours of the 24th of July and by three o'clock in the afternoon the child was born. It was a girl.

"Emma Erica, welcome to the world," said the proud father who was brimming over at having a daughter.

"Philippa, you are the perfect wife. First a boy and then a girl."

"I know. It was just as you ordered, master," smiled Philippa, "look, there's Daddy clamouring to hold the newborn."

Eric passed the baby over to Sir Philip.

"Wow. You are going to be a beauty," crooned Sir Philip, "you've got your father's eyes and colouring and Steffi's mouth and chin. Lucius has Steffi's dark eyes and hair but the rest of him is Eric."

"That is all very interesting," said Lady Saunders, "when they are newborn, one can pick out the bone structure which later you can't because of the puppy fat."

"Daddy, don't you think that Eric has again chosen lovely names. Lucius and Emma, that sounds so good," mused Philippa.

When Eric heard her say that, he felt a little lump in his throat. The café from years ago came up into his mind's eyes.

He now had his own Emma. What he had felt for Lucius, he felt for Emma. The joy of having two children overwhelmed him and two tears of sheer bliss came to his eyes. Philippa saw those tears and her heart filled with gladness. How wonderful that the father of her children was so devoted to them. Such love, as showed in his eyes towards his children, such love he had never directed towards her, but that did not matter, what was important was that he felt it for the little ones.

"Oh Eric," thought Philippa, "I feel that you do have a certain amount of love for me, but the bulk of it goes to the children. That is fine. I feel fortunate in our family and that is how I want it to be. As for me, I love you more than anything in the world, Eric."

In the Western European Department Eric had been put on the desk for Spain. He and the whole family were pleased because that could mean a posting to Spain in the future. Their home life was warm.

The world was agog when on August the 9th, 1974, the American President Richard Nixon was forced to resign.

"What a pity that such an able and intelligent man had brought such a scandal upon himself," commented Philippa.

"Well, he did not follow the eleventh commandment, thou shalt not be found out," nodded Eric.

"Eric, what do you think about going to see the two new films that came out last year?"

"Which ones?"

"The Exorcist and the Last Tango in Paris."

"Lord, no! The former will only be some gobbledegook about the Catholic Church and a horrid attack on the church in general. I could not bear it. As for the Tango, no thank you. Sexual perversions do not interest me. It is said to be very risqué."

The year 1975 began with force. By the first half of the year, three major world events had happened. On the 11th February, Margaret Thatcher defeated Edward Heath. On the 29th April, at the Fall of Saigon, the United States started to evacuate its citizens. On 5th June Anwar Sadat reopened the Suez Canal which had been closed since 1967.

"So much has happened this year already," said Philippa, tucking into her breakfast bacon and eggs. They had bacon and eggs at weekends when Eric was not pressed to hurry to the Office. He enjoyed devouring them at a stately pace. During the week they had omelettes.

"Indeed," replied Eric, "I am pleased by all those changes. I am especially pleased by the election of Mrs Thatcher, a wonderful strong woman. As you know, I can't officially take any political stances except spout what the government of the day wants. However, privately I have my opinions as has everybody else."

The doorbell rang.

"Ah, the proud grandparents are early. As usual."

"Good morning, everyone. Lucius, have you grown since I last saw you a week ago? Emma certainly has. As soon as you have all finished munching, we'll be out with the little ones. The sun is shining and it is almost as warm as in Spain," said Sir Philip giving a kiss and a cuddle to both children.

"In two weeks' time, you will have them for two whole weeks, Daddy, while we are in Austria."

Chapter 22

Katie had again been to Nandita's. She had felt somewhat depressed because Nandita had been pregnant. The couple hoped for a second son. And then she had learned that Eric was back from Paris and the father of a little girl now.

"I am very pleased for them," said Nandita, "it is good that there should be more than one child."

"I think you are right," said Katie.

"How is your manhunt going?" Nandita wanted to know.

"I've been out a few times with different candidates, but nothing special has come out of them. However, I have found bliss in pottery."

"Pottery. You surprise me."

"I surprised myself. I took to it like duck to water. To work with clay gives me intense satisfaction. I think my teacher is quite proud of me."

"Next time we meet, you must show me some of your works. I would love to have one."

"You shall, Nandita, you shall. I am as yet nowhere near to mastering the art of pottery but I'm working my way towards it."

Yes, she had accepted the odd invitation. It had been all right on each occasion but there had been no spark as far as she had been concerned.

What had brought some joy into her life was that an old friendship had been renewed, that with Timmy Day. For her that meant that she would have someone to talk to in a more personal level. She could not do so with her parents nor with her brother. They would only have been stressed. A couple of months ago when she had been visiting her parents, she had come across Timmy. He had become a physiotherapist and worked in Ealing Hospital. He loved his job.

They had gone for a meal together and since then had seen one another roughly every fortnight. They had a good friendship and they could reminisce about school days. Katie appreciated the fact that Timmy had not asked anything about Eric. She needed a bit of a confidante, so one day she approached him.

"Timmy, as you know, I was Eric's girlfriend for eight years. Then that unfortunately came to an end because of his job at the Foreign Office. I am heartbroken."

"Your break-up really surprised me. I heard it from my mother who heard it from yours."

"I thought as much. I get news of Eric through Nandita."

"Shouldn't you let that go, Katie?"

"Maybe I should, but I can't. I've been out with a couple of chaps but there has been no spark."

"That could be because you're still grieving. You probably need some more time. You cannot hurry these things."

"You are right, Timmy. You understand it. For the time being, let pottery be my passion."

Chapter 23

The fact that Eric had been put at the desk for Spain made sense since it was known that he spoke fairly fluent Spanish, thanks to his spouse. He decided also to enrol himself in the Foreign Office Spanish courses at the medium level so as to get to grips with the grammar and language construction. It could well be that he might be sent to Spain as a posting.

He learned that Horace was due to come back from his first posting, which had been China. The two of them, would have a really good chinwag. Cecil and Malcolm had returned from their postings just before Eric. Cecil had been to Russia and Malcolm to Brazil. The dreams of all three had come true.

It was quite funny how Brazil had affected Malcolm, he almost walked in a Rhumba rhythm. And he had married a Brazilian beauty, the lovely Dolores. He had travelled up and down and across the South American continent. He had loved everything, except the earthquakes. Those were frequent and occurred all over. Dolores had some money of her own, so the couple had been able to buy a two-bedroom flat in Earls Court. They had held a party soon after moving in.

At the party, Eric and Cecil got talking. "How was Russia, Cecil?" asked Eric.

"Russia might have been fine, but the Soviet Union wasn't. Grim. What a terrifying world. Nobody can trust anyone. Only authorised people are allowed to talk to foreigners. That goes down even to the level of children. The Russian children are not allowed anywhere near to ours. Tragic.

"That's quite shocking," said Eric, "how can they possibly believe in a system like that?"

"They don't. Nobody believes in the communist crap."

"Was there any fun at all? Places to go?"

"Fun was the opera, ballet, theatre and concerts. Ah yes, and the Moscow State Circus. I saw Swan Lake, Giselle, and the like several times."

"How were you housed?"

"In designated areas. I lived in the huge blocks of flats in Kutuzovsky Prospect next to the Ukraina Hotel. We were swamped by cockroaches! They were everywhere like armies. There was no way of getting rid of them."

"Thank goodness I am not a Russian speaker, Philippa could not cope with that."

"I've been holding you hostage with all my questions, Cecil. I must liberate you to circulate. Just one more question: how did you cope with the winters?"

"Proper warm clothing from underwear down. With no wind, up to twenty degrees was bearable, after that it became horrid.

"Now let's get more drink," said Eric, "when Horace returns from China he will have many tales to tell, I'm sure."

Eric enjoyed his work. At the end of October 1975 he was kept very busy as King Juan Carlos 1 assumed power in Spain. He continued busy as on November 22nd the monarchy restored after 31 years. The Spanish side of his family was most pleased by these developments.

At home all was going well. Lucius and Emma were growing. The Saunders grandparents were young. When Lucius was born, they were 55 and 54 years respectively. They had married very young, when he had been 21 and she 20. They had high energy levels. The children lived in between the parental home and that of the grandparents. It was ideal for everyone.

At the beginning of 1977 Eric was told that he would be posted to Madrid in June. That meant jubilation all round. It would provide a lot of larger family meetings and togetherness.

The family were planning their move. Lucius was now five and Emma would be four in the summer. That meant that the two of them would be at an age to remember Spain well. And it would strengthen their Spanish. Again Eric and Philippa decided to travel by train as it would be fun for the children. Eric had been promoted to a Second

Secretary and they would have a three-bedroom house with a garden.

They settled well int Madrid. The staff at the Embassy were all nice, and there was no fierce Councillor to be worried about. Come September, Lucius would start at the English school, and a year after that, Emma. At the end of October the Embassy was buzzing with work as the President of Catalonia, Josep Tarradellas, returned to Barcelona from exile and the autonomous government of Catalonia, the Generalitat, was restored.

Spain, now being a monarchy, had pageants, and the King was evident in political life. Even though Eric was still quite junior in position, the couple had had the joy of being at some receptions where the King and Queen had been present.

"Daddy, Daddy, did you really see the King and the Queen?" asked Lucius.

"I did, my son, I did."

"Daddy, does the King have a smart uniform?"

"Yes, son, he does."

"Daddy, is the King handsome?" Emma wanted to know.

"The King is a handsome man, my sweet, and the Queen is lovely."

The first holiday the family took was to Cordoba, Sevilla and Malaga in order to see family. Then they continued on "the footsteps of Gerald Brennan, the author whose works on Spain Eric particularly liked. He wanted to see what the present-day Al Pujara would be like. They finished their three-week holiday in Granada, admiring the Alhambra. They did not overdo the culture, they saw to it that the children had plenty of opportunities to play and to swim in the sea. Their Austin Maxi was a comfortable family car.

On future holidays they would tour the Pyrenees, and see Barcelona and its surroundings. Another time they would tour the North West past Salamanca to Santiago de Compostela. Their favourite outings were to Flamenco shows. As Eric had started to learn some flamenco early on in their relationship at Philippa's instigation, he could follow the new courses with some ease. Philippa as well as the children all took lessons in it. They got a lot fun from having little family shows of flamenco and sevillanas.

Sir Philip and Lady Saunders were frequent visitors. Eric loved the family's being together. He had been so starved of normal family life in his childhood home that now he took full advantage of his own. He did make a point of going to see his parents, in secret from the children, twice a year. It had been easy from France and the same applied from Spain. When he visited them, he mainly had to listen to complaints about the neighbourhood and tales from the pub and from the bingo. His parents had no normal curiosity about Eric's life at all.

It was autumn of 1979, and they had been in Madrid over two years. Eric was perusing the Sunday Times as he always did. He was suddenly jolted upright by an article in the arts section. It was about a promising new pottery artist, Kat Claydon, and the successful exhibition she had held in a trendy gallery in Fulham. There was a small photo of two of her works. Eric found the shapes most interesting; somehow they spoke to him. It was uncanny. One of them had soft colours and a kind of unearthly beauty, the other was in black and dark blue and was repulsive. An interesting form, but the way the colours had been applied and the way it slightly slanted, made you dislike it. Curiously enough, Southall came to Eric's mind.

He shook himself. He must be dithering. He had never thought that he would like any modern art at all, yet here he was, seriously interested in the works of this particular artist. Hmm, he'd like to see more of the artist's work. Yes, next week he was in London for three days. That would give him an opportunity to go to the gallery and make enquiries.

As he got to the gallery, he did not need to ask any questions. In the window was a photo of the artist. She was no other than his Katie! She looked beautiful. Eric's heart jumped. All the old feelings were there as they always had been. He still loved Katie deeply. It was as wonderful as it was painful. He went inside to have a brief look. He was unable to stay long as he was so emotionally taken by this discovery.

His Katie. His Katie had become an artist. That was entirely new to him. There had never been any indications that she was gifted in pottery. It must be a mature development. He had thought that he knew all there was to know about Katie, but now he realised that there was so much more to anyone than could be known easily. The closest of people could surprise you.

So far Eric had made no efforts to know what Katie might be doing. Now he decided that he would keep an eye open as to how Kat Claydon was doing. Oh Lord, he needed a drink. He was in London on his own. He needn't worry about anyone seeing him. The last time had been when he had returned from visiting his parents about seven months ago. During those bouts he would say to Philippa "I think I need a bit of space tonight" and then he would sit up late alone in the guest-room, eventually to fall asleep there. He blessed the fact that Philippa never queried anything and never pried. She was the only one who had any inkling about these episodes. Nobody else was in the know.

Chapter 24

While Eric was in Spain, Katie had continued her somewhat monotonous life. In 1977 she had had a bit of luck. She had won a tidy sum at the football pools. It had been enough to buy a two-bedroom flat in Hammersmith. She had chosen that area for the same reason as had Eric all those years ago: it was relatively central with good connections, and the area had stayed cheap. In many parts it was not salubrious, but in some parts it was nice. Her cousin and his mates had come to do the redecorating. They had revamped the kitchen and the bathroom and had painted it magnolia all over as she had requested. A carpet firm had then laid the pink carpet, except in the small bedroom where she had chosen grey lino. That would be her studio for working with clay. Two walls were full of shelves designed to hold weight.

At first, she had dreamt of furnishing it with antiques, as Eric had done, but then she had thought the better of it. She was not Eric. Her tastes were light and modern so she proceeded on those lines. It made a huge difference to her to have her own place and no longer be obliged to live in shared digs. With no rent to pay, her secretary's salary kept her in comfort.

Her proficiency with clay had now begun blossom into mastership. At the end of that year her teacher had helped her to get a small gallery to exhibit her works together with two hopeful painters. The gallery was a greedy wolf, they wanted sixty percent of anything. Katie had had no say in it. She had submitted twelve works of hers.

The big surprise came when in the first four days all of her works had been sold. The gallery asked for more. She had had seven more to give and within the week they had all gone. She had got a nice little sum from that, but what really pleased her was that her work was liked.

The following year the gallery wanted two dozen of her works. She did so, but also upped the price by forty percent, as her teacher had suggested. The teacher had become a friend and an advisor, Katie no longer needed any teaching. The same thing happened as the year before. Within a fortnight all her works had been sold.

The word had gone about. So she was approached by a trendy gallery in Fulham, asking her to exhibit with them the following year. They only charged fifty percent of the sales. This time she doubled her prices. Again, within ten days all her works had gone. The gallery had contacts with journalists and that is how Katie's works had come to be mentioned in the Sunday Times. With her teacher they had invented the name Kat Claydon, they had both felt that Katie Smith did not sound right.

Katie was having lunch with Timmy.

"Katie," said Timmy, "I think you've now had a break-through. You are becoming a name in the art world. I'm so glad for you."

"That's true," smiled Katie, "Kat Claydon is on her way up in the world."

"Having got mentioned in the Sunday Times means that Eric will have seen it. He will be proud."

"Yes, Eric," sighed Katie, her face clouding over, "I wonder whether that would mean anything to him. He is now in Madrid. I know this through Nandita."

"Of course, it would mean the world to him. He has always wished the best for you. Why should he have changed? He didn't stop loving you at any stage."

"Then he should have married me," frothed Katie with disappointment.

"You keep harping on about that matrimony. Even I, with considerably less brain power that Eric, even I can see that a marriage does not work on love alone. The two girlfriends that I've had, I have loved them well, but as for marriage, no way were they suited to me. One of them was a medical student, a budding doctor, and she would not have been happy in the long run to have been married to a mere physiotherapist. You see?"

"Yes, I do see. I see that everything else is of more importance than love."

Chapter 25

Just after Christmas 1980, Eric learned that he was being posted to Caracas. To be a First Secretary there. It was a Spanish-speaking country so there would be no language difficulties.

"We are going to South America in April, to Venezuela," boomed Eric to the family, "What do you think of that?"

"Are there Indians there? And temples?" Lucius wanted to know, who at the age of seven had learned something about the Mayas and the Aztecs.

"I should think so. We will see," replied his father.

"Eric, how come we have been posted to South America?" asked Philippa.

"In the bowels of the Office there is a world map. The promotion board lads put a name on a dart and then throw it at the map. Where the dart lands, that's where the person is sent whose name is on the dart," cackled Eric.

"It comes at the right time for us, Eric," continued Philippa, "Lucius and Emma will profit from seeing the New World while they still don't need to be at boarding school."

"We will still have a fair amount of time for them as I am not yet too senior for all of our time to be taken up by work and social duties," said Eric, "higher up the ladder, it becomes real pressure.

Have you not noticed how our Ambassador here in Madrid is for evermore at some "cat christening"?"

"You do choose some very irreverent phrases, my love, but to answer your question, I have paid attention, and I see that stamina is needed."

"What is the situation as regards our crockery at this stage?"

"Well, Eric, out of twelve settings there are eight of each left and similarly with the glassware. I suggest we keep those for ourselves and buy a load of nice, but cheap stuff. Here in Spain I can get rock bottom prices."

"Brilliant, you are, my spouse. You are the best spouse I ever had."

"Has Daddy had other spouses, then?" enquired Emma with eyes wide in surprise.

"No, he hasn't, stupid," said Lucius, "what he means is that mum's the best mum ever."

"Amen to that," said Eric.

Later that evening the couple sat together.

"Eric, I have been planning a list of places we need to see while across the Atlantic."

"That sounds ominous."

"Rubbish. I'm keen on seeing Brazil, Chile and Argentina. Further north, I'd like to see the Redwood Trees, Grand Canyon and Mississippi River."

"Lord, what a list. I have only six weeks holiday a year. And think of the cost."

"We'll space it over three years. This time don't start to grind on about the price. As you know, father has settled me with money of my own. The holiday fund will come from there. Otherwise we'll stay within your income."

Eric had gathered that to stay within his income was not possible for Philippa. He was aware that a lot of the stuff for the children had not been bought from the bargain basements as Philippa purported them to have been bought. Her bargain basement had a name: Sir Philip. Father and daughter concocted endless ruses to explain certain purchases and cover up the actual expenses.

Eric had had to cave in. He was too busy with work to take time for a major counter campaign. He could foresee that both Lucius and Emma, once they were older, would also frequent the bargain basement. He sighed. In the end, it was better that money was used for something rather than only piling it up.

"Eric, Eric. Have you gone to sleep?"

"Ah, no, Philippa, just in my thoughts."

"Do you know anything about the climate there?"

"Not much, but I've looked into it briefly. I'm afraid it is heat all through the year in Caracas. Twenty-five to thirty degrees Celsius."

"Goodness, that is a bit steep."

"I should imagine that the houses have air-conditioning."

"We are all young enough to cope. And it is a chance to get to know South America."

At the family reunion, the grandparents, who had come for a three week stay in Madrid, were not too pleased because of the distance.

"I've made enquiries about Venezuela," said Sir Philip, "it is at the moment one of the wealthiest countries on that continent, thanks to its oil. That will probably mean that there is not too much crime. But the weather is frightful. Relentless heat."

"I don't think I could cope with any visits there, "said Lady Saunders, "that breaks my heart."

"I don't think your health could support it, Steffi," said her husband, "but we could arrange to go with the young ones on some holidays where the climate is not quite so hot. That is, if they would have us."

"Of course, we would have you," said Eric, "That is a very good idea."

"Philip," said Lady Saunders, "you could go once a year for a few weeks to Caracas. That would give such joy to Lucius and Emma."

"Yes," piped up the children. We want Grandpa to see where we live. And take photos to show you, Grandma."

The preparations for the long journey were intense. Also various vaccinations had to be undergone. This time the whole family would go by plane. Before they left, Eric made a brief visit to see his parents in order to tell them that he would be away abroad with a new job for three to four years. They had been surprised, but showed no interest in the subject. Eric said that he would write to them.

When the family arrived in Venezuela, they were plunged straight away into intense heat. A humid one at that. It took them a while to get used to it, but as Philippa had said, they were all young enough and their bodies were adaptable. They had been given a lovely large four-bedroom house with a large garden. In every room there was an air-conditioning unit. That was a saving grace.

What Sir Philip had said about the economics was correct. The country did seem to be booming and most people seemed to be reasonably well off. The place had a feeling of a permanent party, especially in places like the island of Margarita which overflowed with rich tourists.

"I like Caracas," said Philippa, "the people are friendly and there are smart shops."

"As your father so wisely put it, for the time being, yes. However, the country has not diversified its economy at all. It is totally dependent upon the price of oil. That could have severe repercussions in the future."

"So far they have managed good social programs, health care, education and transport," said Philippa.

"Yes, and people are getting a decent salaries. Well, let's not think of doom and gloom. President Herrera seems to be doing fine so far."

Lucius and Emma thrived at the English school. They were most interested in the country. Lucius showed all signs of becoming a chip off Sir Philip. He had a scientific mind like his grandfather's. Emma was very good at drawing and made many lovely pictures of the nature for her grandmother.

There were many ancient sites of old civilisations and of prehistoric animals. When the family visited Taima-Taima, the youngsters had been impressed by the finding of the bones of the ancient Xenorhinotherium, a cross between a camel and a rhino. It was there that the first human settlement had been discovered, dating from around 14,000 ago.

At Urumaco, the two had become fascinated by the monster guinea pig. This rodent was called Phoberomys Patterson, after the scientist Brian Patterson, who in the 1970's had discovered the remains of the prehistoric animal. The guinea pig had been the size of a buffalo, weighing over 700 kilos. Lucius wanted to know all about it and learned that it had been semi-aquatic and had lived in packs.

"Being so big, it would have been safe," said Emma.

"I'm not so sure. What about the animals for whom it was food? What size would they have been?"

"Please don't worry Emma with the subject of predators, for that is what they are called," said Philippa, "let her enjoy the large guinea pig."

Their time in Venezuela passed very well. They toured as they had planned and Sir Philip came on yearly visits. However, in 1982, the pleasant side of their diplomatic existence underwent a slight hiccup. This was because President Herrera sided with Argentina in its war with the United Kingdom over the Falkland Islands. That caused a certain tension between the Venezuelans and the British.

"The Venezuelans don't think we'll win," said Eric, "and they are not the only ones. The whole world seems to think that we are mad and can but lose. They don't think we have any real power."

"Should we win, against all the odds, the world will change its mind about Britain being weak. Meanwhile the tension towards the British makes itself felt."

"Yes, Philippa. I don't know whether this will happen here, but it could be that the Ambassador will be called home and the Embassy will be put under the care of Switzerland, a neutral country, to look after British affairs. We here become a type of extension of the Swiss Embassy."

"Will it affect much?"

"I don't know, probably not much. We will continue to be as pleasant to everyone as possible."

And the incredible happened, Britain won.

In early 1983, the Venezuelan bolivar suffered abrupt devaluation against the US dollar. It demonstrated the precarious economic situation of the country. There was a respite later that year when the oil prices rose again. So far there had not been any devastating results.

In May that year, when Eric had been in Caracas for three years, the Councillor died in a car accident. That happened only two weeks after the sudden departure of the Second Secretary, who had decided to leave the Service and become a priest.

"This affects our family," said Eric, "as there was a new Ambassador less than a year ago, this means that I am the only one to carry the can at the moment. The two new people that are posted here need time to get to grips with the country. I can see that we shall be here for an extra year."

In fact, it was August 1984 when the Flint family came back to London.

Chapter 26

To be at a home posting was ideal for the family at that stage. Lucius was eleven and Emma ten. In September Lucius started boarding at Westminster school, right in the centre of London. He fitted in well and also had the joy of seeing much of his family. It would be September 1986 when Emma would start boarding at Wycombe Abbey. Again, that would be a success.

At the Office Eric was made an Assistant Head of the department responsible for Sweden among other countries. He decided to learn the language. It might mean he would be posted there as a result. The thought that Swedish was really the main language in the Scandinavian countries meant that later he might get a posting in any one of them. He did not relish the thought of cold Nordic winters but the incessant heat that he had endured in Venezuela did not make him keen on any tropical postings.

In November 1986, Horace was posted home. He had been in New Delhi. After his posting Bangkok the two friends were very pleased to see each other.

"Horace. You are still a bachelor at the age of forty-three," said Eric.

"My dear chap. I was constantly in love with the Siamese women when I was there. I did not

189

know how to choose. But they felt a bit distant. And as for the Indian beauties, they were fire-crackers all right and needless to say, I was constantly in love with them as well. But there was a very big but."

"What do you mean?"

"The 'but' was the extent of a family one would be marrying into. Frightening. I saw it with a couple of colleagues who had yielded and had got wed. With a wife came a couple dozen siblings, cousins, and so on. You name it. Visiting family members came in packs. I like the idea of a quiet wife for me alone."

"Gosh. You are so right. Good man. You escaped any snares."

"And how is life for you, a family man?"

"Lucius is nearly fourteen and Emma is twelve. Lucius is at Westminster as a boarder and Emma is at Wycombe Abbey to follow in Philippa's footsteps. The grandparents are wonderful. Sir Philip dotes on both grandchildren. We lead an active family life with them."

"How lucky for you. You are blessed in having Philippa, a wonderful woman."

"You must come to dinner. We would like to hear about all the tales from your postings. I loved your letters. I'll talk to Philippa and phone you about the dates."

"Splendid. I look forward to that."

For New Year, Eric and Philippa gave a party, and of course Horace was there as well. Philippa had carefully selected three women to invite who were in their early thirties in order to give Horace a chance to find romance. Eric had shaken his head, Horace was bound to see through the ruse, but women were so eternally romance orientated. Most of them hated the thought that any man should remain single. Horace was reasonably good-looking, he had a pair of jolly light-brown eyes and a perky smile which exposed a set of perfect teeth. He was of medium height and slim. He tended to wear comfortable clothes and all his garments seemed a little too big for him. Not for him any figure-hugging sartorial triumphs such as Eric's choice of clothes. Because of his flamenco dancing, Eric was conscious of the beauty of the body and its movements and the clothing to accentuate sex-appeal. He was also aware that he was a singularly attractive man.

"We must find a wife for Horace," said Philippa.

"Must we? The man is perfectly capable of finding himself a wife. And he is only forty-three."

"He is getting long in the tooth, say I. Soon he will become untrainable."

"Is that what women want? A man to train. Into submission, no doubt."

"I have never tried to train you, Eric, much less tried to beat you into submission. I love you just as you are."

"Oh darling, I know that. I hope that I have not tried to do too much leading from my part. Come here, let me kiss you. You make me so happy."

"Any of the three women I specially invited with Horace in mind, any one of them would be a good choice. Girls from a proper background. Out of your crowd of four, only you and Malcolm are family men. I shudder to think that Cecil's first marriage lasted only two years to be followed by an acrimonious divorce."

"He had hardly got married when a mistress promptly appeared in the picture. He has always been a veteran skirt-chaser. As we are talking of him, I heard the other day that he has just left wife number two after four years."

"Goodness gracious. Thank goodness there are no children. I can see though why women fall for him. It is his dark eyes and his dark curly hair plus the Italianate looks he has inherited from his mother. And the charm."

"Yes, he is a handsome man indeed."

At the party, to Philippa's disappointment, Horace had not been interested in any of her three candidates. No doubt Philippa would pursue her efforts, thought Eric. Poor Horace. Let the man enjoy his liberty.

Then something totally unforeseen happened. In April, Horace had invited Eric and Philippa to dinner, a dinner Eric was never to forget.

What had happened? During the early months of the year Horace seemed to have been much occupied by personal life. After one party, where they had all been, Eric and Philippa had asked him to go on with them to dinner at a restaurant, but he had made some excuse about going to see some friends. Then there had been that lunch to which Philippa had asked him to come but he had said that he was busy that Saturday.

"Eric," said Philippa, "Horace has been behaving out of character. He seems very secretive. My hunch is that he has found a woman."

"Hmm. Now that you mention it, I think you may be right. I, too, feel that there is more to him than there was."

"I am dying of curiosity."

"I can see that, my love. We will get to know about it sooner or later. Even though he seems so open, I can sense that the portcullis of his interior is shut."

Indeed, there was a woman in Horace's life. Not just a woman, he had actually fallen in love.

One day at the beginning of February, he had been out with a friend of his who had waxed lyrical about the new exhibition of pottery at a smart gallery in Fulham. In fact his friend had dragged Horace there with him. At the gallery, Horace had been impressed by the wonderful craftsmanship of the artist and the beautiful creations that were there to see. The artist was truly gifted. A middle-aged man with a beard had approached them.

"May I introduce myself, I am Zoltan Landowski, the owner of this gallery. I see you are admiring the pottery. I can assure you that it would profit you well to buy a piece. This is an oncoming artist who will go far. At the moment you can still make a bargain."

"I like them all," said Horace, "but I like particularly the piece called "Yearning". I think I shall buy it."

"Would you like to meet the artist, Kat Claydon, who happens to be here at the moment?"

"Oh, indeed I would."

The owner went to some back rooms and then came out with a woman. As soon as Horace set eyes upon her he was a changed man. It was a "coup de foudre" for him. He fell in love hook, line and sinker.

"May I introduce the artist, Kat Claydon," said the owner.

"Horace Grant. This is a great honour for me, Ms Claydon. Your works have got a sensitivity and grace about them that is quite exceptional. I have just bought the piece called "Yearning". Can you tell me at all what inspired it?"

"Mr Grant, it gives me great pleasure to know that you appreciate my works. "Yearning" came about as I was deeply engrossed in sentiments of yearning and longing for beauty and warmth in life. All my pieces have to do with feeling and emotion. How could it be otherwise, given that I am a woman?"

"Ms Claydon, would it be too much to ask you to take me round the other works to explain them to me?"

"I shall be delighted to do so."

Horace could not take his eyes off Ms Claydon. She was a beauty. A beauty in a subtle way, in a non-frightening manner. One could not tell her age. Early thirties was Horace's guess. Lovely hazel eyes, finely arched brows, flawless complexion and a full mouth with a sweet expression. Her long hair had been tied back with a red ribbon. She was small with an hour-glass figure. She was dressed in a brown skirt and a caramel-coloured twin-set. She wore interesting jewellery, a pendant which was obviously one of her own works. She had red shoes with a small heel which picked up the colour of the red ribbon in her hair.

Horace was mesmerised by her. Now that love had hit him, it had hit him hard. He could not find his easy-going patter. He could not get any funny phrases out. It took all of his courage to ask her if she would accept an invitation out.

To his great relief and joy, Ms Claydon had accepted his invitation to lunch the following Saturday. He had asked what type of restaurant she liked, and as result he had booked a table at a fancy Italian restaurant. On Saturday morning Horace overslept and did not wake till nine. He jumped out of bed like a scalded cat and rushed into the bathroom to start an extensive grooming session. He even endured a cold shower to finish with to get the circulation really going. He needn't have bothered, his circulation was in over-drive anyway. He took great care with everything and when he was dressing, for the first time in his life, he felt sorry that his entire wardrobe consisted of comfortable clothes. Silly he, he should have gone to the shops. He put on a bit more aftershave than usual. With his grey suit he put on a shirt with light-blue and pink stripes to go with a light-blue tie. He wanted to look young and perky and not like a fossilised old toad. He had always avoided "The Handbag" fashion, however worthy it was.

He was early at the restaurant. When he saw Katie arrive, his knees felt weak.

"Ms Claydon, what a pleasure it is to see you. Let me take your coat. I chose a table by the window, are you happy with that?"

"Oh, very much so, thank you."

Thy found that conversation flowed easily. Early on it became evident to Horace that Katie did not have a solid educational background, but that did not worry him in the least. He was a second son, a spare rather than an heir, and he did not parade airs and graces. He found Katie amusing and a lot of fun. What did it matter that she was not a brain-box? He was overwhelmed with pleasure when she said,

"Mr Grant. I think it would be preferable to be on first name terms. My real name is Katie Smith, Kat Claydon is only an artist name."

"Thank you very much for that. I am Horace. I think you have chosen your artist name well, Claydon is perfect as you work with clay."

The lunch ended much too soon for Horace. However, on Wednesday Katie had agreed to go for a dinner. Thus began Horace's slow romance. He hardly dared to touch her, so precious was she to him. He could sense that she liked him very much, but would she ever feel something more? They saw one another a couple of times a week and Horace felt as if he were on burning hot coals. He decided that he needed help to know in which direction to steer. He had better introduce Katie to Eric and Philippa so that they could get to know the intended, and then Eric would be in a position to guide him through the pitfalls of love.

After all, he had landed a wife successfully. At the same time Horace wanted to keep Katie a secret for a while. A secret just for him. So he decided to arrange a surprise dinner party where all parties would meet. He would leave who was coming unknown, to be found out on the evening. It was to be a memorable evening. What he did not know then was that his dinner party would become one of the most memorable ones ever, but only from a negative point of view. He had forgotten the principle: do not ask a question to which you do not have the answer.

Chapter 27

Eric and Philippa were getting ready for Horace's dinner party.

"Eric, when Horace asked us to come to this dinner party in order to meet someone he'd like to introduce to us, did he say who?"

"No, but I'm sure it must be his new lady love. He has been behaving in the classic way that a man in love behaves. He has the look of a sheep. And he has spruced himself up with a new wardrobe. He has brought an electric shaver and a bottle of aftershave to the office, for the times when he goes out straight after work. This has been going on since February and now we are end June."

"This is obviously not a passing flame."

"No, Philippa. He would not introduce us to a passing flame. What for? I think the man might even be planning to sacrifice himself on the altar of matrimony. I know Horace well-enough to know that it must be serious."

Katie was the first to arrive at Horace's surprise dinner. She looked lovely in a silver dress with a bottle-green bolero. Silver shoes and silver hair decorations. Her hair fell to her shoulders and the ends had been slightly curled. Her lipstick gave a touch of red. She wore bottle-green earrings and a bracelet to match, all of which she had made herself. She looked elegant and yet approachable.

Like a hearth one wants to return to and in the light of which one wants to relax, thought Horace. As he stood there speechless and wide-eyed, Katie gave a sweet smile and said,

"Horace, do please relax. Come here, and you may kiss my cheek."

Horace was choking with emotion at that request. So far he had only touched her hand, and that had been at the gallery when they were being introduced. He breathed in her perfume.

And then the doorbell rang again. Eric and Philippa came in. Horace turned to say, "May I introduce…" when Katie cried out with a voice full of joy and ecstasy, "Eric. Eric. How wonderful to see you."

And she dashed to kiss him on both cheeks. Horace and Philippa were left staring. It was clear that those two knew each other, and more than well at that, one could not help seeing.

As Eric saw Katie he wished that the ground would sink under him. What a devastating surprise. To see Katie suddenly after so many years, sixteen to be precise, was a joy and a horror. A lot of things were bound to come out. Only, pray, nothing to link him with Southall.

Here was Katie, beaming at seeing him. And she had dashed to him. Philippa was bound to take a dim view of that. And what about Horace? He was no fool, he would see that Eric and Katie had been an item. Eric had managed to steel his arms to his sides so that he did not touch Katie. But he had had to bow politely to receive the greeting pecks. And her arms had been around him. Groan. Katie, as usual, had not used her brain. She had acted instinctively. Groan. Aloud he managed to say,

"What a lovely surprise to see you, Katie," then, turning to the other two, he said, "Katie and I are old friends from when I was in Hammersmith and she in Shepherd's Bush. She was in Iffley road sharing with two friends. May I introduce my wife, Philippa."

"How do you do," said Philippa rather stiffly and with the warmth of an iceberg. This effect was even accentuated by her ice-blue outfit where the diamonds at her ears and wrist glinted like icicles. A rhapsody of winter, chilling the air.

Horace was having kittens. The evening had already turned into a nightmare and it had not yet even begun. Katie was evidently a former girlfriend of Eric's. Horace was vividly reminded of the rouge and the lipstick that he had found in Eric's shower room all those years ago. The worst was the look of love in Katie's eyes as she had seen Eric. Goodness me, the woman was still in love with him. With a rival like Eric, he, Horace, had no chances at all.

And good Lord, there was Philippa. The poor woman had not deserved this. Where was his behaviour as a host? He would try to smooth over what could be smoothed. His surprise dinner had not only turned into a true surprise, it had turned into a disaster. An avoidable disaster at that. All the fault of himself, Horace. If he had mentioned who had been invited, the different parties could have pulled out of a meeting. In fact, none of them would have come. Now thanks to himself the evening had to be lived through by some polite miracle of proper behaviour. Grim.

"Now, dear friends, further introductions are not necessary. I've got some champagne in the fridge."

He brought his guests to the living room, then he had a brainwave as to how to help at least in a small way.

"Philippa, before you settle yourself, would you like to come to see that small Chinese painting that I have mentioned to you? I'd really like you to see it. I have it in my bedroom."

Philippa went with Horace. The bedroom was at some distance. In his flat, the lounge was at the end and there was a long corridor on either side of which were the kitchen/dining-room, his study and last his bedroom and bathroom. This way Eric and Katie would have five or six minutes in which to concoct whatever story they saw fit to trot out. That would help to prevent horrible talk at cross-purposes.

It showed how intelligent and kind Horace was. Eric had at once understood and was grateful to his friend. As soon as the two had gone, Eric said, "Katie. I must beg you never to reveal to anyone that we two grew up in Southall. That would kill me. It would destroy my whole being. Can I count on you?"

"Eric, of course you can count on me. I won't say anything about it. But Horace knows that I come from Southall."

"But not that I come from there. It would cause my poor wife intense grief if she knew that you are the only one who has been in my life all those years. She has not deserved that."

"Eric. I would never hurt you, you know that. I love you today as I loved you then."

"Dearest Katie, you know that you will always remain in my heart. I thank you for those wonderful years. I am sorry that it did not work out for us. My fault, I know. Please help me through this evening, try to concentrate on Horace. No talk about the past."

"Oh darling," whispered Katie, "I'll do my best. And also, there is no closeness between me and Horace. I am unable to get close to anyone but you."

The other two were already coming back.

"Horace has a wonderful pottery artwork in his bedroom, done by you, Katie. How come we have none of Katie's pottery, as you and she are old friends?"

"Ah, may I explain," said Katie, "in those days I had not yet discovered my interest in pottery. It is sixteen years ago."

"It may be sixteen years ago, you bloody cow," thought Philippa, "but you are ogling my Eric as if he belonged to you. I can see from your whole demeanour that you are still in love with him. As

202

for Eric, he is unreadable when he puts on his mask. But I think he has got over you. Curse Horace for having arranged a surprise dinner."

Horace was indeed sweating blood. It taught him never ever again to make any surprises for anyone. Any future surprises by him would be the calculated outcome from a thorough research into every aspect of the matter in question.

He would remember the words: time spent in reconnaissance is rarely lost. Thank goodness it was only a cold supper and therefore he was not holding anyone hostage for longer than they wanted to stay.

The evening limped forward with difficulty. It was mainly Eric and Horace talking about what the papers said. A bit was talked about pottery and the art world. As soon as politeness allowed, Philippa got up to go.

"Thank you, Horace, for a lovely evening and it has been so interesting to meet an old friend of Eric's. I am sorry to leave before coffee but I need an early night because I have not been too well lately."

Goodbyes were said, and Eric and Philippa fled.

Katie could only observe how relieved Horace was once the door closed behind the couple. He looked as if a heavy weight had been lifted from him. Only then had he dared to look at Katie. All through the dinner he had kept his eyes mainly on his plate.

"Horace, what are you frightened of?"

"Well, hmm…"

"That I have been Eric's girlfriend? And why would that be? Please give a straight answer, I beg you."

"Because I am in love with you and I don't think that I have any chances. I don't have Eric's qualities."

"Horace. For an intelligent man you are saying stupid things. Thank you for feeling love for me. That is such a precious gift. However, Eric is no rival to you. And from the other side, you are no rival to him. As far as I am concerned, Eric has never had any rivals nor will he ever have any. I love Eric to this day. You saw my reactions when I saw him. Over the years, I have wished that I could forget him, but that has not been possible for me. I am very fond of you, Horace, but I am not in love with you. It would be wonderful if we could be friends."

"Surely we can. It makes me happy that you want my friendship. You are a wonderful woman, Katie, so kind and sweet."

While saying that, Horace realised that he loved Katie so much that he would want her happiness, even with another man. He would not make himself into a problem for her. Let her dream of Eric if that was what fulfilled her. And suddenly he had an intuition, the beautiful pottery works came as a result of her love for Eric. That piece "Yearning" was Katie's yearning for Eric. What her face could perhaps hide, her hands could not. Her feelings came out in the pottery. And the world was much richer for it.

As soon as Eric and Philippa were at home, she flew at him,

"Katie was a former girlfriend of yours. That was clear."

"Most unfortunately clear."

"What have you got to say? She was all over you."

"She was not all over me. She only gave me two pecks."

"Even a blind man could see that she's still head over heels over you."

"I can't help that. It ended sixteen years ago. For heaven's sake, please stop exaggerating. You know full well that women tend to go for me, and that without any encouragement from my part. And very tediously, women do tend to carry the torch for me for quite a while. Yes, before I got to know you, I had three girlfriends, if you must know," lied Eric, "and Katie was the last. I saw no point in telling you that before we met I had some affairs. Of short duration. What is so terrible about that? I had not taken any monastic vows. Since I met you, I have not looked at another woman."

"You could have told me."

"Why? What would have been gained by it? Under no circumstances did I allow myself to hurt you by unnecessary and unimportant stories of former girlfriends. It seems to be a feminine trait to want to blurt out details of that kind. I've known some men who have left their girlfriends the moment they started to wax lyrical about some exes. Such accounts are pure folly. Why should a chap wish to know that their present loved one has bedded some other fellows. It goes against the grain."

"All right. All right. I get your point. The evening was appalling. I only wanted to get out."

"You did manage a perfect show of an iceberg personified. I am grateful that your good sense prevailed and that you did not make the evening even more unpleasant for poor Horace."

"The idiot deserves a spanking. I hope this has cured him of any yearning for surprises."

Eric lay long awake. Thank heavens the worst had been averted. No mention of Southall. If Philippa had known, she would have put two and two together and understood Eric had to be still in love with the one and only woman for him who had been there since childhood. That would have been a partial misunderstanding, because though Eric had remained firmly in love with Katie, he actually did love Philippa. But the latter would not have understood that. She had gathered that Eric loved their two children more than her and she had accepted that. But another woman – no. All hell would have broken loose.

All was now saved as Philippa had believed his story that Katie had been but one of three short-term affairs. She had not liked the idea that he had had any affairs at all, but she could not hold it against him, especially as she had been no virgin herself. The thought that there had been only three affairs would eventually calm her down. She was no doubt contented that she had managed to worm out his past secrets. She had always had a curiosity about the subject. Precisely because he had not told her anything at all about it. Now she would relax under the impression of having found out. Eric sighed. Women seemed to be tarred with the brush of Bluebeard's Wife.

The friendship between Katie and Horace worked out well in the end. Horace happened to like the cinema, as did she, and the two of them went to see most of the new films. It was nice for Katie to have Horace also as a friend as well as Timmy. Through Horace she learned about the diplomatic world.

One day Horace said, "Katie, I am most interested in your pottery, I understand where the beautiful soft pieces come from, but where do the ferocious ones come from?"

"Must be childhood, I think."

"But you told me that you had a warm family life."

"That yes. But the surroundings and the neighbours were frightful. As you are interested, would you like to come with me on Saturday to visit my parents."

"I'd love to. Shall we drive there?"

"No, not in your posh car."

Horace had never been to Southall before. What a different world it presented from the centre. The large blocks of tenement flats were ugly and dirty. At Katie's parents' it was neat and clean inside. Katie made the introductions.

"How nice to meet you, Mr Grant," said Mrs Smith, "Katie has been telling me that you are interested in her art."

"I am indeed, Mrs Smith. Katie is a gifted artist."

"By the way, Katie, Dad's not here because he got a free ticket to football from Mr Day, who could not go. He sends his love."

Mrs Smith got the tea ready and the biscuits.

"Oh dear, I've run out of milk."

"I'll go and get it," said Katie.

When she had left, Mrs Smith looked questioningly at Horace." I understand that you are only a friend, Mr Grant."

"That is so, Mrs Smith."

Mrs Smith sighed.

Horace changed the subject.

"You have some nice photos on the mantelpiece. Can I have a look? Ah, here is Katie with her cousin. They look very much alike."

"And here is a school photo of Katie when she was sixteen. Do you recognise her?"

"Oh yes, Mrs Smith, there she is in the second row on the right-hand side. A very pretty girl who is even prettier today."

"Katie was part of a little group of friends," said Mrs Smith looking at the school photo, "such nice children. For so many years Katie thought she would be marrying her childhood sweetheart. But it was not to be. I'm so glad she has found pottery."

At that Katie returned.

"I've been admiring family photos," said Horace.

"Now, let's have our tea."

In the evening Horace sat pensively sipping some brandy. That visit to Southall had been an eye-opener. In the school photo he had recognised Eric. It showed him how very closed Eric was. Nobody at work seemed to know much about him. And certainly not that he had come from tenement flats in Southall.

Now he understood Katie. From childhood on she and Eric had been together till Eric had married. Yes, till 1971. A life-time. It was clear that Katie had not forgotten him. The same must apply to Eric. Why, why had that relationship broken? Horace could not find an answer. Eric was complicated.

He had married Philippa. Not only for money, that was clear to Horace, for Eric was truly fond of his wife. But had he ever been in love with her? No, he could not have been, mused Horace.

The man was carrying some heavy burden. In spite of it, he was managing well both at work and at home. That took strength. It would be imperative that Eric should not get a whiff about Horace's visit to Southall. If Eric knew that Horace knew, he would never speak to Horace again. Yet Eric's background in Southall in no way diminished Horace's friendship nor admiration for his friend, in fact it increased it no end.

Horace saw another thing. The fact that the can of worms had been opened thanks to his dinner party had probably prevented an even worse situation. It had stopped his dream of marriage to Katie in its tracks. Knowing what he knew now, they had all been saved. In the course of time, and with his continued courting of Katie, it could have resulted in her saying yes in the end. Perhaps even out of sheer loneliness. It would have been infinitely worse to find out later in life that one had married the love of one's best friend's life. Their friendship would have broken never to return. And to have by one's side a wife who was in love with her former lover, that would have been a killer. Katie had not been a fleeting flame in Eric's life – no, she had been his one and only. Horace had learned that from the photo in Southall and the few words by Mrs Smith. What he could not fathom was why on earth had Eric left Katie? There would have to be a reason somewhere deep in Eric's psyche. Horace could not come to grips with that. It must have been a very powerful force, to make Eric leave Katie.

What, wondered Horace, were Eric's feelings as a result of that dinner? A good question. Horace had a partial answer to it. He had realised that seeing Katie after sixteen years would have brought up to the front all the old memories. A yearning that had probably by then receded to the back burner would now have leapt to the forefront. A rekindled passion would rage inside Eric as it would rage inside Katie. How painful. Eric had it much easier than Katie, for he had the solace of his children. Katie was alone. Horace would be a stalwart friend to her, and he would explain to Eric that he was only a friend. Eric need not feel pained that Horace was in any way after "his girl". Eric could have coped, in theory, with the fact that Katie might be bedding someone, but he would not be able to cope with knowing who the person was. And certainly not if it was an old friend.

Chapter 28

It took quite a while before Eric's and Horace's friendship got back to normal. In the end Horace had had to say,

"Look, Eric. I find it pretty bad that you begrudge any life to a woman whom you purport to love. Is she to bury herself into loneliness by your statue? Do be reasonable. I am just a friend to her. And I think she needs one. I know that Timmy Day is another one and an Indian girl whose name I forget.

I am not torturing you by incessant stories about Katie. If you want to know anything then ask me, and I'll tell what I can.

We men don't often talk about matters of the heart, but let me just say that I really do understand the emotional plight you have been under for so long, and still are. However, since you chose your path, now you must follow it the best you can. You are a lucky man to have such a lovely family."

"Oh Horace, please forgive my behaviour to you. It was quite unmerited. But you understand why. All is well between us. Also, my dear friend, Philippa has decided to forgive you your surprise dinner."

"I humbly bow at such grace. Tell her that I have been prostrate with grief at having caused her pain and that only now do I dare to hold up my head. Tell…"

"Oh shut up, Horace. It's a storm in a teacup."

Life in the office continued its exciting path. The Diplomatic Service was never dull. There was always something going on in some corner of the world. Eric enjoyed learning Swedish. He found the pronunciation difficult at first but eventually he got used to the sing-song of it. The practical side of it was that with Swedish one could get by anywhere in the Scandinavian countries, and also Finland. Eric, who was a monarchist, loved the fact that Sweden and Norway were monarchies. Where there was a court, life was ever so much fancier. He loved pomp and ceremony with every fibre of his being. He had a collection of magazines about royal weddings, funerals, coronations and special anniversary feasts. In his children he found a wonderful audience to share his enthusiasm with and who thus learned to love pomp and ceremony just like their father. Each magazine was a fairy tale, except for being a real one. Philippa left him to his hobby. In her opinion, it was rather over the top.

Eric had been kept busy with his Swedish desk from almost the beginning. On the 28th of February, 1986, there had been real flurry. The Swedish Prime Minister, Olof Palme, had been shot dead. It was a major mystery. Almost in its footsteps, in March, Eric had noted that the Swedish AB Bofors had signed a $15 billion contract with

India. The arms trade continued to blossom everywhere, thought Eric.

He had had a hunch that he would be posted to Sweden and thus he crammed himself with knowledge about the country. He found it fascinating that Stockholm was built on an archipelago of fourteen islands woven together by fifty bridges. The Swedes seemed to be fervent. Eighty-five percent of them were members of the Lutheran church of Sweden. Of note was that the very first IKEA store had opened in 1958 at Almhult, and now it was a huge concern. What made Eric shake his head was to learn that in 1979 they had outlawed the spanking of children. How were parents supposed to keep law and order? He himself had on several occasions spanked Lucius, and Philippa had done the same with Emma. Eric firmly believed that the Good Book was right in saying "the man who loves his son does not spare the rod".

The year 1986 had held a lot of romance. The courtship by Prince Andrew of Sarah Ferguson had the world papers and magazines selling at the rate of knots. And then on the 23rd of July their wedding had taken place at Westminster Abbey. The whole Flint family had been glued to the box.

"Mami. Mami, "cried Emma, "all the ladies are wearing beautiful clothes."

"So they should, they are all guests at an important wedding."

"Oh, look, that pale yellow and white outfit is gorgeous. And so's the purple one. Look. The red hat is good but the jacket is boring I hate boring clothes."

"You pay a lot of attention to women's clothes, Emma."

"Sure I do, Mami, I shall become a fashion designer."

"What a boring job," commented Lucius unhelpfully.

"Just ignore your brother," said Eric.

"Ah, here comes the bride," crooned Emma. "Her dress is all right, but it should be more jazzy. At least it does not make her pale into insignificance, as did the over-sized, over-frilled grimmo made for Princess Diana. But that was not her fault. She knows how to dress exquisitely."

"The bride looks very jolly," said Lucius, "They should have a fun marriage."

"To be married to a Royal will not be easy," said Philippa, "but at least she will have another young woman around her, I mean Princess Diana."

In October 1987, Eric was told that he would be posted as a Councillor to Stockholm the following May. When he told this to the family, both Lucius and Emma were jubilant.

"We shall see the midnight sun. And the Aurora Borealis. Ski-ing and skating, galore!" enthused Lucius.

"And there is Abba," added Emma.

215

"Don't forget the King and the Queen, court etiquette and all the wonderful outfits, Emma, at the functions," smiled Eric.

"We will need real furs," said Philippa, adding a practical note.

"Oh and saunas," said Lucius, "I hear that in the North they roll in the snow after saunas."

"Well, son, I'll look forward to seeing you do the same," smiled Eric.

"I bet he will," interjected Sir Philip, who was, as usual, on a visit together with his wife. The whole family were together so often that it would have made sense for them to live all in the same house.

"Daddy's been to Sweden on several occasions," said Philippa.

"I have indeed, the summers are delightful but the winters are horrid, over six months of ice and snow. It can be heavy."

"But we are still..." started Philippa.

"Young enough to cope," Eric finished the sentence for her.

Chapter 29

After that surprise dinner of Horace's, Katie's feelings had blossomed again. She dreamt of Eric more frequently. She had seen him, she had touched him and she had kissed him. She had seen in his eyes, during those few minutes they had had alone, that her love was returned. This meeting had in no way depressed her, it had galvanised her love to burn yet more brightly. He had not forgotten her. She still meant something to him. He had not rejected her, he had only put her aside.

If Eric had wanted her to be his mistress, Katie would have been perfectly happy. But he was too decent a man to do that. For that, too, Katie adored him. The news about Eric's family life continued to trickle through Nandita. Horace was too honourable a man to tell any tales about his friend. Katie respected him for that. In summer 1988 she lost Horace's company because he had been sent to China as a Councillor. He was very happy; his career too was moving along well.

Katie was again visiting Nandita.

"Hello, Katie, do hurry in from the cold."

"In November it is supposed to be cold, so never mind."

"You know, Nandita," said Katie as she settled down comfortably on the sofa, "it is quite remarkable how I have perked up after seeing Eric at that dinner."

"That is so surprising. I would have thought you would be down in the dumps for a long time."

"No, Nandita. I saw in his eyes that he still loves me. He said that I will always remain in his heart. Oh Nandita, he was even more handsome than in his youth."

"The main thing is that you are not grieving."

Nandita did not voice her real thoughts upon the matter. Her friend would not have wanted to hear them. She thought herself that Katie's obsession with Eric was sick. And now after an absence of sixteen years the poor woman was gushing again like a lovesick teenager. Dear me. She had not allowed any other boyfriends into her life. At least she had started a livelier existence since her success at pottery. She made friends, she went out. Nandita still shuddered when she thought of the account that Katie had given her of that dinner. It was a miracle that it had not been worse. Nandita felt primarily sorry for Philippa, who had taken the hardest blow. No doubt Eric would have concocted some story by which to save his bacon. That was as sure as sure could be. Anyway, it was clear that Katie wanted to stay cocooned in her love for Eric.

"Are there any news about Eric?"

"I thought Horace was your source of information."

"Oh no, he never has been. Also, don't forget that he was posted to China eight weeks ago. As a Councillor, he said."

"Then you would not have heard that Eric has been posted to Stockholm next May. The Foreign Office is certainly using his language skills."

"I shall think of him as a polar-bear," said Katie dreamily.

As a result, her pottery began to have a Nordic flavour of icebergs and icicles and snowflakes. She was having a big exhibition in March. The gallery was over the moon at the versatility of her works. The exhibition was well advertised and all items were expensive. Kat Claydon was a name.

What Katie was not to know was that Eric, who had seen the advertisements, went secretly to see the exhibition. He was mightily impressed by Katie's skill. He had been touched, for his instincts told him that all of her creativity was mainly due to him. He bought two small, but exquisite pieces. Small because he needed to be able to hide them. He paid in cash, having prepared himself with a suitable sum. When they asked whether he could give his name and address, he wrote down: Patrick Jones, 104 South Parade, Crosby.

Chapter 30

In May 1988, Eric and Philippa arrived in Stockholm. The weather was wonderful and the days so long. Philippa had gone to the trouble of learning some basic Swedish so that she could cope with daily life. In the so-called polite society everyone seemed to speak French, which made it easy for the couple. They had been given a lovely, centrally located large house, with entertaining in view. The dining room seated twenty-two. There were two living rooms, separated by double doors which could be kept open. There were five bedrooms with en-suite facilities. They had brought a cook/housekeeper with them. A cleaning lady for two days a week was employed locally.

As the winter came along, Philippa found it difficult to endure it. Her headaches had got worse in Sweden, she was sure of that. For the past year she had had headaches from time to time, but since they had come to Sweden, these aches had intensified. She had not bothered Eric with it. The weather seemed to have no effect on Eric, but for her it was a nightmare. Life was otherwise pleasant though somewhat stiff. The eternal and overwhelming rules of etiquette made most occasions into obstacle courses. One had to remember what to do and what not to do. That year the Swedish film "Pelle the Conqueror" had won the Palme d'Or at Cannes Festival. It was talked about for months.

Back home the early months of 1989 were full of gloom because of the December disaster of the Pan Am Flight 103 which was blown up over Lockerbie. Then in April British football got a bad name thanks to the Hillborough disaster. These topics of conversation did not produce any pleasant talk at the social occasions.

Matters perked up in the summer. In June Pope John Paul 2nd visited Sweden. Eric and Philippa were among the guests at one of the receptions.

Their second winter had started early with very low temperatures. Philippa tried to keep a brave face, but it tired her enormously. For a Nordic Christmas Sir Philip and his wife came for a three week stay from the 22nd of December till the 12th of January.

Fun reigned supreme. Eric, Sir Philip, Lucius and Emma threw themselves into cross-country skiing. Sir Philip had taken to skis like duck to water. He had an excellent natural technique and kept up with the younger folk without a problem. Lady Saunders stayed at home keeping Philippa company. The evenings were spent with family games and home performances of flamenco and the sevillanas. Lady Saunders was very good at sevillanas.

"Grandpa, I shall become a physicist like you," said Lucius.

"Good, I can see that you have all the aptitudes necessary," answered Sir Philip, "but there will be hurdles to overcome."

"And I shall be in the fashion world," said Emma.

"Darling," said Philippa, "do bring your fashion sketch books here for your grandparents to see."

"Sure. I'll get them at once."

"I wish she would go to university," sighed Philippa.

"What for?" said Eric, "she seems truly talented in fashion. I'll insist that she takes a business course, nevertheless. She will need to know how to run her future business empire."

Emma came back with the sketches.

"These are excellent," said Lady Saunders, "and you have a special style of your own. A sense of line, shape and how the material falls. I am impressed."

"I know nothing about women's fashions," said Sir Philip, "only that the three women in my life always look wonderful."

"I am looking forward to that New Year Dance which is being held for the young people, which you told us about, Daddy. In fact I shall be wearing one of my own creations. Pink silk with turquoise and silver decorations. A boat neck, sleeves till the elbows, skirt billowing slightly from below the hips. Just over three quarter length. Silver shoes and silver handbag."

"You are obviously planning to be the queen of the ball," said Lucius, "you just might succeed."

He looked at his sister appreciatively. Emma, at the age of sixteen showed all the signs of becoming a beauty. Her eyes were unforgettable, large, light-blue and luminous. She had thick nearly black eyelashes that curved up naturally and the same colour arched eyebrows. The eyes were nearly Eric's but they were definitely those of Eric's mother. From her Emma had also inherited her thick, dark-blond hair. For Eric it was a special sensation to see the eyes of his mother look at him with love – through the eyes of his daughter.

In the new year, the ladies wanted to go to the sales. The cold did not worry them at all under those circumstances. A few days later they went on a second hunt in the shops and came back laden with parcels.

"Lucius, come and help your grandmother to take off her coat," shouted Sir Philip while helping Philippa.

Suddenly, Philippa gave a twitch, and then, without any sound, she collapsed. Sir Philip had caught her fall. He laid her down gently.

"Philippa darling, are you all right?" he asked with mounting worry.

Her eyes were open, but they had no expression in them. Her father's fingers went to her pulse – nothing! A terrible wail escaped from Sir Philip. No, this could not be. His daughter could not be dead.

"Mami, wake up," said Lucius, patting her cheek, "We need brandy."

Lady Saunders had gathered what had happened. She needed to stay strong for the sake of her husband and grandchildren. Sir Philip had gone as white as a sheet. He was hardly taking in the reality. He was totally unable to cope with the thought that his beloved daughter lay there dead. Lucius too was in denial, he wanted to believe that his mother had only fainted. And what about Emma? The girl stood there, rooted to the spot, still with her coat on, just staring. Lady Saunders realised that it was deep shock. She addressed herself first to Lucius,

"Lucius, go phone your father. Right now. Tell him to call an emergency doctor and come home at once. I repeat, at once. Say your mother is seriously ill."

Lucius went to do so.

Then she addressed Emma, taking her hand and said,

"Emma, darling, come here to the chair with me. Now sit down. We can deal with your coat later."

"Daddy. We need Daddy. What's wrong with Mami?"

"Your Mami is not well, darling. Daddy will be here in a minute."

"Grandpa, is Mami waking yet?" called Lucius, returning.

"Philippa! Philippa! Apple of my eye. You can't leave me," wailed Sir Philip, "oh Lord above, not this, let it not be true. I can't face a life without my little one. Steffi! Do something!"

Sir Philip had broken down completely. He sat by Philippa's body, holding her head in his lap and wailing from the bottom of his heart. Lady Saunders saw that her husband was just as much in shock as Emma. She herself had to prop herself up for the sake of the living ones. She, the mother, had to keep calm whilst looking at the dead body of her one and only child. She could hear in her head an inner voice which said, "Mama, stay strong for my children". She would not let her daughter down, she was now next in line to be a mother to the two motherless children. She would find the strength to comfort them. They would probably be much easier than her husband. No parent was equipped to cope with the death of their children. That was the worst that could happen to anyone.

Lucius had joined his grandfather on the floor, and he was wailing as much as Sir Philip.

It was only about ten minutes, though it seemed like an eternity, till Eric got home. Lady Saunders went towards him,

"Philippa is dead."

The terrible scene in front of his eyes told Eric that such a catastrophe had indeed happened.

As Emma saw her father, she lifted her head and whispered,

"Daddy, Daddy. Help. What's happened to Mami?"

She got up, but as she did so, she fainted. Eric managed to catch her fall.

"Emma. Emma darling. Estephania, get some water. Emma, Daddy's here. Lucius, come over here to help me with Emma."

Lady Saunders returned with some water. Emma had begun to get some colour. In a docile manner she swallowed a few mouthfuls of water.

"Mami?" she whispered.

"Mami's gone, Emma, Mami's in heaven…" Lucius' voice broke.

Eric put his arms around his children.

"Daddy's here. I am here for you. We need the whole family to comfort one another. Now I hear that the doctor has arrived. Lucius, hold Emma while I go to talk to him."

The doctor saw an appalling scene. Before anything else, Emma and Sir Philip needed administering to. It took a lot of effort to make Sir Philip let go of Philippa's body, but the doctor needed to make his examinations.

"How is it possible that my wife could just drop dead? She was only fifty and in good health," asked Eric.

"There could be a myriad of reasons, replied the doctor, "an autopsy will have to be conducted. Only then will we know the reason. I'll call an ambulance but now we need to get the grandfather and also your daughter to bed. I can see that the sedatives are beginning to work.

The doctor was very efficient and after caring for Emma and Sir Philip, he said that he would leave pills for the others to be taken as necessary. Then Emma was escorted to her room and Sir Philip into his, both of whom were now beginning to fall asleep.

Eric, Lady Saunders and Lucius went into the small drawing room. Eric phoned the Embassy to tell them what had happened. The Ambassador was appalled. He was an efficient man and he arranged for the Head of Chancery to step into whatever needed doing. Eric was not to be disturbed by any work matters. Nobody was to barge into the Flint household without previously phoning to get permission. London would have to be told. The autopsy would delay the transport of the body back home. There were the grandparents and the two children, now motherless at a delicate age. The Ambassador, who was very fond of Eric, felt most distressed for Eric's plight.

From the work point of view, would Eric be able to stay on in Stockholm? If not, it would make it difficult at the Embassy. Eric was in many ways the Ambassador's right-hand man. The Head of Chancery was infernally slow and ponderous. A good man, but infuriating. At anything sudden, the man was bad at coping. However, he was religious and so could probably give Eric the support that was needed, as Eric was a regular church-goer as well. Oh yes, the Anglican Chaplain would have to be told.

In the drawing-room Eric was mopping up his tears. His loss was enormous. His support during all the years was gone. The effect on their children was devastating, especially as their mother had died in front of them. How would Lucius cope, he who had been so close to his mother? He himself would be able to calm Emma down. She was a Daddy's girl. How would the studies in school continue? He would have to explain that the two would have to do well for the sake of their mother's memory. The schools were good, so they would be able to deal with stressed young. In situations like this, a lot of understanding was needed. Sir Philip would never be able to cope. He and Philippa had been two peas in the pod. The old man would never be the same again.

Lady Saunders would know that. She sat there quietly weeping, keeping herself calm. Lucius had by now stopped his crying and wailing. Now would come the period of fury. That of denial. That of questioning. Wanting to put the blame on something.

"Has mother been ill? And nobody told me? How could this happen?"

"No, son. Your mother has not been ill, but she has been rather tired lately. She tends to be tired during the winters."

"Bloody winters! They've been too much for her. Curse this posting. If she had not had to suffer these cold winters, she would have remained alive."

"We don't know yet what killed her," said Lady Saunders, "we have to wait for the result. And Lucius, death does happen, nobody knows the time when it comes to them, but one day we all have to go."

"Mother was young."

"Yes, she was young. She should not have died so early. I am her mother, don't forget, she was my baby girl. But the positive in this is that she did not suffer at all. And she had led a very happy life, thanks to her loving husband and two wonderful children. Oh Lucius, her love has not left anybody, only her body has gone. Try to think of it in that way. I shall have an extremely heavy role with her father. Philip will not be able to cope."

"Estephania", said Eric," I'm afraid you may be right. Philip is in a terrible state. I admire you. You are controlling yourself for the sake of others. And you are the mother."

"My grief will be grieved in another way. Philippa would want her children to thrive and not be bogged down by too much sorrow. You, Eric, and I, are here to give strength to the rest."

Eric was truly sad at losing Philippa. They had had a good marriage; they had got on well with each other. She had been a stalwart support in every sense. He had loved her very well, more than he had thought he could. The two children were the most precious gift from her. The grandparents had been ideal; their whole family life had been exemplary. Now the rest of them would have to make the best of the situation. They still had each other and formed a family. Eric would have to assume the role of a mother and a father. He would have to help Lady Saunders to prop up Sir Philip for the sake of the children.

The funeral had to be arranged as soon as they had finished the autopsy. He was himself wracked by the question, what on earth had killed Philippa?

"Estephania, I suggest that we do not change any of the travel arrangements. You and Philip go back on the twelfth. I shall accompany Lucius and Emma to their schools in order to have a proper talk with the Heads. I shall look into the funeral, the grave, the headstone, and so on. I will consult you two in the matter. I think it should be a family effort. It is now the ninth, so we still have some time all together."

The autopsy did not take long. Philippa had died of a cerebral aneurism. Eric was reminded that lately she had complained of some headaches. The aneurism had lurked for some time in her body, a bit like a time-bomb, and nobody had had any idea of its existence. If it had been found out, then an operation could have saved her, but that was by no means certain. Her death had been instantaneous; she had not suffered at all.

To know that did not help the family grief. If Philippa had felt something, she had not said anything much, nor often, and thus nothing could be known, but she probably had been unaware of anything serious being wrong.

The effect on Lucius was to make him grow up with a jolt. Life was uncertain, anything could happen at any moment. Sorrow could hit at any time. One needed to treasure what one had, it could be taken away in an instant. He decided that for his mother's memory's sake he would study the best he could, he would come out with straight A's; he would make her proud. He would be the best grandson his grandfather could wish for. His father was strong and would support his sister.

As for Emma, she clung closer than ever to her father. She needed his protective shield. Grandfather in this case was useless, in fact he was a big burden to his wife. But the family kept together, and with time their sorrow would become bearable.

Chapter 31

It was a good decision by Eric to complete his tour of Stockholm in spite of its being the place of the family disaster. He was already well-anchored in Sweden for over two years so he would not need to undertake any new subjects.

At first, it felt very odd to be alone. Eric had got used to having conversations with Philippa in the evenings. Now he did a lot of reading and also listened to classical music. His entertaining duties were carried out by the professional caterers that the couple had employed before. Thank heavens he was busy at work.

One marked change was that women flocked to him in droves. At dinner parties there was almost invariably a single woman between thirty and forty to be his dinner partner. Society obviously was trying to marry him off. No way. He needed his grieving time.

Lucius and Emma were doing well at school. They were very conscious of the fact that their father should be given no problems from their direction. At half-terms, there were Sir Philip and Lady Saunders. With Philippa gone, Sir Philip had turned towards his wife and had become far more dependent on her. He continued to pamper the grandchildren.

In London, when Katie learned from Nandita that Eric was a widower, her hopes rose immediately.

"What a pity that Eric still has a couple of years to remain in Sweden," she said to Nandita, "now would have been the time for me to comfort him."

"Just as well that he's not here," her friend replied, "It would have done you no good. The man needs to get over his sorrow and start to re-orientate his life. Even if it was not the greatest of love marriages, the couple were married for nearly twenty years. That binds people together. He must get used to being on his own. Also, don't forget the two children. How do you think they would have taken to you comforting their father the moment their mother was dead? They would have got rid of you most effectively."

"I didn't think of that. You are right, if I got into the bad books of his children, then I will have no chance with Eric. I will have to be patient."

"I can see and hear that you are planning a campaign to get Eric firmly in your clutches."

"Yes. And? So what? With his being a widower, why should I not have chances? It is my dream to be his wife."

"Yes, it has always been your dream. One day it may yet come true."

"Oh Nandita. This opens a completely new time for me."

Another new creative period in pottery would now begin, thought Nandita. She was curious as to what the new shapes would be like. Katie had given her as a present one of her works named "Childhood Play" in tones of red and pink. Nandita admired Katie's skill in being able to make even the thinnest of thin forms in clay, to suit whatever shape she wanted.

Katie had been in correspondence with Horace. They exchanged letters about twice a year. Plus there were a number of cards from his travels. He had heard about Philippa's death from Eric. What a tragedy, thought Horace, those poor children. It would be very difficult for Eric to be two parents at once, but mercifully there were active and supportive grandparents to help him.

And then his thoughts turned to Katie. This might change everything. Maybe at last she would have her chance. They were only forty-four years old, on the young side of middle age. A few years of grieving would first have to be surmounted, but then, life had to go on. And why would Eric not now use his opportunity to get Katie? One would see.

Eric came back to London in May 1992. He was pleased to be in his real home. He loved the house in Chelsea. He had been back about a week when he made his obligatory visit to his parents. It had been the same old tiring thing. After an hour he got up to go. It was only eight o'clock, and the evenings were light.

As he passed the old flat of the Patels and then turned into the main courtyard, he found himself facing Katie. Thus the two of them met each other again on the estate of their youth. It was like an electric shock for them when they saw each other. As their eyes met, they felt the same old irresistible pull towards each other as they had felt in their youth. Their hearts were pounding. In one fell swoop, all the years seemed to have been wiped away. They were there for each other.

The few words, "Katie, my love" and "Eric", spoke volumes. As always, they turned together to walk away from the Estate, and only when they had turned the corner of the next building did Eric take Katie's hand. That holding of her hand had always been a complete love declaration. And so it was now.

Eric escorted Katie to his car.

"Where to?"

"Where else but to Hammersmith?"

Eric's eyebrows shot up.

"Chancellor's road. I've been there since 1977. And Eric, no talking, concentrate on the driving. Eyes only on the road."

It was easier said than done, but Eric closed his mind to anything but the traffic, for both their sakes. He could feel Katie's presence. It felt they were one.

Katie's heart was brimming over at being together with Eric again. It was a heady feeling. They were on their way to be truly united. Oh Eric.

When they finally got to her flat, the door had hardly had time to close when they fell into each other's arms. For a long time they stood there stroking and kissing one another. In between Eric kept saying, "Katie, I love you" and she responded with the same. Then Katie said,

"There is something I need you to do with me."

She went to her bedroom and came out holding an exquisite piece of pottery in various shades of blue. She beckoned Eric to follow her to the kitchen, and once there, she said,

"Now please hold this piece with me and help me to fling it on the floor with strength. Broken pottery means happiness."

Eric was surprised, but he complied with her request. The piece broke into smithereens. Katie smiled, holding his hands and closing her eyes. Eric could feel how important the breaking of the crockery had been for her.

What she did not tell him was that the piece had been called "Sorrow" and that she had had it for twenty years. Also, in her mind was a story that she had heard somewhere, which told that in ancient Egypt a couple getting married broke a vase together. All old things were gone, and new life was to begin. Whether that was only a story or whether it was true did not matter to Katie, for her this was her marriage ceremony to Eric. A visual and tangible sign. She would keep one small piece and Eric would keep another. As she gave him his piece she said,

"We each keep a piece of this happiness."

Eric smiled and found it lovely. His Katie had always been full of ideas.

Then Katie opened a bottle of wine and gave it to Eric, saying, "Please bring it to the bedroom, I'll bring the glasses."

They both had a sip and then started to undress. Eric was just about to fling his clothes off but Katie said smilingly, "No, Eric. Fold your clothes neatly as you always have done. Flinging is for me."

Eric had to laugh. Katie was so sweet. She had always found his meticulous folding of his clothes funny. They were mentally in their youth, and it had to be exactly the same. And it was, except that now the precautionary measures were no longer needed. She could really feel and experience her Eric. They were like two playful puppies; they had played together since they were small. The playfulness made bearable the force of their deep feelings which were raging like wildfire.

Their night together was more than wonderful. The joy of being together was indescribable. Both could at last release all the pent-up passions that had mounted over the years. Only now did they become fully aware of how much they had missed one another. It was a vindication of the saying "old love does not rust". They realised that neither had fallen in love with anyone else. They were unbreakably tied to one another; their childhood love had matured first into youthful love and then into adult love. They understood one another, they supported one another. They were fascinated by one another. Neither had to pretend anything in each other's company and they were most naturally courteous and caring to each other. It was sheer bliss. And now they were both free!

Chapter 32

At the Office, Eric had been made the Head of the European Integration Department, which dealt with the future European Union. He found it fascinating. Already at the beginning of June he was plunged into much work as Britain was dealing with the replies of various countries as to whether they accepted or rejected the Maastricht Treaty. Denmark had just rejected it, and Ireland had accepted . Having known for a while that he would be heading the business of integration, Eric had made a point of reading the Maastricht Treaty. It had been unreadable. It actually had made no sense. However, how many people would even try to read it? Most people would put their own interpretations into the matter, which was unfortunately obfuscated by the media. Eric was perturbed by the increasing type of covert mendacity that was creeping into the press. In any newspaper, the news was slanted according to which political party any paper was leaning towards. On the whole everything was becoming more and more confused. Many significant happenings, either at home or abroad, were either not reported or only skimmed over in small paragraphs. Preferably at the back. How were the young to orientate?

This brought the thought of education to Eric's mind. He had striven towards excellence all his life. These days excellence seemed to be frowned upon. From what he read, he had come to the conclusion that education was moving towards the speed of the slowest in classes. It was said to be unkind to single out any of those who could not really cope with learning. How that could benefit the children escaped Eric. Surely it would make more sense to strive to get all children up to the fastest level that each was capable of. Thank heavens that Lucius and Emma had not suffered from this new trend. He knew that they were forward movers just like him.

He was a happy man, he was advancing in his profession and now he again had the love of his life. They both felt that this was a continuation of their youth. They fell into the same pattern of behaviour, going to the cinema, pubs and dancing. They had an easy journey to see one another, only a few stops on the District Line between Hammersmith and Sloane Square.

Katie had happily told him all about her life during their years apart. She was very curious to know how Eric's life had been. He told her about the different countries that he had served in, but almost nothing about his personal life. Nothing about what he had felt. He saw no reason to come up with information about his married history. That disappointed Katie a bit, but she did not press him with questions. After all, what mattered was their future.

Katie waxed lyrical to Nandita.

"We are together again. Just think. I hardly know how to think straight, I'm so wrapped up in Eric. We are closer than ever now. It shows that true love does not wilt. I somehow knew that we'd be together in the end."

"You have taken a new glow, Katie. You were always beautiful but now you are even more so. Happiness is the best embellisher there is. I'm so glad to see you happy."

"He really loves me. It is not only sex."

"It never was only sex. You two have been devoted to each other since childhood."

"It's only been two weeks. I'm waiting to see what his house is like. I bet it will be muted elegance. He's always gone in for that. But he does like my pottery, nevertheless."

"Who wouldn't like your art? You are a big name by now and deservedly so. Your pieces vary from stage to stage and in your hands clay seems to be light almost like paper. I'm so proud of your present to me. It is one of my most treasured items."

Eric had no-one to confide in. Even if he had had, he would have refrained from passing on any personal information. Other people did not need to know about him and Katie. In the course of time they would work out what their relationship was going to be. Why should others nose about in it?

When Katie went to Eric's house, she sighed in admiration. As she had expected, it was the elegant, underplayed luxury of another century.

241

Antique furniture and ornaments. The colour scheme surprised her, it was light. Beige, white and yellow were dominant which kept the house from being sombre. She could see that no expense had been spared, but it was not advertised. She got a surprise when she saw Eric's study. There on his desk were two of her works. One of them was called "The Kiss" and the other "Theatre".

"Eric, when did you get those two pieces?"

"A few years back, as you well know."

"They are tiny but special."

"I know. I knew at once when I saw them to what they referred. Our first kiss and the outing to Richmond Theatre."

"You are right. I wondered who had bought them. Your name was not on the list of purchasers."

"Darling, at the time I was not at liberty to divulge my name. I wrote Patrick Jones. Till I was widowed, I kept the pieces in a locked drawer in my study. I took them out from time to time to reminisce. I hope this does not make you angry."

"Oh Eric, why should it? I'm glad that they meant something to you. I'm so glad you have them. At home I have other versions of them, which I'll show you."

On the whole, they met at Katie's place. Eric felt at ease there which he did not when they were in his house. Katie understood that in some way Philippa's ghost was there. More to the point was the fact that Eric did not want to advertise his new

242

relationship to the neighbours. And definitely not yet to the children. Only two years had passed since they had lost their mother. Also, Sir Philip was in the habit of popping by occasionally without warning and under no circumstances did Eric want him to know about Katie. Sir Philip would have been filled with righteous wrath, that Eric was sure of.

When the summer holidays were nearing, Eric said to Katie,

"Darling, once Lucius and Emma are at home, I'll have to curtail my visits to you. We will not be able to go out as much as before."

"So you want to keep me a secret?"

"For the time being, yes. It has only been two years since they lost their mother, and that is not a long time when a mother is in question. Surely you understand that?"

"You are right. We don't want to worry them too soon."

"Sweetheart, come September, we shall be free again."

When he thought about it, Eric surprised himself at the fact that he still found that Katie had to be kept a secret. Was he frightened? And if yes, then of what? In a way he was alarmed by the strength of his feelings for her. Why? For a long time he had thought that he would never be able to love anyone with the same intensity as he loved Lucius and Emma, yet he found himself caring for Katie with equal strength. Why did he not like that thought? It was probably because it gave him the feeling that he was allowing Katie to usurp the place of the children. He would need to think it over carefully and take his time. But not yet. He wanted to enjoy full euphoria for quite a while more, as he had lacked it for so long.

To be with Katie was relaxing and invigorating. From the time when they were children, Katie had been the one to give him that affection which he craved from his parents. He had been a child parched for love. He could not understand what the reason could be that neither his father nor mother had loved him. He knew that his mother's pregnancy with him had caused the early marriage. That would have caused some resentment in anyone, but in most cases it did not poison the life of a child. He wondered whether his mother had considered him to be her ball-and-chain which doomed her to imprisonment by a man she did not love. His mother must have felt trapped, and she had been trapped. Youthful follies could so easily end up being shadows for the rest of one's life. Lack of love caused intense suffering. All people yearned for it. Yet it was the one thing that was considered less important than all other matters. People tried to ignore that, but curiously enough, the lack of love made people's lives into a misery. It was the most prized feeling in the Good Book, the most elevating passages had been written about it; the Song of Songs glowed with beauty and passion.

Yet, especially in real relationships, it was on the back burner.

His thoughts went to Philippa. His poor wife. Did he miss her? Not really, not really her person, but he did miss the interesting conversations about politics and world happenings that he had been able to have with her. Eric was devoted to daily history, in other words to various happenings that were shaping the world. As for Philippa, he had made sure that she would not think that she was anything but central to his life. He had seen to it that he was chivalrous in her direction and he had created a picture of blissful harmony. It was a picture of an ideal union. And yes, Philippa had been happy, his efforts had produced good fruit. He owed her that.

But personally? He had felt like a dry leaf. He had had to be constantly on his guard, constantly on his best behaviour and constantly to remember to say and do what was expected of him. His own person, in his inner core, had not been loved. It had been his outer mask that had received such adulation. To keep being loved he needed to achieve. This he had gathered. Philippa would have fallen out of love with him the moment she had seen any of his tenement background being imported into her life. Then she would have despised him. Only by Katie was he loved as he was.

Philippa had been a wonderful woman, and he had respected her qualities. Unfortunately, all her qualities had not made him love her. Like and admire, that yes, but she had not filled his inner yearning. They had not been two halves of one entity. No wonder he needed to get drunk from time to time.

Chapter 33

Over the summer holidays, Eric had missed the frequency of Katie's company. They had managed to meet only once a week and they had not spent any nights together. During the three weeks Eric had holidayed with the children in Spain, they had only had phone calls.

Katie had poured this out to Timmy.

"I miss Eric so much, Timmy," she said as they were sitting outside at an Italian restaurant in Chiswick.

"I can understand that, but there are the two children to consider. You must allow time."

"I wonder how I coped with all those years without him? Now a few weeks seems an eternity."

"That is how love behaves, Katie. On that subject, I have news for you. I have fallen in love."

"How marvellous. Who is she?"

"She is one of the new theatre nurses. A Norwegian girl called Astrid. She is thirty-eight and has been divorced for five years. Her husband has custody of their one son aged seventeen. This so that the boy can complete school in Oslo."

"Has there been much rancour?"

"Luckily no. The couple just grew more and more apart. Her English is good because from the age of four to eight years old she was in England with her parents."

"So you are smitten?"

As a matter of fact, yes. I am serious about her. The son will soon be leading his own life, so that is unlikely to cause any difficulties. By the way, I bumped into Nandita last week. She has made her clan ever so proud of her through her three sons."

"I know. I see her regularly. I wouldn't be surprised if there would yet be another child. This time she would want a girl. The amusing thing is that her father also is panting for granddaughter."

In the autumn, Eric's and Katie's bliss continued. They were having the time of their lives. He took a Thursday and a Friday off in early October and took Katie to York. The weather was glorious, a type of Indian summer, and the two of them loved it. They had gone by train in first class and had had a good breakfast. Both had felt like a married couple.

Nearing Christmas there was sad news in the country. On the 9th December, the Prince and Princess of Wales publicly announced their separation.

"A fairy tale come to grief," sighed Eric.

"What I have heard is that Charles had not exactly been faithful to his poor wife. Camilla's been in the background."

"Katie, what is good for the goose is good for the gander. The two seem to have led their own lives. What is so sad is that a family break-up affects the children."

"But they were so unhappy with one another. Life must have been terrible."

"Oh yes? How terrible exactly? Theirs are amongst the highest titles in the land. They are not stuck nose to nose in a one-bedroom council flat. They have everything that over ninety percent of people in the world lack, and then here they are, destroying the happiness of their children because of their selfish aims. It is deplorable."

Eric felt righteously indignant. Here he was, doing everything for the benefit and contentment of the two children he had put into this world - even to the extent of having to keep his relationship with Katie a secret. With Christmas nearing, he was very conscious of the fact that it would be celebrated without Katie. However, he felt that a minimum of three to four years needed to pass before he could divulge that he had another woman. What weighed heavily in all this heavily was that Sir Philip knew that a childhood friend had been in Eric's life and he'd know at once that Katie was that friend. Sir Philip was very likely to think that Eric might have got together with Katie as soon as he had returned from Stockholm. Be that as it may, Sir Philip would appreciate Eric's sense of propriety in that several years would have passed before Katie was trotted out to the children.

The Spring continued their harmonious relationship. The last week in May and the first in June Eric took Katie on a holiday to Portugal, to the

Algarve. It was sunshine, blue skies and the sea. Katie was most interested in the colourful pottery made by the Portuguese.

"The shapes may be a bit rough," she explained to Eric, "but it is all traditional. I like it very much."

As a result, a few mugs and plates were purchased.

"We have come far, you and I," said Katie one evening.

Eric's mood dropped.

"You can say that again."

"Who'd have thought in the old days that…"

"Katie, please drop the old days. You know I can't bear them."

Katie realised her mistake as she saw Eric gulp his wine and order another bottle. Was this going to be one of those evenings? Yes, it was. After yet another bottle she suggested that they go up to their room and order any drinks there. It was a wise move.

"Oh Katie, the old days never vanish completely. I am still at a stage of having to hide everything. It is at times bloody difficult. I want to be completely free, but I am not yet even near to free."

His shoulders sagged. Would he ever be free?

"But darling, you are free," said Katie, stroking his hair.

"Katie, I don't want to lose you."

"I don't want to be lost. Why would you lose me? I'm here for you."

That evening eventually came to an end with Eric falling asleep. Katie was left somewhat nonplussed as to what could still be eating oppressing him.

Chapter 34

Then the summer was gone. Eric had again been with the children to Spain, together with Sir Philip and Lady Saunders. The autumn was turning into winter, and in November Eric had much to do as the Maastricht treaty took effect, formally establishing the European Union.

Katie decided to tackle Eric about the meeting with his children.

"Eric, I feel that the time has come that you introduce me to the children. Christmas would be a good time."

"Darling, Christmas is a family feast. It would not be appropriate to introduce someone new, especially as then the thought of a potential step-mother would be introduced."

Katie's heart missed a beat. She was bowled over. This was the very first time that Eric had indicated that he might be thinking of a marriage with her. Oh bliss! So he did want to marry her. She would not press him. Give him time, and her patience would be rewarded. She went to kiss and hug him. She was the happiest she had ever been.

"We can do it another time," she said.

"Darling, we'll spend New Year together. Lucius and Emma are with their friends for a few days, so we can live it up."

New Year 1994 started well, thought Katie. Soon Eric was bound to pop the question and then introduce her to the children. Eric could feel her expectation. Again, it should have filled him with delight, but actually it did not. He was dragging his heels. He could not understand why he had such a reluctance for the children to get to know Katie. The reason was of course the same as ever, he was not sure about a marriage with Katie.

In April, Katie had a big exhibition. The success of it was exhilarating to her. She had been approached by several galleries in the centre of London. Now she was beginning to earn serious money from it, so she could consider giving up her secretarial work and concentrate on art. Eric was very proud of her. The exhibition had been open four days, when Lucius and Emma, who had been spending a long weekend with their father, gave him a surprise.

"Daddy, Lucius and I have been to the new exhibition of pottery that is so raved about, aand with reason. The artist, Kat Claydon, is wonderful. We notice that you've actually got two of her works in your study."

"Ah, yes," stammered Eric, "I've been aware of the artist for some years. Wonderful creations she produces. That's why I got two of them."

"Just as well you got them years ago. Her prices are seriously high, quite rightly so."

"Well, I'm glad you had a good outing. We'll eat out today, collecting your grandparents on the way."

Eric had felt hot under the collar when Lucius and Emma had mentioned the exhibition. For a moment he had thought whether to open up a way for the "great meeting" by mentioning that he knew the artist fairly well. But he had not done so, feeling that it was for a later time. He felt that the Kat should not yet be let out of the bag. He had also begun to wonder how much more delay Katie would tolerate.

His hunch was correct. Katie was beginning to feel irked by his constant prevarications. This was not an affair to her. Any time with Eric had never been an affair. It had always been a preparatory time which would lead to marriage.

"Eric, I'm beginning to feel seriously worried by the secrecy that you're still holding to. Do you think that Lucius and Emma would dislike me? Why should they?"

"They would not dislike you. But your presence in my life could worry them. Till summer, Lucius is busy getting his BA at the university and Emma's course in business studies lasts till July also. At this last stage I think it would be unwise to rock the boat of their perceived security. Should they get bad marks at this late stage, I would blame it on myself. Young people have strong and often simple emotions, I'm sure you would not wish to disturb them either."

Eric was skilfully producing highly plausible excuses for delaying any commitments. He was also "forcing" Katie to see reason.

"I see what you mean. No, I would not wish to take on such a responsibility potentially of ruining the marks of two young people. You would blame me forever. But after that there are no more excuses."

"As a peace offering, can I take you to Paris on the channel tunnel that opens in May?"

"Great. That would be fun."

In the end, the meeting so feared by Eric, came by unexpectedly. It was the end of September, and Eric had wanted to see some old artistic film which was being shown at the Institut Francais.

"Let's go together, Eric."

"But it will be in French."

"Never mind. I'll get the gist. What is it called?"

"Hiroshima, Mon Amour."

They went to South Kensington and had lunch at an Italian restaurant. Then they went for the two o'clock show. At that hour, the cinema was only about half -full. They chose a seat about middle distance from the screen on the right-hand aisle by the wall. The film was no doubt very good, it had won several prizes, but the subject matter of Hiroshima being annihilated by the atomic bomb was most depressing. Katie found herself bored to the core. She started to nudge towards Eric. He was in a receptive mood and nudged her back. Soon the two of them were nudging and kissing like two teenagers.

When the film ended and the lights came on as they were getting out of their seats, Eric felt a pat on his shoulder.

"Hi, Dad. Fancy seeing you here."

It was Lucius. Eric wished that the earth had swallowed him. To his intense fury, he felt himself blushing. This was terrible. What would his son think? He must have seen how his father was nudging and kissing with Katie. Eric's secret was out. He had no choice but to introduce his son to Katie as the boy stood rooted to the spot.

"Ah Katie, may I introduce my son Lucius to you?"

"Lucius, this is Miss Smith, an old friend of mine."

"Oh, but you are the artist Kat Claydon," said Lucius excitedly, "My sister and I have been to your exhibition. It was marvellous."

"Thank you for your kind words. My real name is Katie Smith. I know your father of old. I'm so glad to meet you at last. I've heard ever so much about you. You seem to enjoy Cambridge."

"Yes, indeed, Miss Smith. May I ask whether you are a devotee of French films and how you liked the film?"

"Oh, I know nothing about French films. We only came here because Eric wanted to."

Eric was sweating blood. He had seen the look in his son's eyes when he appraised Katie. There had been appreciation and admiration in it from the masculine point of view. He had seen the beauty and felt the sex-appeal of his father's companion. As for his father's words about a Miss Smith and an old friend, Lucius was bound to doubt both statements. After all, he had seen all that cuddling. He would have figured out that here was father's latest. He had to get rid of Lucius quickly before there was any more conversation.

However, his son was intelligent and polite and promptly said,

"Please do not let me keep you any further. I'm here with Jerome, and we're going to meet friends. Goodbye, Miss Smith. So long, Dad."

"What a handsome son you have, Eric. I am delighted to have met him at last."

"He is a good boy," said Eric, "Let's get out of here. We'll have a pint at the pub before going home."

With an iron will Eric controlled himself. He did not want Katie to see how embarrassed he had been by this encounter. What a horrible thing to happen. Damn that film. He now hated "Hiroshima, Mon Amour" with venom because it had brought about that dreadful meeting. Oh Lord, Lucius was bound to tell Emma. She would be full of questions. It did not bear thinking about.

If only he had not been kissing and cuddling in the cinema all would be well. He could have got off with "old friend". As it was, Lucius was not an idiot. It was as clear to him as it had been to the whole cinema audience that there was a loving couple. A close couple. There was no getting away from that.

After a quick pint, Eric hurried home. During that pint he had had to endure the intense irritation of seeing Katie purr and grind on about how the boy was so similar to him and almost as handsome. He was fully aware and indeed proud of the fact that his son was handsome and intelligent. And similar to himself. This was one time when Eric was glad to see Katie depart.

On his way home he pondered. From now on he would not take Katie anywhere central or to an area where his children might be found. No interesting films would be on the agenda. Any dancing clubs would be limited to near Hammersmith or Shepherd's Bush. The only safe place was Katie's flat.

The inevitable happened, just as Eric had foreseen.

"Dad. Lucius tells me that you've got a woman!" Emma's eyes were full of curiosity, "Sex on legs, so I understand."

Eric winced. "I wish you wouldn't use such words, Emma."

"I'm not all that surprised, Dad, you are a handsome man not yet fifty and you've been a widower for four years. Something like that was bound to happen. Who is the said Miss Smith, and where did you meet her?"

"Well, darling, Katie Smith and I knew each other when we were young. We were at the same school. I bumped into her some time ago, we went to have a drink and talk about old times and then slowly we got a bit closer. Katie is unmarried."

"This is all most interesting. I want to meet her. I want to know who is in my Dad's life. I hope that you are not being 'lured'.

"I am not being 'lured', Emma. I am a grown man and I know my mind. Sweetheart, there is nothing to worry about. I do like to have some female company from time to time."

"What is this about female company?" Lucius had walked in.

"Son, you just couldn't keep your mouth shut," seethed Eric.

"Was it a big secret? What for? To my knowledge you have not taken monastic vows and a man like you in his prime is bound to want some female company. Especially after four years of widowhood. Emma and I have been wondering when the day would come that you'd meet someone."

"My dears, since this matter has now arisen, let me assure you that it is nothing serious, nothing that you should worry about."

"You mean that it is only an affair? How can you be so sure, Dad? Daughters of Eve have always had a knack."

"Well, I shall not get 'knacked' to use your word. I am very fond of Katie, but that is as far as it goes. She will stay a friend of mine for the time it suits us both. Then what will happen, I do not know. On the whole, my career fulfils me. Perhaps I shall give up hankering after the female of the species and take up dominoes."

"I shall still want to meet her, Dad," repeated Emma.

"All in good time, sweetheart."

The day ended pleasantly with a game of Scrabble that Eric suggested.

Chapter 35

As Christmas neared, Eric again felt nervous. He felt that he had managed a number of Christmases like obstacle courses, that since being together with Katie. His former enthusiasm for the festive period had changed into panic. That coming Christmas he was saved from Katie's wrath by the fact that Lady Saunders had insisted on their going to Spain that year.

After the New Year, Emma asked,

"Are you still together with Katie?"

"Yes, I am," her father replied.

"Don't you think it is about time for me to meet her? You've been very cagey about the whole affair. Why?"

"Why should I burden you and Lucius with my private life…?"

Eric got no further.

"Don't try to prevaricate with diplomatic verbiage, Dad, I can see through it. Don't forget I grew up with it."

In the end Eric had to capitulate and promise to arrange a luncheon at the beginning of February.

Katie was most excited by the thought of the luncheon and the fact that she would at long last meet Emma. Eric had booked a table at a smart restaurant in Chelsea. Katie was to go first for drinks at the house and then they'd go to eat. She would finally get to know both Lucius and Emma properly. She was aware that this was her big test in life. If approved of, or at least not objected to, then all would be plain sailing towards matrimony.

The important thing that Eric had stressed to Katie was that his children had been told that Eric's parents were dead. In order to spare them, he had said. Katie had felt outraged at the idea that anyone could pretend that their parents were dead. She felt that it showed a cold and hard side in Eric, a side of him that she did not know well. It would take her a bit of time to come to terms with that. He had pointed out to her that he had always visited his parents regularly. Yes, he had; Katie knew that through her own parents.

"But Eric, if your parents knew they had grandchildren, wouldn't that change them? A new way could begin."

"At what cost? You are looking at life through rose-tinted spectacles. And if they didn't change, then what? For me to have two thoroughly upset children on my hands? The stakes of that gamble are too high, with a totally uncertain outcome."

"Do you think that you know your parents through and through? I don't see how you could. Often we don't know our nearest and dearest as well as we'd like to think. Look at us, I had no idea that you had such a secret."

"Katie, it is not for you to judge. Also, it is not for you to say anything about it. It is my decision concerning my life and the life of my children. You have no right to destroy that."

"You don't need to worry. I'll not say anything. However, I somehow think that you may have come to far too simple a solution."

How to wear her hair and what to wear occupied her mind ferociously. She had to make sure that her appearance left nothing to criticize. She did not want any spokes in the wheel of her future. Eric had told her to be smart but at the same time serious. Emma was in the fashion industry so she would judge her severely. The dress had to fit a picture of a future step-mother, worthy to be at her father's side. No open sex-appeal. Not too elderly. What a bind!

In the end, she decided on the blue one she had worn for two parties in honour of her exhibitions. It was an elegant, expensive model for which she had splashed out. Never mind if it had no sex-appeal at all. What Katie forgot was that she herself had sex-appeal. She did not need any dress to point it out.

She dressed her hair in a low bun with pink hair decorations. At her age, no flowing locks. So many women of an advanced age still kept flowing locks, thinking that it added to their sex-appeal. Sadly, such a look only showed their age, an old face with flowing locks only looked silly and desperate and even more aged. The blue dress had white decorations at the neck and at the sleeves and a skirt that reached mid-calf. The decorations at the top were perky. A pink handbag and shoes. She looked fresh and young. She wore her camel coat, a recent luxury.

She was nervous when she arrived at the house. Eric opened the door and then took her to the drawing room where Lucius and Emma were waiting. Katie was again struck by Lucius' good looks, but she was bowled over by Emma. She was one of the loveliest girls Katie had ever seen. Her long blond hair was held on either side of her head by combs from which it cascaded to her mid-back. A full mouth and Eric's gorgeous eyes! She was dressed in an elegant pale-green two-piece with a pencil skirt.

Eric made the introductions and Lucius served the drinks. Lucius was most taken by Katie, and the two of them got on well. As for Emma, though she was perfectly polite and friendly, she remained distant. Eric was doing his best to cover up the dissonance emanating from his daughter. He had seen at once that Emma was very wary of Katie. Dear me, and there was still that luncheon to be lived through!

The restaurant Eric had chosen was furbished with bright colours, the curtains were green with red flowers, the table-cloths green, and the napkins had lovely red flowers. As they settled down, Katie exclaimed,

"Oh, I like these colourful serviettes. What a super idea."

"They are nice indeed," said Lucius, who had noticed Emma's eyebrows go up.

"Would you like an aperitif?" enquired Eric.

They all decided to have a sherry, except Eric who had a Campari soda.

"May I taste that?" asked Katie.

"Sure, but I don't think you'll like it, "said Eric.

"Oh Lord, no. It's like bitter mouthwash."

"Well-described," said Lucius, "I can't bear it either."

Then they studied the menus.

"I see that they've got a sausage dish as well. At home when we were having our tea in the evenings, Dad was very keen on sausages."

Then the ordering was done. White wine with the first course and red with the main. The conversation was a bit laboured. Somehow it got to the ancient Egyptians thanks to Katie's pottery.

"Egyptian women seem to have been so attractive," said Katie.

"I'm sure they were, and still are today, in a sultry, dark way," said Emma, "but they could be dangerous."

"Really? Why?" asked Katie.

"Think of Potiphar's wife."

"What happened there?" Katie was curious.

"She was keen on young men."

"Has Mr Potiphar found out about that?" asked Katie.

"I'm pretty convinced that he has," said Emma with a light smirk.

"Listen. Let's leave such a subject alone," said Eric firmly, "I don't like discussions about other people's affairs."

Eric was bailing Katie out.

After a while the conversation turned to music.

"How do you like Haydn?" asked Emma in an innocent manner.

"I don't know any Heidi," said Katie.

"Of course you wouldn't. She is one of Emma's fashion friends with a bit of a name," said Eric, giving his daughter a glance of rage.

He was not having the girl insult Katie. Emma read his glance correctly, and realised that her father was seriously annoyed. If she continued in that manner, there would be repercussions. So, she resolved to leave early, pleading a head-ache or something and go straight after the main course. Indeed, before they had reached coffee, Emma said that she was feeling most unwell and would the others please excuse her. The girl left.

Her departure was a relief to Katie. The rest of the luncheon went well, or so she thought. But because of her nerves, Katie had had a bit too much to drink, which had made her tipsy and giggly. It also loosened her tongue, a fact that enraged Eric. Another unforeseen development was that Lucius could not take his eyes off Katie nor disguise how charmed he was by her. Eric was appalled.

266

Katie prattled happily,

"Eric and I know this super dance joint in Kensington. We love to twirl the nights away. Your father is such a good dancer, Lucius."

"Yes he is. In fact we all are. Dancing has always been one of the family interests. Father is excellent at sevillanas and pretty good at flamenco."

"There were dancing lessons even in Southall," said Katie.

Eric froze. He had to stop her in her tracks.

"I seem to recollect your telling me that one of your Indian friends took dancing lessons there. The area is known to be very Indian."

He looked piercingly at Katie, and she realised her gaffe.

"Yes, yes, that's what I meant," she blurted.

"Now do tell us of your future plans for exhibitions," said Eric, turning the subject to a safer ground.

"I love your creations, Katie," said Lucius.

"I'm so glad. Oh Eric, could I have another brandy and another coffee as well? This is so good."

"But of course."

Eric was sweating in agony. Katie was sitting there like a growing mushroom. She sensed that he wanted to shift her, but in her tipsy state she had become obstinate. She would not give in this time. She enjoyed Lucius' company. They got on well.

"Katie, you have beautiful hands. I can imagine them working up forms," said Lucius.

Dear me, the boy was waxing lyrical and paying unnecessary compliments. And slightly risqué compliments at that. He was almost flirting with her. Eric was livid, the lunch was going from bad to worse.

"Were you not supposed to go to some meeting this afternoon?" said Eric, hoping that the wretch would take his cue and leave.

"No, Dad. That's next week. I am entirely free."

What a nail in the coffin of this lunch, thought Eric. He had no choice but to live it through. It was a white-knuckle effort for him to keep his cool. Lucius continued to be rooted to his chair in spite of the glacial looks his father was sending in his direction. Finally, but finally, the luncheon came to an end. Eric bundled Katie into a pre-paid taxi. Then he asked Lucius to go home to see how Emma was. He himself was going for a walk.

When Eric got home, he got a barrage from his daughter.

"Good Lord, Dad. How could you? What a complete ignoramus. Which gutter did you dig her out from?"

"You are being very rude, Emma."

"Dad, you are too good for a woman of her class. It is very plain that she is not really educated. What can you possibly have in common with her except sex?"

"Oi. Oi. I will not be spoken to in such a manner. Not even by my daughter, and especially not by her."

"What a bitch you are, Emma," said Lucius, "I think Katie is lovely."

"That was pretty clear. You drooled over her like a dog. The whole restaurant could see it except father. Where were your wits, brother? The woman is supposed to be father's girlfriend, after all."

"Stop, both of you. This has gone far enough. I will hear no more," roared Eric.

Emma was not going to be put off.

"I'm sorry if I was rude. But I am upset by such a relationship for you, father. It was quite clear that Katie thinks that she already owns you. She was mentioning that you two have future plans. What plans? She believes you are going to marry her."

Emma looked most anxious.

"At this point I'm not thinking of any marriage," said Eric.

"I do hope so, Daddy. She is beautiful, yes, but have you thought at all what life would be like with her? On many instances you'd be blushing with shame. She has all to gain from a marriage, and you have all to lose."

Tears had come to Emma's eyes. She was not blustering any longer. Real fear had got hold of her as she had realised what Katie meant for Eric. She had sensed that the union was far stronger than it appeared. And she sensed that Katie posed a possible danger for her father.

Eric saw that the girl had sussed out his own dilemma. He went to hug her.

"Please, darling, don't cry. Let me repeat that I am not thinking of any marriage at the moment. What the future holds I don't know. But rest assured that I do know what I am doing. Please credit your father with some brains. Now, both of you, please leave me to ruminate in peace."

Eric went into his study. It was unendingly sad that he did not feel ready to marry Katie yet. That happiness was there for him to take, but he was not taking it. He was running away from it.

"I should end it right now," he thought, "but I want her by my side as long as I can. Selfish or not, I'll keep her till I'm going abroad again. I'll tell her at the last minute. It is cowardly, but so be it."

Chapter 36

After that luncheon, Eric was more passionate than ever with Katie and saw her more frequently. She took this as a good sign which showed that all was well with the relationship in spite of Emma being unkeen. At the end of the day, thought Katie, why should adult children have any say in the affairs of their parents? They would soon be leaving the family nest to lead lives of their own. Lucius liked her, so that was half the battle won. The daughter was still a Daddy's girl, but she would grow out of it, certainly once a serious boyfriend had been found. Daddy would find himself on a lower pedestal.

In May, Eric took Katie on a two week holiday to his beloved Spain. They flew there and then hired a car. Eric was keen to make their tour "in the footsteps of Gerald Brennan", whose books he particularly liked. They went to the Sierra Nevada, Al Pujara, Granada, Sevilla and finished in Cordoba.

It had been an exhilarating trip. Now Katie understood why he was so passionate about Spain, the countryside, the flamenco, the guitar. His enthusiasm woke an interest in Katie. This had been their first cultural tour, and this time Katie had appreciated the magnificence of the churches and cathedrals, the fortresses ad the palaces. She had been captivated by the Alhambra. The imposing and majestic heights of the mountains had almost made her swoon. The views had bowled her over. How lovely the sea was and the air was perfumed by luscious vegetation everywhere around.

Back home Katie's euphoria over Spain continued. She got books from the library on Spain. Her pottery took on a flair of Southern spice. All this pleased Eric and he was there to answer her many questions.

When September arrived, there was another fateful luncheon. Katie had been in the centre of London to discuss her spring exhibition at one of the top galleries. Afterwards she was ambling by Leicester Square, and as it was getting towards twelve thirty, she decided to lunch at an Italian restaurant.

As she went in, she saw Lucius. He waved and beckoned to her.

"Hello, Katie. How nice to see you. Would you like to join me for lunch?"

"Hello, Lucius. Yes, I'd like that very much."

The two were pleased to see one another, and soon conversation was flowing. The young man sat looking at Katie admiringly. What a lovely, warm woman she was. He could fully understand his father's passion for this woman. What surprised him was that his father had not indicated in any way that he might be keen to marry her. His father should have snapped her up, thought Lucius.

"What do you think of Dad's new posting?" he asked, assuming that his father would have told Katie about it. "Just think, Ambassador to Denmark."

Katie had gone pale. She was in shock. Her hands trembled and tears came to her eyes. Lucius was appalled.

"Good Lord, has he not told you about it?" he gasped.

Katie could only shake her head as she got out her handkerchief and was then racked by sobs. Lucius was on hot coals – he had been an idiot. Never assume anything. His thoughtless words had caused this terrible distress in this kind woman. She must feel cheated to the core. Lamely he tried to alleviate the situation.

"Katie, dear, he only told us a couple of days ago. He obviously hasn't had time to tell you yet. "

Katie sobbed even more. Only yesterday she had been with Eric.

"Please don't cry. I'm sure that when next you see him, he will tell you the happy news."

It would be news but it would not be happy, went through Katie's mind. It came to her clearly that Eric had said nothing about it because he had not wanted to upset her. And she would only have been upset in case he would not be taking her with him. Her hopes were dashed.

Lucius could see that Katie had realised that Eric would not be taking her with him. How awful, it was plain to see how much she loved Eric. It had been him, Lucius, he would never have let Katie go. Oh dear, he seemed to have been smitten as well as his father. That was a silly thing from him, and he would see to it that he gave it no opportunity to develop.

It was regrettable that his father had not mentioned anything about his posting to Katie. However, the man was within his rights to have made that decision. He had a duty to tell his family, but he had actually no duty to tell it to anyone else. Lucius realised that Katie was so upset because it meant that Eric was not going to marry her and take her with him. From what His father had said to him and Emma that he was not considering any permanent relationships for the moment, it meant that at least he would not have filled Katie with false hopes.

She obviously saw it differently. In Lucius' meagre experience of women, the one girlfriend he had had in his life so far, had after a mere ten months started to become possessive and had begun to make hints about permanence. That had frightened him off. The girl had been livid and had accused him of lifting her hopes. How dare he disappoint her so! It had been a salutary lesson. Woe betide a man who does not see that a woman will invariably want to be the big Number One in a man's life, with marriage as the next step.

Going out and having sex was fun. So why the hell did the female of the species not leave it at that? No, the dreaded matrimony loomed large in their books.

It seemed that even mature women did not escape that curse. Here was Katie, obviously having expected Eric to marry her. Well, why should he? If he did not feel ready to take such a step, why should he be blamed? Unless he had mentioned marriage to Katie. His father could be considered a victim of a kind of pursuit. He was the real victim whilst Katie was only a victim in her own eyes. She had built a castle in the air and when it collapsed, she blamed Eric instead of blaming her foolish expectations. She could have stipulated her terms, but she had not done so. Eric's terms were not marriage-based.

It seemed that most women had a leaning towards making themselves into badly treated and cheated innocent victims, blaming the males. If only they had realised that once a man was ready to marry, then they would approach their desired goals with a firm decision to do their best in the fold of family life.

Katie seemed to recover.

"I'm glad that your father has been offered his Ambassadorship. It is well-merited, he is such a bright man. He has finally reached the goal he has always wanted. Forgive my silly tears. It is quite right that your father should tell his family first about such matters."

"You are a very special kind of friend to him, rest assured."

"I've had the great joy of being that to him. I've known him all my life."

"What was my father like as a child? He himself does not talk about the early days."

What a difficult question. What would Eric want her to say? What would he want her not to say? Any continuing friendship with Eric depended now upon her answers. She had better get them right.

"Unfortunately, he had a difficult childhood. His parents were not very good at bringing up a child. I think there were shouting matches. However, he was the star pupil of our school. He more or less educated himself as his parents were not much help. Money of course was tight. Already at the age of seven he was doing little jobs to get pocket money. Please don't ask me anything more about his past. It is not for me to say, and I might have got things wrong. It is your father that you should ask."

"I understand. You are right. It is not for me to go behind my father's back. But just one more thing. Were you just friends or also sweethearts? "You do not have to answer."

"That I will answer. Oh Lucius, it was love. Your father is the love of my life. He is my first and only love. We were sweethearts till he got his grade 9 at the Foreign Office."

Lucius did mental calculation. Goodness me, his father had been about twenty-five at that time.

Eric's leaving her must have broken her heart. What a sad fate. He tried to sooth her.

"Katie, but now you two are together again."

A distant look came into her eyes.

"For the time being anyway. And the future, as in the famous song by Doris Day, "Que sera, sera"."

"Let me say, Katie, that should you and father decide to get married at any stage, I have nothing against it."

"Thank you, Lucius. I don't think I would have the same reaction from your sister."

"She's always been a jealous daddy's girl. After mother's death, Emma became a protective mother-hen to our father. Believe me, she should not find even a Princess of the land good enough for him. She thinks that she fulfils the roles of a wife and a mother. But Emma has not yet fallen in love herself. When that day arrives, it will be "goodbye Daddy" and she will swan away with her loved one. Father of course realises this and enjoys for the time being the role of being the only object of Emma's adoration. It is lovely, but it won't last. I myself feel strongly that Dad needs to concentrate on his own relationships. Later on, Emma won't pose a problem for you."

You are so positive. It makes me feel better. Now, let's enjoy our meal, and I'd like you to tell me about your own plans."

A few days later, Sir Philip popped in one evening. After a suitable period of small talk, Sir Philip addressed the matter he had come to talk about.

"I hear from Emma that you've got a woman in your life. Someone called Katie Smith who was at school with you. Do I take it that she is the same woman you were with for those eight years?"

"My private life seems to have been announced to the papers!" raged Eric, "This meddling is intolerable. I'm annoyed, though not surprised, that Emma saw fit to come and bleat about it at your door. What does she expect you to do?"

"Calm down, Eric. It seems normal to me that families talk to each other about matters affecting them."

"Gossip! That's all that it is," Eric spat the words, "I happen to be a fully grown man who does know what he is doing. Is it of some special importance to others that the lady in question happens to be a former flame of mine?"

"As a matter of fact, yes. It is of importance to me. You left her for Philippa."

"I've never regretted that step. I did my best by her."

"I know you did, Eric, and I thank you for it. And before you get any more annoyed with me, let me assure you of my appreciation that you have let several years pass before telling the children anything."

"The family seem to be running my life for me! No doubt Emma has been telling you that she'd never forgive me if I married Katie now?"

"She did say words to that effect, but they are not to be taken seriously. But now that you mention marriage, how serious is this relationship? Especially in view of your promotion to Ambassadorship in Denmark next September."

Eric had begun to fidget. He needed a drink and he wanted to get rid of Sir Philip. The man had hit a raw spot.

"And Estephania, she no doubt has an opinion as well?"

"Yes. She feels that you've done wonderfully as regards Philippa and that now you should be left in peace to decide for yourself."

"A wise woman. I think that by now we have said all that there is to say, don't you think?"

"Oh indeed. Please forgive this intrusion. I'll see myself out."

As soon as Sir Philip had left, Eric got the whisky bottle out. Tomorrow was Sunday, he would miss church.

Chapter 37

Eric, who was unaware of the lunch talk between Lucius and Katie, continued happily without saying anything about his posting. He had decided not to say anything till the springtime. He did feel that sometimes Katie looked at him quizzically but he did not know how to interpret it. Katie for her part had decided not to spoil anything. They were still having the time of their life, so why cut it short? Should all end in tears, there would be plenty of time to cry then.

During the year, Eric had been kept busy in his department, what with the UK's reluctance to join the Schengen Agreement, which eased cross-border travel, having gone into effect. Now that he had been notified about his posting to Denmark, he promptly took up learning Danish. His Swedish would help him a long way but he wanted a certain proficiency in Danish. He had just under a year to get to grips with it.

Again a Christmas was looming which was to be celebrated without Katie but he was planning to take her to Scotland for a week, when they would celebrate the coming of New Year 1996. He had noticed that Katie had not mentioned anything about a Christmas meeting. He wondered how come she was so docile about it but had found no real explanation. The main thing was that the question of Christmas was not souring everything.

His children were doing well. Lucius, the budding physicist, was employed in a research team by one of the great multi-national pharmaceuticals. Emma was in the fashion school. After a year there, she was planning on opening her own business, Emma Erica Fashions. The setting up of the business would be provided by the "Bargain Basement", i.e. Sir Philip. It was clear that that was the case as Eric had not been approached with any demands for money. He had also noticed that grandfather and grand-daughter were often closeted and had the appearance of being as thick as thieves. One could see how they were plotting.

In June, Eric took Katie on a holiday to Italy. They did Venice, Siena and Florence. Five days in each place. Eric reckoned that the holiday would make it easier to approach Katie with the bad news afterwards. That was a serious miscalculation. Already, when he had suggested the holiday, Katie had begun to wonder whether he would approach the dreaded subject of his posting while they were there. Probably not, because he would have had to know that such a move would spoil the whole trip. She was really surprised that so far nothing had been said.

It was the end of June and Eric was at Katie's.

"Darling, I've got something to tell you."
Katie looked up.

"I've been promoted. I've been made Ambassador to Denmark. This from September on."

"Congratulations, Eric, that is wonderful. And how long have you known about it?"

Katie's face had remained expressionless. That took Eric by surprise.

"For a little while."

"Why not tell me earlier?"

"I wasn't ready to."

"Does this affect me in any way, Eric?"

"Well, yes, in a way it does. We will be apart."

"So you're not taking me with you, are you?"

"I've weighed the matter up in so many ways, but it is best if I go alone."

"What has our relationship been all about, Eric? It has been intense enough to have lulled me into thinking that there might be a future for us."

"I have not lied to you about anything, and I have not made any false promises."

"You have indeed kept yourself most carefully from any promises. I cannot throw in your teeth that you have led me down the garden path. But everything that has happened between us has pointed towards marriage."

It struck Katie's mind that Eric still did not consider her suitable to be his wife. He seemed blind to the fact that she no longer was the uninformed girl of the early days. He didn't seem to see that she too, had risen above the dreaded Southall. She was an acclaimed and famous artist in her own right. She had as much 'career' as he had. He was successful, but so was she. Katie would have wanted to throw that at him, but thought the better of it. Their relationship had always been fragile, so fragile that it would not survive any attack. And also, she truly loved Eric, so why say something really hurtful to him? He'd figure everything out in his own time.

"Oh God, Katie. I cannot marry you. I'm not ready for such a step. But it does not mean that I don't love you."

"You call it love that you don't want to marry me? I find that so insincere and downright hypocritical."

"But I do love you."

"Yes, a tiny teeny little bit. I am a comfortable bedwarmer. A convenient station to relieve tension. How marvellous! You obviously think that you've made my day. Do I need to be grateful as well?"

"I know that you're upset. I knew that you would be. That's why I didn't tell you earlier."

"Why tell at all? You could have just departed one day, perhaps having had the grace to leave a little note saying, "I am leaving you". That would have made me feel no worse than now."

"You're being unreasonable…"

"Unreasonable?" hissed Katie, interrupting him, "I think I'm being bloody reasonable in having such a measured and controlled discussion about the fact that you are dropping me like a hot potato."

"You have always harped on marriage…"

"Stop right there! In our type of close relationship, any woman at all would have started to think that it was leading to something permanent."

"You are berating me for not proposing?" Eric looked belligerent.

"In a way perhaps I am. I honestly thought that I mattered to you enough for you to want to marry me. My heart is freezing over at the thought that in the end I have not been sufficiently important to you. That realisation sends shivers up my spine. It freezes my emotions. I'm not even able to scream or shout. To you I am a nobody."

"Katie, I don't want to uproot you…"

"Spare me such insincerities, they are insulting."

"I'm not trying to insult you. We can carry on as always and make visits."

Katie was beyond tears. To feel that she did not really matter to Eric was killing her inside. No, she would not be his little bit of fluff. As no marriage was forthcoming, there was no point in their relationship continuing. She would not be able to. The pain was far too acute. It would only be a burning and searing fire to be with him with no future.

When they had found each other again and they were both free, Katie really believed that marriage was awaiting her. What was preventing him? She was by now a well-known artist. She was not a nobody. She knew that he should want to marry her, but something was in the way. What? Till Eric found the reason why and then dealt with it, there was no future for them. That was why Katie had to put a stop to it, right now.

"Eric. Under those circumstances I don't want to be in your life. You know that you mean the world to me. I'm afraid that for me it is either a marriage or nothing at all."

"Katie, it doesn't have to be like that. A lot of couples are together without a marriage."

"I am not a lot of couples. I am me. You have a choice to make. Now. This very day. I've given you years in which to make up your mind. There is no more time for you. The last grains of sand are falling."

"Darling, I'm not ready to take such a step."

"Thank you for giving me a straight answer. Now we two must part. Thank you for loving me at all and for all the kindnesses on your part. I shall treasure them in my memory. We shall not now go to the restaurant. Instead, you will go home. And then I don't want any contact at all. A clean break is the kindest for both of us. No, don't try to come near, have some respect for me. This is goodbye, Eric. Let us at least be dignified about it."

Eric was amazed at Katie's composure. It was as if she had rehearsed it. He had expected a terrible tearful scene. But he did not know that she had had all those months to wait for the axe to fall. What she definitely did not want was to beg a man to marry her who did not want to do so. Her anxiety and fear showed in the pottery that she had created during those months. They were powerful pieces showing an inner turmoil. What she did not know at that moment was that those works would be selling as fast as she could produce them. Now she just stood there, calm and pale and composed. Her dreams had broken into shards.

Eric decided not to prolong the agony.

"Well, I had better go then, Katie. I think we both need a lot more time to consider out situation. Goodbye for now, Katie."

"Goodbye, Eric."

Then he was gone. Katie felt almost inanimate. Tears would have helped her, but none were forthcoming. She did what was best under the circumstances: she watched various comedies. Later on, she took a sleeping pill in order to have an unbroken night. She thought of Scarlett O'Hara saying, "After all, tomorrow is another day."

Chapter 38

Eric allowed two weeks to pass before phoning Katie. He reckoned that by then her fury would have abated. He got the answering machine and left a message. After a week he made another call. Again, he got the answering machine. Things were beginning to look serious. After another ten days he made a third attempt. He left a shot message. As time passed, he gathered that she was not going to answer. She had meant what she said.

Indeed, Katie had found each message deeply upsetting. She was going through a very difficult emotional time and could barely keep her wits together. There was no point to Eric's love messages when he had decided that there was nothing further for them in the future. She would have to start to lead a new life with new expectations. Easier said than done. Once she knew that he had left for Denmark, only then would she start to feel easier. It would help her to know that he was at a distance.

This time Katie did not run straight to Nandita. She waited till September had passed, and then she poured her heart out to Timmy.

"Timmy, Eric has left me again."

"This doesn't come as a surprise to me. As time passed and he did not introduce you to the children, I began to have my doubts. What's the matter with the man?"

"I don't know. There is something in his mind that prevents him from marrying me. It is no longer that I'm not much more educated than I was before. I am now a name and have my own standing."

"It is a pity. You two are so ideally suited."

"I've neglected you a bit since Eric's return. Tell me, what's going on in your life?"

"Astrid and I got quietly wed eight months ago and to our great surprise, and delight, she is now pregnant."

"How wonderful for you, Timmy. I wish you both all happiness."

Later that week a parcel arrived for Timmy. The couple gasped in admiration when they opened it. There was a beautiful work by Katie.

For Eric, the rift was so much easier to bear. He was going to a new posting, new happenings and new people. Each posting was a type of adventure and settling in took a lot of time so there was not much time left to brood. He had been to one of his self-imposed obligatory visits to his parents in August. His mother smoked more than ever. It was a wonder that the Grim Reaper had not yet come to collect her. But then, thought Eric, being so smoked and pickled, she would probably make it to a hundred. His father had sobered up somewhat and had not been as offensive as usual.

Once Eric got to Copenhagen, there was the ceremony of presenting the credentials. The job of Ambassador could be described as being an icon of the Queen. To be the head of post was extremely satisfying for him.

As in Stockholm, after he had been widowed, the same syndrome appeared at functions. His dinner partners were almost invariably single women between the ages of thirty-eight and forty-five. As always, he was charming and polite, he even invited some of them out with him, but nothing ever went further. Inside himself he felt wedded to Katie.

Back home, Emma had fallen in love. She was now twenty-three. The loved one was twelve years older though he did not look his age. He was a stockbroker. As Eric was at his posting, it fell to Sir Philip to listen to all the adulations of the young man.

"Grandpa, Charles is taking me to dinner at a place called Sarrastro's. I've never been there before, but he says it is fun. It is not stuffed with codgers. Now I must think what to wear."

"Sweetheart, you always look stunning. You're in the fashion industry so you know exactly what to wear."

"That's true, Grandpa. I've been out with him four times. I can't wait to be in his arms."

"What do you mean, Popsikins?"

"He kissed me on our third date."

289

"That's fast work. You no doubt encouraged him, what?"

"Of course. He is such a handsome man. I think that I'm in love."

"Handsome is not everything. Take your time about love. Think what your father would think. He's counting on me to take care of you in his absence."

"Father would tut tut, purse his lips and make sarcastic comments. He's good at those. Finds the right arrows. I can't speak to him as I can with you. Because I can talk to you openly, you can advise me so much better than father, to whom nothing can be told."

"I see. But back to your young man. Don't encourage him too much. He might go into over-drive."

"No, no, grandpa. Charles behaves properly."

"Emma. I don't want you to get hurt."

"I plan to noose and to net him. I intend to marry him."

"By the time you have noosed and netted him, the poor man will have nothing to say. When will you allow me to meet him?"

"Not quite yet. He must not be frightened off. In May, just two months' time, he is taking me to the Russian Ball. That would be an ideal time. I'll ask Charles for drinks with all of us as he comes to collect me."

"Excellent. I can't wait."

As a result, Sir Philip put out all his antennae in order to know what there was to know about Charles Antonio Williams. He even paid a private eye! He was most careful that nobody knew of his machinations. He knew that both Emma and his wife would have skinned him alive. In his mind he justified his actions by thinking that Eric would certainly have approved as he was a man well-practised in reconnaissance. As all reports were favourable, Sir Philip relaxed.

Later, Emma had a chat with her brother.

"Lucius, I had a chat with Grandpa about Charles."

"Ah, did you? And what did you tell him?"

"Not much, that's for sure. Don't want to upset the old thing. After all, he comes from another century."

"That was wise. But tell me, how is Charles?"

"He's an ace in bed, I can tell you. Comes from the Sicilian background of his mother. And I know, thanks to the 'recommended reading' suggested by Daddy. Do you remember when he took us aside one day and said, "As I am the mother and father in this family, now that you have both reached the age of eighteen and nineteen respectively, I feel the need to advise you on sex. Don't look so startled. I'm not going to do the teaching, but I've got two books of recommended reading upon the subject which I'd like you to read.

291

One is on the medical side of it and the other is about sexual psychology. These books will give you the necessary information. I don't want you two to rely on the rubbish you may have heard behind the bicycle shed or in the girls' dormitories."

"I remember that scene well. Typical father. To have waited till we were nearly adult! By then it was old hat! But full marks for father, he tackled a thorny subject which most parents never even touch. Emma, I see that you have gone to bed with Charles. Where is this leading?"

"Oh, to marriage, brother dear. To marriage. That is why I let Charles stew for four long months before bedding him. Let the hunter hunt. He is wonderful. I adore his dark hair and eyes. They glow. And his hairy arms and legs. Hairy legs always does it for me."

"You'd get the same result from a fur coat."

"Don't be ridiculous. It is the action. Charles is indefatigable."

"He'd need to be with you."

"Soon he will propose. I know it in my bones."

"I shall be waiting for the announcement."

"You will, dear brother, you will. In the not too distant future."

Chapter 39

Lucius had been dragged to the drinks before the Russian Ball. Emma wanted the whole family to meet Charles. Lucius gathered that his sister must regard her relationship as going towards the permanent, why otherwise subject the young man to an invitation to a crocodile pond? Grandpa especially could be a ferocious beast behind all that jovial mask of his. Also very protective. So far father had been told nothing. Emma had said that that depended upon these drinks and how Charles got on with everyone.

His sister looked fetching. The ball-gown she had designed was made of peach-coloured brocade. What she called a boat-neck was jagged like icicles, with the thin middle-plunge pointing downwards a bit deeper than the rest, so as to show a whiff of cleavage. Small sleeves with jagged edges. Around the hips the fabric appeared to be twisted into a kind of plait whose diagonal lines enhanced an hour-glass shape. The broad skirt was not quite full-length which enabled the red patent-leather high-heels to be seen. Her big red earrings, together with the red shoes, created an electric effect. No wonder that her business was going well.

Charles arrived. Emma flew to open the door.

"This is Charles. May I introduce my grandparents and my brother, Lucius."

Hands were shaken in the continental style because Lady Saunders liked it. The housemaid served the drinks.

"The Russian Ball sounds wonderfully old-fashioned. I am surprised they have it. On the whole balls seem to have remained only in Vienna," said Sir Philip.

"It is most wonderfully old-fashioned. Proper dancing to a dance orchestra. Later in the evening a Cossack band will play and perform. And I want Emma to learn sabrage."

"What's that?" asked Emma.

"It is the art of opening champagne bottles with a sword."

"Charles, how exciting," enthused Emma, "I never knew such a thing existed."

"Well, my dear, I shall look forward to hearing all about it, "said Sir Philip.

"Lucius, when you finally get a girlfriend, that is where you should take her."

"That sounds like a good idea, sis."

Then the young couple left.

"What a pleasant young man," commented Lady Saunders.

"Sis has chosen well. She is doing a swell job in disguising how crazy she is about Charles. Good for her."

"I have a feeling this might end in wedding bells," mused Sir Philip. "Emma tells me that later in the summer she intends to take Charles to Copenhagen to meet father."

"Well, then it is serious indeed," said Lucius.

After the Ball, Eric got to hear about Charles. He phoned Sir Philip.

"What is the whipper-snapper in my daughter's life like?"

"Relax, Eric. Emma has chosen well. Charles Williams is a very pleasant young man. I'm sure you will approve."

"My approval will count for nothing. The young these days don't listen to their parents."

"Did they ever? I remember when Philippa dragged you in front of my eyes. Her mind was firmly made up, no matter what I might have said."

"Well, yes. It was most nerve-racking for me. I feared that you would have pulverised me."

"It turned out to be wonderful for all of us. We have two splendid youngsters as a result, Lucius and Emma."

"I shall look forward to eventually meeting the young man."

"Oh, you will, you will."

In August Emma and Charles went to Copenhagen. Eric and Charles liked one another on sight. The very next day at breakfast Emma said,

"Daddy, Charles and I got engaged last night. May he now move into the same bedroom with me? Once back in London he will get me a rock for my paw. I'd like pink morganite surrounded by light-blue Ceylonese sapphires. We'll have it made."

"Congratulations, my dears. Welcome into the family, Charles. Champagne bottles will be opened at lunch. Emma, my treasure, come and give your Daddy a hug."

Great joy reigned supreme.

For Eric it was a new sensation to think about wedding plans. Emma's wedding made Eric think about his own missed wedding with Katie. He could have walked up the aisle and then stood there with his best man to wait for the bride. But he had chosen not to. It made him feel a little wistful to see how others were going into the bliss of matrimony. He was not entirely sure whether he had done the right thing by himself. Being in Denmark was not a hardship post, there was mercifully not much going on, so actually, Katie would have coped. Her decision of no contact was hard for Eric to bear. However, he could understand that she was not up to it.

As for the plans, as Eric was in Copenhagen, he wisely appointed Lady Saunders to undertake the task of wedding planning. She was a practical woman who would inject some common sense into the plans which Sir Philip did his best to take over. He was a true mother-hen. He loved being closeted with Emma and to talk till the cows came home about the arrangements, ceremonies, colours, food, guest-list and so on. Without Lady Saunders's input, the whole wedding would have ballooned into an impossibility.

Emma did not want any delay, and so a winter wedding was planned for February. The church favoured by Sir Philip was St Magnus the Martyr. To make sure that the church would be sufficiently warm, he negotiated a special payment which meant that the heating system there would be roaring at full strength from early morning on. For him it was important that the bride need not wear a coat.

The two had also decided that they did not want an almighty bunfight, so no more than a hundred guests were invited. Charles of course was consulted, but he did not feel that he was up to such plans and was more than happy to leave it all to others. On top of that he did not want to be seen to meddle in any way. Let the enthusiasts loose!

When the day of the wedding arrived, Eric felt almost as nervous as the bride. His little girl had grown up so quickly and now she was going to be a married woman. It was lovely to think how harmonious the young couple seemed to be; the bride looked so happy it was heart-warming.

Emma's dress was simplicity itself. It was Empire in style with short sleeves and a square neck-line. It was a full-length gown made of a double layer of soft silk-chiffon which cascaded beautifully from the high waist-line under the bust where it was gathered by a band of small white silk flowers. The same silk flowers were around the high bun of her hair from which flowed the veil made of extra thin chiffon with more of the same flowers. Her only jewellery was an antique bracelet which her mother had worn at her own wedding and which had initially been given to her by her father. A touch of silver eye-shadow and warm-pink lipstick completed her looks.

Father and daughter coming up the aisle were a lovely sight together. Sir Philip had to wipe a tear from his eye, he was so moved. He would have the fourth dance with the bride, the first ones going to the groom, then to Eric, then to Charles' father and then it was himself. Sir Philip purred and was already planning to be at the front of the Pram Pushers' Brigade for his great-grandchild. He had missed for some time the days of playing in the mud, crawling around and stuffing oneself with ice-creams!

Chapter 40

By May Emma was expecting. The child was expected in February 1999. Sir Philip, as ever, fussed no end.

"In his previous life Philip must have been a nanny," said Lady Saunders, "he is indefatigable with children."

"Charles's parents will have to battle with him firmly. They are ever so keen on a grandchild. Charles' two brothers are not yet married, but then, they are seven and eleven years his junior. This is the first grandchild." said Emma.

Katie knew about Emma's marriage through the births, deaths and marriages columns in the papers. Emma would now be concentrating on her husband and on her own life instead of that of her father. Once she'd had a child, her father would be on the back burner. That was how life went. To Katie this had no specific significance since she was no longer with Eric, but her sad mood had not lifted with time.

She remembered how the young Eric had sought solace from the church and that it had helped him. One of Katie's friends frequented Holy Trinity Brompton and had suggested that Katie go there one Sunday to see what it was like. Why not, in the end? What had she got to lose? So she went. It was a revelation to her. It was warm and friendly. The singing had been beautiful and the sermon had given cause to think. Afterwards she had been asked to stay for coffee and meet a few people. She had done so.

A new era began for her. She felt at home in the HTB, and within half a year she had been baptised and confirmed. Going there on Sundays lifted her spirits and gave her inner strength. She made some very nice friends and took part in various little trips and activities. The burden she was carrying because of Eric was beginning to lift slowly.

It was important that her spirits had lifted, for she was going to be faced with another ordeal. It was her mother. The poor woman had started to suffer from dementia already three years ago and now it was rapidly worsening.

"Katie, I cannot cope with your Mum anymore," said her Dad, "She is a danger to her own self. I think the time has come for a nursing home."

"Yes, Dad. You've done wonders so far. I'll do some searching and find a good one for her. I can afford to pay for it. What about you, where would you like to be?"

"Katie, I don't want to move anywhere. I've had a good life here and here I want to stay till I'm carried out feet first."

The nursing home was arranged and Katie saw how her father took on a new lease of life thanks to having had the burden of a seriously sick wife lifted from him.

Time was passing. The year 2000 had arrived. At the beginning of January, while Eric was still on his Christmas break in London, Lucius said that he would like the family to get to know Amanda, whom he had met that autumn.

"Fancy big brother bringing home a woman," said heavily pregnant Emma, "all I know is that her name is Amanda Prescott. Otherwise Lucius has not breathed a word."

"We are all curious," answered Eric.

When Lucius arrived with Amanda, it was as if unease had walked in. She was tall and thin, with dark hair in a bob style. Small, grey piercing eyes glowered from behind a long fringe. She had a pretty mouth but it was petulant mouth. Spelt trouble. Not the choice the family had at all expected.

"How very nice to meet you, Amanda. I am Lucius' father and here are his grandparents, Sir Philip and Lady Saunders and his sister Emma with her husband Charles."

The group settled themselves for drinks.

The conversation flowed with difficulty. It took Eric all his diplomatic skills to get a general conversation going at all. Sir Philip, most unlike him, was mainly silent. Lady Saunders did her best to cover up for him. It was important that Lucius did not feel anything awkward. Luckily he was so wrapped up with every word and gesture of Amanda's that he did not notice anything amiss. Eric was charm itself, and Emma, taking her cue from her father, prattled happily about fashions.

The drinks did not last long. When Lucius and Amanda had departed, the rest of them sighed with relief and looked at each other.

"What a prissy know-all. Being a lawyer, that woman thinks that we are only some apprentices, but more to the point, that she knows better. What the hell has hit my brother?"

"She certainly rules over Lucius. It was a bit as if she was teacher and he the pupil. He is like wax in her hands," said Eric.

"I can't think what attracted him to her, Dad. Thin as a rake, fine, but did you see the eyes? If looks could kill, we were toast. She's got some chip on her shoulder. A big one."

"You are probably right, my sweet. There was something odd about her."

"She did rather emanate a discontent," said Lady Saunders, "and I'm pretty sure she did not like any of us."

"She was curiously suspicious, for want of a better word, and her guard was up," said Eric.

"She's got some agenda as regards Lucius," said Sir Philip, "I think she wants to net him. For reasons we don't yet know. I dislike her intensely."

"Loathsome creature." Emma had bared her teeth.

"Pray God that this is not serious," said Lady Saunders.

"Amen to that," said the other three in unison.

Eric was deep in thought over Amanda. She was not what he had expected Lucius to choose. But then, he mused, history was full of most unlikely unions. One never really knew what attracted people together. Lucius deserved a softer type of woman. Eric, who had the ability to read character, had seen that his son's choice was a hard cookie. A fleeting thought came to him whether Lucius in some way was trying to emulate Eric in the choice of wife. If so, the boy had miscalculated. King Edward the 8th and Wallis Simpson came to his mind. It was a mystery what had attracted the King to this woman, to the extent of abdication. Eric could not understand how any man was capable of giving up a position for the sake of so-called love. It did not make sense to him.

Here was his son, on his way to matrimony with a difficult woman. However, Lucius obviously saw her from another angle. So, for better or for worse, Amanda would be joining the family group. Whatever the result would be, the best had to be made of it. He himself was a most family-orientated man; he felt that his efforts in life were not only for himself but also for the launching of his children.

In February Emma gave birth to a healthy baby boy who was named Daniel Philip. Crooning over the baby, Sir Philip said,

"He's got your eyes and eyebrows, Steffi."

"And your nose, Philip. I think his mouth and chin are from Charles's mother."

"He'll be a lady killer," cackled Sir Philip.

"Grandpa, don't put him with other women yet. I want to enjoy my precious baby boy for some time. Now pass me my handsome."

Charles and his parents were over the moon. This, their first grandchild had been much awaited.

Eric had been unable to get to London for the birth, a fact that disappointed him, but work dictated his movements. He would see his grandson after Easter, when he returned for a home posting.

He had had to content himself with a phone call.

"My sweetheart, so many congratulations. I'm giving little Daniel a big bear hug in my thoughts. Does he look like me?"

"Daddy, he's got a lot from you, but the family committee here has pronounced that he mainly takes after Grandma and Charles's mother."

"Is Grandpa fussing?"

"But of course. That goes without saying."

Upon his return after three years, Eric was made an Assistant Under-Secretary. He was pleased. That gave him time before he would, he hoped, get another Ambassadorship. He felt a bit sorry to have missed the great opening of the Oresund Bridge between Denmark and Sweden which would occur in the summer. During his stay in Denmark, nothing earth-shattering had happened there, and now he was ready for something else.

Come September, there was more family news. Lucius announced his future engagement to Amanda. A grand party was held. The coming bride looked satisfied. She kept glancing at the large diamond ring she was wearing. For the party she wore a severe grey dress with silver jewellery. She did not look like a bundle of fun. But Lucius was happy.

The following weekend the rest of the family got together.

"Did you see how smug that cow looked?" seethed Emma.

"She looked mighty triumphant, she couldn't hide it," said Sir Philip."

"Now we've got the wedding next May," said Lady Saunders.

"At least that is organised by her parents," pointed out Eric.

"I bet I'll be asked to design her gown," Emma was nearly frothing at the mouth, "I know what I'd like to design."

"Darling," said Charles, "go easy on that. Think of Lucius."

"Emma dear," said Eric, "may I suggest that you leave all the suggestions of style for Amanda to decide. Then there will be no come-back on you."

"Daddy, you are a fox. And as intelligent as you are handsome."

"Lucius also is very handsome, but I don't think Amanda is marrying him for his looks. The whole thing smells of money," said Sir Philip with a sombre look.

"From now on we'll be stuck with family reunions with that cow," Emma continued seething.

"That is so, provided that she is at all keen to keep up relations. A fact which I severely doubt," said Eric.

"We must make the best out of it," said Lady Saunders, who with her common sense had grasped that that was the only way forward.

For Christmas Amanda arranged for her and Lucius to be with her parents. For New Year they would come to see the rest of the family. And as Emma had predicted, Amanda did ask her to design the wedding gown. She was most conscious that in May 2001 there would be a Mrs Flint!

Emma had listened to her father well, and when Amanda came to talk about designs, she immediately said,

"Dear Amanda, I am only the designer, I can but carry out your wishes. Do please explain how you visualize your wedding dress. I can then tackle the practicalities."

"How very sensible of you. I have indeed very special notions as to what effect I would like to produce. I consider a marriage an extremely serious step in life, in fact one of the most serious, if not

306

THE most serious. This should be reflected in the gown. I want no flesh to show. I do not want to look like a flibbertigibbet or some hopeful fairy princess. Sober straight lines and a stouter type of fabric, perhaps brocade, sounds suitable."

"How very right you are. On top of that, such a style would suit your shape as well."

The two women continued their discussion.

That evening Emma hurtled to talk to Sir Philip and Lady Saunders.

"Boy, what a creation the cow will be wearing. I hate the fact that I've got to design it. It goes against the grain to be associated with anything so awful. However, it will have style. Even if it kills me."

"How can a wedding dress possibly be awful?" Sir Philip wanted to know.

"Think of a stiff paper packet. A thin one. Full length, stiff brocade, absolutely straight. Long thin sleeves even over the wrist line. Just about the fingers visible. After all, the woman will have to be able to eat at the banquet. A stand up stiff collar round the shoulder line. A sort of extra wall. The thick brocade to go along the body like a sausage skin. As there is hardly a bust-line, the whole effect is definitely a package."

"And that is what she wanted?" Lady Saunders exclaimed.

"Absolutely. She explained in detail how she wanted her dress to reflect he serious step a marriage was. I followed Dad's advice and

307

immediately asked her what she wanted. I made no suggestions at all."

"Well, Popsikins, you've made us curious. I agree with you that under all circumstances, the dress must have a style. In your business, it is style that matters, am I right? This monstrosity will show your ability to create versatile models for every taste. Good for business."

"Is there a veil?" asked Lady Saunders.

"Not what you'd call a veil. A round tower like a hat from which protrudes some stiff gauze till the shoulders."

Sir Philip's shoulders were heaving, and a laugh even escaped his wife.

Chapter 41

Eric had had a busy week. It was Friday and he was relaxing with a small sherry. The doorbell rang. Eric guessed who it was before even opening the door.

"Dear father-in-law, to what do I owe this honour?"

"Oh, shush, Eric. We need to talk."

"This sounds ominous. When you turn up on your own, it means something tedious. Am I right?"

"I am here to stop tedium from arriving at our door."

"Please come and settle yourself comfortably. What can I offer you? Sherry, whisky or brandy?"

"A brandy will do fine."

Eric went to comply. As he gave Sir Philip his glass, he asked,

"Now, what is this all about?"

"Eric, the impending marriage has given me to think. I have bad premonitions about it. If nothing else, it was the design of the dreaded wedding dress that brought the realisation of a potential future problem, if not divorce, to my mind."

"Unfortunately I must share your view."

"That woman is after our money, believe you me. I can smell it," Sir Philip snuffled with his nose like a dog.

"Please continue."

"I've decided that under no circumstances will I allow her to get a hold of my pennies. Not one. She will be able to bleed Lucius dry, but not me. I am changing my Will. The half going to Lucius will be put into a trust for him and any future children of his. Them only. Upon any divorce, she won't get anything."

"What a sensible idea, Philip. You are so right to do so. I'm glad you came here to talk, for I shall do exactly the same. Now that the housing market is picking up so fast, this house is worth a fortune. And yours in Knightsbridge will have an astronomical price tag."

"Exactly. As you are aware, I did settle good sums for Lucius and Emma at their twenty-first birthdays."

"I gathered that you must have done something of that ilk. Something must have set up Emma's business."

"I hope it does not annoy you that I have always feathered the nest of the family members. To me family is sacrosanct, and we have a flourishing one. It saddens me how family life is being eroded in this world. Some finance helps to keep the worst problems away. Also, Eric, I am settling sums in advance to my great-grandchildren."

"Dear Philip, how very kind and thoughtful of you. We all love and admire you greatly."

When Sir Philip had gone, Eric decided the very next week to see his lawyers and set up a trust.

At the same time, he hoped and prayed that Lucius' marriage would not turn out too badly.

In May, the wedding of Lucius and Amanda was lived through. It had been in St Albans. Sir Philip had hired a limousine for the day to keep everyone comfortable. As Amanda appeared on the arm of her father, Emma observed the other guests. As she had guessed, there were a number of raised eyebrows and suppressed smiles. The dress created a sensation all right. All went as planned and eventually the family could relax in the limousine, safely on their way home. After the honeymoon in the South of France, the couple would settle in Islington.

By June, Emma was pregnant again. The next child was expected towards the end of January 2002. A baby boy came into the world on the 27th of January and was named Dominic Philip.

Lady Saunders, who always followed with a beady eye the features of the newly born, pronounced that Dominic seemed to have Charles's mother's eyes but that the rest of him was pure Eric.

"Lucky you, Philip," said Lady Saunders, "now you have two youngsters to crawl and mess about with. I can tell you that you are the muckiest child in the playground."

"That's why washing-machines were invented," laughed her husband.

The greatest of the family news was yet to come. Eric had known about this for some time, but he wanted to surprise the family with two pieces of good news at the same time. The first was that he was being made the Ambassador to Spain as from the following May, and the second was that he was being knighted and it would appear in the announcements of the New Year's Honours. Till he said anything he wanted to see it in print with his own eyes. He knew that Sir Philip would be combing through the said names, as he did every year. This year was no exception. There was a huge shout from Sir Philip,

"Look what I've found! What a magnificent surprise! You old fox, Eric, not breathing a word about it before!"

"What? What? What is going on," the others were shouting.

"My dears, Eric has been knighted."

"Daddy. How wonderful. Just think that now there will be two Sirs in the family. Congratulations." Emma ran to hug her father.

"My boy, that is an honour well merited," said Sir Philip, "I shall enjoy calling you Sir Eric."

"And I shall start calling you Sir Philip."

"I know," said Emma, "You can be Sir E and Sir P."

"I've got another bit of news as well. I've been made Ambassador to Spain from May."

"Magnificent, we are so proud of you," said Lady Saunders. "You will be in some way home from home and we can have the to-ing and fro-ing as we did during your first posting there."

Eric's greatest dream had come true. He had managed the nearly impossible. He had put all his energies into hard work all his life and now he was finally reaping the rewards. To be ambassador to a country that was a monarchy gave him immense satisfaction, and that it was Spain on top of everything, was the icing on the cake. There would be the pomp and ceremony that he loved, and he'd need a diplomatic uniform. All so wonderfully old-fashioned.

Oh, if only Katie knew. But of course she would know. She would see it in the papers. He knew that she would be pleased and happy for him. And indeed she was. Eric received a letter of congratulations from her. He was touched; contact at last! He decided to start a tentative approach towards her through correspondence, not too much so as not to frighten her that he might be taking advantage of her, but just the occasional short letter and Christmas card.

He had instinctively chosen the right method. Katie was also in need of contact with him. Over the years she had mellowed, and she had learned not to resent her dreams not coming true. Eric had never stopped loving her, but he had not been able to marry her. She should not have held it against him. A person can only do what they can. And whether the reason was honourable or not so honourable, that had to be left with the person concerned. He

313

had done the right thing never to talk to her about a marriage. It had been she who had hankered. However, once a marriage had definitely been put aside, it had been the right move not to continue as an affair. An affair would have been too hurtful. It would have spoilt their happiness.

Now, for both of them, a new time was slowly coming. It was as if a new morn was appearing, and the very first rays of sun were beginning to light up the background. The night was not totally dark anymore. For both, their inner feelings and longings were beginning to surface and surmount the exterior carapace of worldliness. The exterior was beginning to matter less, especially for Eric. He had to admit it to himself that, without Katie, he was not a happy man.

All through their separation, he had followed the life and success of Kat Claydon. He knew that she had successful exhibitions in Hamburg and in Amsterdam. He was proud of her. He had often wondered what her private life was like and whether she had found another man. So far nothing had been written in the papers about the artist having any special relationships.

Now through their correspondence, they were giving each other a chance.

In the family, Lucius had got a daughter in March 2003. For Easter, Eric had been in London to see the family and thus he was introduced to his grand-daughter, Irene Philippa. Lucius had been adamant that the second name of the child be Philippa and Amanda had had to cave in. What Eric could make out about his son's marriage was that his son had woken up to reality but was doing the right thing by all. The child would help. The young man would probably throw himself heavily into work and thus avoid what could be avoided. The main thing to be avoided was of course a divorce as it was so detrimental to the children. It remained to be hoped that there would be no special quarrels between the couple so that a modus vivendi could be established.

Emma's two boys, Daniel and Dominic, were now three and one year respectively. Sir Philip was in his element with the little ones. He might be eighty-five but he had the energy levels of a much younger man. His wife sometimes wondered whether her husband might be overdoing it.

"Is there much contact between you and Lucius?" asked Eric.

"Not as much as we are used to, but some yes. I make a point of being pleasant to Amanda. Grandpa is unable to do that. I should think that now that they have a child, there could be a new lease of life between the cousins. However, we meet with Lucius for lunch from time to time, in secret from her."

"Well done. Keep as much contact as possible. Lucius needs that. I can see that he has woken up from his dreams. But he is doing the decent thing. Choosing a spouse is one of the most difficult things, and it is one of the most important ones as it determines one's whole life. Without children, one can separate to lead new lives but once a child is there, then one is tied to the other parent for life! With a divorce, the child is the ground trampled upon."

"Daddy, I'm pregnant again."

"Congratulations. You and Charles are busy beavers in the line of child production. I suppose you want a girl?"

"Yes, Daddy, we do. The baby is due in the summer."

On the 19th of July, 2004, Helen Estephania came into the world. Eric happened to be in England for a holiday at that time, so he was pacing the corridors together with Charles, Charles's, father, and Sir Philip. The women sat calmly waiting. When the baby was there, as soon as he could, Sir Philip wanted to hold the little one. He was so moved that he got tears of joy in his eyes.

"My dearest Emma, you have yet again given your family such a wonderful present. Bless you, my child."

With so much happiness all around, it is inevitable that some sorrow be mixed in with it. Most unexpectedly, in October 2005, Sir Philip had a sudden major heart-attack and died on the spot. He died in the happiest possible way, he had been preparing the pram to take Helen, Daniel and

Dominic out. Emma heard the crash and then saw her grandfather lying on the floor.

She was out of her mind. It reminded her too starkly of the sight of her mother, lying dead on the floor. Luckily the nanny was there to call for assistance and then to call Charles, who came home immediately. Emma had to be sedated. This was as big a blow to her as had been the loss of her mother. Sir Philip had in a way taken the role of Philippa, and Emma had relied on him all her life. Charles did his best to calm her, but failed.

It took a very long time for Emma to get to grips at all. She was inconsolable. In the end Lady Saunders had to have a serious word with her.

"Grandfather was taken far too early," cried Emma," he was in best of health. Now I have nobody to confide in. I miss him so terribly, Grandma."

"Emma, pull yourself together. You've got your husband to stand by you. He is giving you support. You need to think of your three children. Some control for their sakes would not go amiss. Let me tell you, my dear, your grandfather would not approve of such a sorrowing. I knew him intimately; we had been married for sixty-six years. A life-time. He was not taken early, the man was eighty-seven after all. I am happy that my Philip was taken so suddenly and in the middle of doing what he best liked to do. It was merciful that he was taken before he became debilitated in any way. Sitting in a wheelchair would have been worse than death to him. I am sustained by all the happy years he gave me. Believe me, Emma, Grandfather would not wish us to sorrow like this. His love is here all around us."

"Oh Grandmother, you are wise. Yes, you are right. I just miss him no longer being around."

"Time heals, my child. And I am still here. You can come to me anytime with anything you wish to talk about. You know that you are in my heart."

"Thank you, Grandma. Your words have helped me."

Chapter 42

With the death of Sir Philip, Eric felt that an era had come to an end. He found himself genuinely sorrowing over him. The departure of his much-loved father-in-law left him in a turmoil. The old man had had such a zest for life, such a sunny disposition and had been kindness personified. Eric had learned much from him and both Lucius and Emma had had an exceptional grandfather who spent time with them. To give of one's time, that was the biggest present one could give. Eric was much taken by various thoughts and felt an acute need to confide in someone. Who did he have? He needed Katie. He sat and penned a long emotional letter to her. He needed inner help.

He was not mistaken in her. When Katie received the letter, she could feel how lonely Eric was on the inside, how he needed comforting and being cared for. His outer success had only partially fulfilled him.

She replied in an instinctive way, not worrying how well her letter was constructed or what fancy language to use. It came from her heart. To Eric it was five pages of beauty. Her love for him shone through. Eric said a prayer for her, his Katie who, in spite of the harsh cruelty he had meted out to her, still loved him and had not turned against him.

He realised that though it was late in life, it was not too late. They were both alive. There was still a chance for them, provided that he himself undertook to build it up again. He would start with a frequent, honest and open correspondence. He had less than a year to stay in Madrid before his retirement. The correspondence would help them both towards an eventual meeting.

Eric started to assess his life. He had cultivated his exterior persona and felt that there he had succeeded to near perfection. As to his inner self, what had he done? It started to become clear to him that he had left that side of himself parched. Had he been right in assuming that people would only love him for his perfections? Yes, he had. His marriage might have given him more happiness if he had given Philippa the chance of knowing him better. The poor woman had never known him properly. If he could have exposed to her some of the interior hurts caused by his parents, she might have been able to alleviate the hurt. Or at least the brooding resentment.

He had of never stopped to consider his parents' behaviour from their point of view. Not that he condoned cruelty to children. But to think as to what might have caused it. The couple, stuck in a marriage, stuck in Southall, stuck in poverty and both with very little education, they probably did not know better. He had never enquired about his parents' childhood. There could have been factors that contributed to all that misery. In the summer, when he would be on a visit to the children, he would go and talk to his parents properly and ask questions. He was reminded of what Katie had said about the fact that often people did not really know much about their nearest and dearest. He was bound to learn at least something. Should his mother be in a suitable stage of inebriation, which she usually was, she would be garrulous. Then he could turn the direction of any conversation as he wished. He felt guilty at hiding from his parents the fact that there were two grandchildren and four great-grandchildren. So far he had reasoned that the best for the younger generation, as well for his parents, was to be ignorant of the existence of the others.

The barren inner marriage that he had created had not enabled his inner feelings to mature. But he had been frightened. Fear was such a strong emotion that very little could beat it. Only love had that power. And of all feelings love was the most blessed one. He had longed to drink from that well, but instead he had run for cover and avoided it.

He began to understand that he had a great capacity to love. As had anyone. He loved his two children and their offspring deeply. And his love was returned. However, children cannot give the type of love that a spouse can. Only with a spouse can one be really fulfilled. A spouse, is another person who is not only another body, but another spirit in harmony with one's own. Honest deep confidences needed to be exchanged. One has to open most of the seven gates guarding one's inner personality. When that happens, a true union can take place and the two can complement one another. He could now understand that that was the meaning of marriage.

He still had the great treasure that was Katie. He would start a slow process to nurture and heal that relationship. Their long separation made it a bit complicated, so he would have to tread carefully. Before any actual meeting, the relationship needed to be repaired.

There was no point in going on a trip to meet her. No, once they were together again, he needed to be there for her and not disappear from sight yet again. Katie had wanted all or nothing. She would have her all. He would offer all that he could give. He would humbly ask her to marry him. He would be there with a definite decision. He wanted to love her and cosset her, to be a support where needed and give her happiness.

His Katie. He prayed that they would have years and years and years together. They would have the same old fun together as always. She was bound to say yes to his proposal, she would not pretend or artificially make herself hard to get. That reply to his letter showed clearly that all the old love was there.

The dread of Southall and the fact that they came from there, was beginning to crack. He began to see that if one is too tied to the past, then it stultifies all possible moves forward. One had to be able to let go, especially of the bad things in life. He saw how he had almost been wedded to his dread of the place, and in the end, what for? Did it matter that they both came from Southall? Not in the least. Did it matter that Katie was not as well educated as himself? Not in the least. Why had he looked down on her? What stupidity! Katie had probably given more to the world that he had through his hard work. His job had given joy to no-one, Katie's art had given joy to so many. Oh Katie, forgive me.

Eric needed his own life with Katie. He did not want to become a pitied solitary soul that his children felt obliged to visit. He also knew in his bones that they would more than welcome their father's not breathing down their necks. He remembered that it had been Sir Philip who had been Emma's confidante, not himself. He needed nobody's permission to lead his own life, and he would definitely not ask for it. What he did in his life would only be announced after the fact. He did not meddle in the life of his adult children, and they had no right to meddle in his. Not that they would, they were both far too intelligent.

What now mattered was how Katie would react.

As Eric was thinking of Katie, so she was thinking of him. That letter from Eric had thrown her life apart. It had been an existence rather than a life. It had been through her turning to the Church and finding faith that her inner bitterness and anger had started to melt away. She had eventually got to the stage that she prayed for Eric's happiness, in whatever form and with whichever woman he would find it. Her possessiveness had gone. That brought inner harmony to her. Now that they had started their correspondence, she would hold nothing back; she would just see where it would lead them.

Chapter 43

Eric was on his way to visit his parents. It was August, and the weather had been a bit thundery from time to time. Today, it was warm and humid but no rain.

He was wondering in his mind as to how the visit would turn out. After his great soul-searching, he was now able to envisage this visit without hatred. Usually he had hated any visits and had only stayed for an hour each time. He had felt entitled to his wrath. He had now realised how awful a life with hatred was. Hatred was a horrible force, it spread around getting bigger and bigger till it enveloped most areas of life. Eventually most things got poisoned by it. This time Eric was not sitting rigid with suppressed nerves. He wanted to understand.

As he was going through the door, he heard his mother call,

"Is that you, Tom? You're back early."

"Mother, it's me, Eric. I'm here to visit again."

Eric looked at his mother with new eyes. The hair-dye and the war-paint were there, but through that he saw a frail, aged, vulnerable woman. Vulnerable? Eric's heart missed a beat. His dreaded mother, a vulnerable woman? Yes, but this was the first time that he had looked at her without preconceived judgment.

His mother was in the kitchen, putting on the kettle.

"Sit down, Mum, I'll do the tea. I've brought a gin and a brandy for you and also a hundred cigarettes. Shall I put some brandy in your tea?"

"Oh, that sounds good."

His mother actually had a little smile on her face.

Eric brought the tea, sugar, milk and cups.

"How have you been, Mum?"

"Me usual self, son. In the past few weeks I've been thinking that your visit was due sometime soon."

What! So his mother actually paid attention to his visits. And waited for him to come. He now thanked the Lord that he had come to visit his parents twice yearly, except for that period when he had been in Venezuela. He now had learned that his visits had been important.

"You've lost weight since I last saw you, Mum."

"So I have. Good job too not to carry too much weight. But me boobs are as usual. They've always been the pride of the estate."

"Mum. We've never really talked about your or Dad's family. I'm curious to know something about your childhoods."

"Oh Eric. Those stories are best avoided."

"Oh come on, I'll pour you a drink and then tell me something at least. Let's start with Dad."

His mother's eyes were looking into some distant horizon. She was looking into the past. The way the evening light fell upon her showed off her bone-structure and face very well. Eric realised that his mother was a very beautiful woman still. In her younger years she would have been stunning. Then why had she covered herself in all that make-up? Suddenly, the answer came to Eric. His mother had wanted to cover up her vulnerability. A mask was there. Just like he, Eric, always wore a mask.

"Well, Eric, Dad's father was a hard man. He had done time. He did not even need to be drunk in order to swipe a good one at Tom. Terrified, your father was. He bears the scars on his body to this day."

Eric was stunned. He had not expected that. It explained a lot.

"I'm so sorry to hear that," he said, having gone quite pale.

"It's just as well that the man died when Tom was only twelve. Otherwise your Dad might have been killed with the escalating violence."

What a horror story! No wonder that his Dad had taken to alcohol.

"That explains why Dad was so often in the pub. But what about yourself? You've never spoken about your parents."

"Son, what has got into you? What has brought about this curiosity? You've never asked before."

"No, and I regret that. Please carry on, tell me."

"I'm not sure that I should. Some things are best kept hidden."

"Oh, go on, Mum."

"I don't know who my father was. Me mum ran a sort of house of ill repute. She had five girls under her. It was disgusting what I grew up in. I ran off at the age of fifteen after one of the punters raped me. With mum's blessing as she wanted the money, and there was a tidy sum for "plucking the cherry"."

Eric was hot under the collar. A cold rage filled him. He was truly shocked. His poor mother, she had lived in hell.

"Yes," continued his mother, "I did odd cleaning jobs and worked in a pub. From time to time I had to grant some favours in order to survive. When I met your Dad, he saved me. He had a steady job and he said that he'd take care of me. At first we were in love, but somehow your father could not really bring out his feelings. I began to feel lost. And then I was pregnant with you. Tom and I needed to get married."

Eric was in tears.

"Good Lord. A grown man in tears. I knew I should not have told you."

"Mum, let me give you a hug." And Eric proceeded to do so.

He held his mother and stroked her gently. She patted him back. In Eric, all his hatred of

Southall had vanished; understanding had taken its place. His parents had not been able to overcome the result of their childhood traumas. They had wanted to rebel but they had not known how. Their own self-respect had been smashed. They had not had anyone to help them heal so they had been unable to mature into any ability to love. They had not been able to surmount the past. What a curse! It came in a flash to Eric that he too had been stuck in his past, the past as he had perceived it to be. He knew now that a life could not be properly lived if one was stuck brooding about the past.

"Oh mother. I wish I had been a better son for you."

"Now, now. Don't take it so. Dad and I made our own mistakes too. You've always come to see us regularly. Not many kids do that."

The evening was deepening. It was the evening when mother and son had found each other. As his mother sat quietly smoking her cigarettes, Eric lit them for her. They exchanged the odd little smiles. Their speech had dried up for a while as each was in their thoughts.

Then the door was heard. Eric's father had come home.

"Hello, son. This is a surprise."

"Hello, Dad. Nice to see you. Mum said that you were beginning to expect my visit."

"That's true. The other day Babs said that you'd show up soon. I'll go and get some beer out of the fridge."

Eric saw that his father was looking quite well. He had obviously continued to curb his alcohol intake for some time, as Eric had thought on a previous visit.

"I'm still working abroad for a bit," said Eric, "but I'll be back in less than three months. Then I'll come and see you again. I think the time has come that we see each other a bit more often."

"What a thought. What have you two been talking about?"

"Old family matters, Tom. It was time it got said."

"You haven't told it all, have you?"

"Yes, Tom. What happened, has happened. Nothing can be changed. Our son wanted to know about us. I think he has the right to know."

"Mum. Dad. This has been the most important meeting for us. I can only say that I admire you both for having managed to come out of horrible situations so well."

"You know, son, Southall and this estate have been good for us. We have not needed to move. It has been steady. We've had our ups and downs, but who hasn't? And you seem to have done well. We've never thanked you before, but let me do so now. Thanks for the two hundred pounds you have left for us on each visit. You've done that for ten years now. The money has not gone amiss."

"When I got to working age, I left you and was not here to contribute. I hope that that has made up for it a bit."

"More than made up, Eric," said his mother.

"Mum, do you have any recent photos of yourselves? I'd like to have one."

"Tom, would you bring the blue photo box here. We've got some from two years ago when we attended Brenda's wedding. They sent us a few photos afterwards."

How fortunate, felt Eric. There were four pictures. They were professionally taken and Eric's parents came out well.

"May I keep this one?"

"Sure, son. You keep it."

Then there was small talk about the estate and the neighbours and football. When it was nine-thirty, Eric left so as not to tire his parents. The miraculous had happened, for the first time he had enjoyed his visit, and he was not running to escape as quickly as he could.

When he got home, he sat ruminating. The question uppermost in his mind was the one whether he still should keep his parents a secret from his children and vice versa. Also he was weighing in his mind whether he had been right to have done so in the first place. He came to the conclusion that it had been the right thing to do and also that the same reasons which had made it a secret, still applied.

The past of his parents was too horrible for his children to know. What would they gain from the knowledge? They could not have visited

Southall without a sense of shame coming in. Whether that was right or wrong was not the issue here. It was a statement of fact. If the Southall background had come to the knowledge of their peers, both Lucius and Emma would have been castigated. The young can be cruel. Again, the right or wrong of it was not under question. It was for him, Eric, to carry the can of his past.

He had managed a happy lifestyle for his children, unburdened by a dark past, and that was what they were entitled to keep. Let them keep that little bit of an ideal world. Whether he would be able to share his background with anyone ever, was a question. But he did not have to answer that now. He was on his way to try to get close to Katie again, this time with the full intention of marrying her. Would she accept him? He prayed that she would. He had at long last managed to put his demons behind him, he was no longer shackled to his past. Hopefully, he would be accepted, he was by now a bit of a grey-whiskers, except that he was vain enough to disguise it with colour.

The thought of hair-colour made him cackle. What a new subject to discuss with his mother!

Chapter 44

Through their letters, Eric and Katie understood that they were on their way to being united again. Eric was coming home on the 8th of November. "I shall be back in the evening, give me time to snooze the next morning, and in the afternoon I'll phone you," he had written.

In the end, it was Katie who phoned Eric. His phone rang at three in the afternoon.

"Eric! Please come at once to Southall. Come by the Underground to Ealing Broadway and then take a taxi. There is not a minute to be wasted. There is a fire. Something terrible is happening."

Eric hurtled out as fast as he could.

What had happened was that Katie had gone to have lunch with her father. Suddenly there had been a terrible commotion on the estate.

"Fire! Fire!" voices were shouting. Katie had dashed out to see. Oh my God! The smoke was coming from the flat of Eric's parents. She phoned at once. The fire brigade was there in ten minutes. Ten long minutes which enabled the fire really to take hold. The conflagration grew to momentous proportions. It took some time for the firemen till the flames were mastered.

"Is there anyone left alive? Katie screamed.

The firemen looked at her and shook their heads. That meant that Eric's parents were dead. Katie was shaken by sobs. She suffered for Eric.

This was a terrible homecoming for him. What a terrible end to his parents. Whatever they may have been like, that is not what he would have wished for them.

When Eric arrived, he went straight to hug Katie. Then he talked to the firemen.

"This is my parents' flat. I am their only son. Are they alive?"

"No, unfortunately there is no-one alive in the flat. The men are bringing two bodies out just now." The charred remains were dreadful to see. Eric and Katie both felt nauseous.

"Oh no, no. Katie, this is intolerable. My poor parents."

He broke into sobs.

"How, how did this happen?" he managed to stammer.

"Sir, what caused the fire in the first place has to be established. The couple were asphyxiated by the fumes. It would have rendered them unconscious and thus unable to save themselves. They were found sitting on the sofa. The whole place is thoroughly burned out. There was so much inflammable material there, - the carpets, the curtains, the soft furnishings."

The authorities, the police and the fire brigade did their jobs. Eric was asked if he was in state to be able to go and fill in some paperwork.

"I'll come with you, said Katie, "It's best to get it done quickly."

Eric had never imagined that he would feel so sorry at his parents' death, but he was deeply saddened by it. An era had gone. What the poet had said came to his mind, "only love and death change everything". True indeed.

"Eric, I have my car here. May I suggest that we go to my place? I don't think you would want to be alone."

During the drive there was no conversation. Eric sobbed quietly into his handkerchief. When they arrived in her flat, Eric said,

"Katie darling, may I stay?"

"Of course, my love. I'll fix us a drink, and later we'll have something to eat. But first, would you want to phone your children?"

"I will do so to alert them to the fact that I'm not at home. Otherwise they'll wonder."

"Eric, I am so sorry for all this."

"I have a small consolation in this disaster. At least I had made a sort of peace with my parents last summer when I was briefly in London. My father came home a bit later, which gave me some time alone with my mother. We talked in a manner we had never talked before, going over various happenings and as a result we both felt that we had got closer. I went impulsively to give her a hug, to which she said, "You old man giving me a hug," but I think she was pleased. When my father came in we talked a bit about the events in Southall, and then I left.

You know, Katie, that visit made me feel good for the first time. I thank the Lord that I had that opportunity."

"You did the right thing. That memory will help you. Now come here and sit down."

Then they went to sit on the sofa, as in old times. Words were not flowing because too much had happened in too short a time. They had to come to terms inwardly first. Katie felt that it might be a good thing to leave Eric to brood alone in silence. She was right. Eric's entire life was going on in his mind, especially his childhood.

"Eric, do you mind if I go into my workroom? Handling clay calms me down."

He nodded.

Katie was in many ways exploding inside. To see her beloved in shock at that appalling scene of the fire, with his parents dead, took its toll on her. She felt unendingly sad for him. She needed to create those feelings in clay. As she worked, her thoughts were confused. How would this affect Eric? How would it affect their budding relationship? Was there a future? She prayed as her hands were working the clay.

After a while she heard Eric move. He was coming towards her. As he looked at her sitting there with her hands in the clay, his heart swelled with love. His Katie. His beloved Katie. He touched her gently on the shoulder. She looked up.

"Katie, I love you. You are my one and only beloved. Will you marry me? Say yes, say yes, say yes."

"Yes. It is yes. It has been yes all my life."

"My sweetheart, you are the most wonderful thing that has happened to me. You've been my support always. My heart is bursting with feelings."

"You can kiss me once I have finished this shape. Till then you'll have to patient yourself."

"I can always nibble at your neck, can't I?" said Eric and proceeded to do so.

"Eric, you are tickling me. The shape is changing. Dear me, it has collapsed."

"Good. Clean your hands and come to give me some attention. Your future husband is in need of cosseting."

"I'm only marrying you in order to become Lady Flint."

"But of course. Why else? That is understood. Fine by me, as long as you become Lady Flint."

The two playful puppies were there again. It was heart-warming. They were wrapped up in each other, looking to their future, ready to support one another. Real, true joy filled their hearts.

The next morning they slept late and did not wake up till after nine.

"Good morning, future Lady Flint. Has my one and only slept well?"

"Sir Eric, I have indeed. The thought of that title gave me the best sleep ever. Your prowess has not diminished at all, it is as strong as ever. Would you like to have my famous breakfast omelette?

"Sounds super. Have you got strawberry jam as well?"

"I surely do. All the old ingredients are there. Like the Wise Virgins, I have kept myself prepared for the Bridegroom."

Eric laughed. Then he dug himself further into the bedding.

"Would you allow this exhausted traveller a few more winks?"

"You lazy toad. I'll call when it's all ready."

After breakfast when they were dressed, Katie asked,

"Do you by any chance have that small piece of broken pottery that I gave you all those years ago?"

"As a matter of fact, I do. It lives in my wallet."

"Good, now come and watch me work."

Katie created a small vase of very thin clay. The shape was original.

"It has a broad bottom to prevent it from keeling over. Now, give me your shard."

He did so. She put it inside the vase and then put her own shard into it as well. Then she sealed the top.

"I shall now put it into the small kiln I have here. It is sufficient for the job. This vase signifies our union."

"You have amazing ideas. I so admire you. Now, where would you like to get wed?"

"At Holy Trinity Brompton."

"That is news indeed. I had no idea that you had come into the faith."

"Yes, a number of years ago. My strength to cope with life without you came from what faith has given me. It showed me the path, it comforted me. As a result I am very happy."

"I'm so pleased for you Katie."

"We shall have a proper church wedding."

"This weekend the children are coming to see me. I would like you to be there."

"I look forward to that."

On that Sunday afternoon, when everybody was assembled, Eric said,

"I have an announcement to make. Katie and I are engaged to be married."

"Congratulations, father," said Lucius and Emma with one voice.

"We shall be married at the beginning of June at the Holy Trinity Brompton, on the first Saturday of the month. We were lucky that we got the date, but there was a cancellation. Usually the place is booked a year in advance. We intend to have a medium bun-fight, that is, no more than a hundred guests. And Charles, would you like to be my best man?"

"With great pleasure," answered Charles.

Emma went to Katie.

"Oh Katie, father looks so happy. Would you like me to design your wedding dress?"

"Yes, please. I'm grateful for your suggestion. I shall be proud to wear an Emma Erica creation."

"Do think about the style. I've already got ideas in my head."

When Katie went to see Emma about the dress, the latter said,

"Katie, let's make it a really special style. Tell me roughly what you have in mind."

"I have actually given it a lot of thought. I'm not sure whether it would suit me, but I've always been an admirer of Erte. Ever since a friend of mine gave an artbook of his as a present."

"Splendid. That's just the stuff I wanted to hear. Erte has so many versatile models, one of them is bound to suit you down to the ground. I'll hunt out the style that will suit you. I am a professional in this."

"Something suitable for my age and something that would suit a Lady Flint. Your father must not be disappointed."

"As a fabric, what would you prefer, brocade or velvet?"

"Definitely velvet."

"We'll have dark cream, which will suit your skin colour and hair to perfection. And we'll trim it with a light-brown walnut colour. That will give it sex-appeal."

"Oh dear."

"Don't worry. It will only be a hint, but an important one. I want to bring out what a desirable woman you are. And Katie, I'd like to say to you how very sorry I am for my nasty behaviour towards you on our first meeting. I do hope that you forgive me."

"Oh Emma, it is all forgotten. Don't worry."

"I can assure you that you'll look wonderful. You don't think that I would design anything but the best for my father's lovely future wife? He has such a happy look on his face. So heart-warming. You two will be very happy."

Christmas was celebrated by Katie and Eric with the children. Katie enjoyed the family feel and the hustle and bustle. She was amused to see Eric in the role of a grandfather. He was copying Sir Philip and was doing so successfully. When the young crowd had left, he sighed with relief.

"It is exhausting being a grandfather. I'm doing my best and I hope the little ones had a good time."

"You did well, Eric. Everyone was happy."

Finally the much-awaited wedding day arrived. When Eric saw Katie advance on the arm of her father, he smiled warmly. She was a picture of the 1920's elegance. He recognised the Erte influence on the design and congratulated his daughter in his mind upon the result.

It was a muted down Erte to suit Katie, and the silk velvet gave it softness and added to its femininity. It was not ornate, but it had style very much printed on it. The dress was full-length with a waist-line around which was tied a broad belt, tied in a bow, the ends of which reached the hips. The skirt widened slightly towards the bottom. The neckline was in the shape of a low V and the sleeves were till the elbows. Over the shoulders was a cape of see-through organza, falling to the elbows. On her head was a small hat with a broad walnut colour bow, the same as round the waist. From it cascaded a veil in the same thin organza which was full-length at the back but which was shorter at the sides, only reaching the hips. It would not bother her when dancing. The edges of the veil were embroidered in a geometric Erte design. Her hair, which reached only just to the shoulders, had been slightly curled which lightened the straight lines of the dress. Katie looked wonderful in it.

At long last, the ceremony was over, and the priest pronounced them to be man and wife. Eric gave Katie a quick peck on the cheek for the benefit of those who expected the kiss. Then off to the party. The couple may have been sixty each but they felt like Spring chickens and behaved as such at the party afterwards. Jollity reigned supreme.

The honeymoon was a cruise in the Caribbean which the bride had wanted to do. Eric had never been on a cruise before so they both regarded it as an adventure. They had each other and that was all that mattered. The ocean liner was impressive. They had a lovely cabin with a sitting corner, a dining area and a balcony. It amazed them how large the ship was and how very ornate.

It was the second day of the voyage and all around them was only the vast ocean. The sea air was like the most wonderful perfume. They had decided to eat in their cabin and then sit on the balcony and watch the sun set. Eric insisted that they open a champagne bottle. The bubbles were so much fun to watch, and the golden liquid was like nectar. They clinked glasses.

"To my bride."

"To my husband."

In the sky there were a few wisps of very high clouds which began to change colour with the setting of the sun. The soft orange pink hues were magnificent. A warm glow permeated the atmosphere. Katie in her pink and white dress looked like a flower. Eric looked at her with tenderness.

"Lady Flint, what are you thinking about?"

"About the Creation, Sir Eric, and the wonder of the world."

"To me you are the greatest wonder," said Eric, kissing her hand.

"Remember when as children we talked about Never Never Land. We have finally arrived there."

"Yes, my beloved. Our never, never ending love has only just started, and we are sailing into bliss. Before I embrace you, my bride, let me read you a few lines from the Song of Songs:

"You have stolen my heart, my sister, my bride;
You have stolen my heart
With one glance of your eyes,
With one jewel of your necklace.
How delightful is your love, my sister, my bride!
I have come into my garden, my sister, my bride;
I have gathered my myrrh with my spice,
I have eaten my honeycomb and my honey,
I have drunk my wine and my milk."

The water reflected a picture of human happiness."

Printed in Poland
by Amazon Fulfillment
Poland Sp. z o.o., Wrocław